# The Spoils of War

JOHN FINCH was born in Liverpool and brought up in the South Yorkshire coalfields. After the war he went to London and worked for a while as secretary to the sculptor, Jacob Epstein. He had a variety of occupations, including a short but hectic period as a crime reporter, before returning to the North where he met and married his wife. He has always been a writer, and at this time he became one of the first three writers to join *Coronation Street* during its first weeks on television. He also produced the series before returning to writing with *A Family at War* and *Sam*, and later *This Year, Next Year*. *Cuddon Return*, his first novel, was published in 1978.

KEITH MILES was born and brought up in Wales. He read History at Oxford and lectured in the subject for some years before becoming a full-time freelance writer. He has written several plays for radio, television and the stage and has contributed to many series and serials. He has published a novel, some short stories, and a critical study of the German author, Gunter Grass.

Keith Miles is married and has two children.

# KEITH MILES

# The Spoils of War

*Based on the Granada Television
series by John Finch*

FONTANA/COLLINS

First published in 1980 by Fontana Books

This novelization
© John Finch and Keith Miles 1980

Made and printed in Great Britain by
William Collins Sons and Co Ltd Glasgow

# CHAPTER ONE

Everyone has his own idea about how the war in Europe actually ended. For some it was when the Russians marched into Berlin, for others it was when Adolf Hitler raised a Walther pistol to his head and pulled the trigger, and for others again it was when a bespectacled Montgomery formally accepted the surrender of all enemy forces in North West Germany. There were those who dated it from the second that Churchill began his broadcast to the nation on V.E.-Day, those who knew it by their first proper night's sleep in years, and those who believed that the darkness was finally over only when the lights came on again. A few claimed to recognize it at once by its sense of anti-climax.

Captain Blake Hayward of the 11th Armoured Division had no doubts on the subject. He could pin down the ending of the war to a precise moment in May, 1945, because of a memorable event—his Commanding Officer smiled at him. Nothing short of victory could have coaxed a smile out of that grim, impassive face and Blake was delighted. In his excitement he found himself grinning back at his C.O. and trying to salute.

'Steady on, sir,' warned his companion.

'Aouw!'

Blake had forgotten that his wounded arm was being dressed and that it was not yet capable of saluting, even on such an historic occasion. He watched his C.O. walk on past and did his best to ignore the steady throb of pain he was now getting. As the bandaging continued, he began to think about the implications of that smile. If the war really was over, he might soon be able to get back home.

'All finished, sir. Slip your arm back into the sling.'

'Oh right. . . .'

'Easy does it,' advised the young medic, helping him. 'You'll need to have the dressing changed in a couple of days.'

'How long before I can get rid of this damn sling?'

'A few weeks yet, sir. You'll just have to grin and bear it.'

'Been doing that ever since I joined the Army!' They laughed. 'As long as I get home in one piece.'

'You will,' assured the other, tidying away the scissors and the bandages. 'Where is home, sir?'

'Doubt if you'll have heard of the place. Nobody else has.'

'Try me.'

'Whitstanton.' Blake did not give him chance to reply. 'There. I told you.'

'But I have heard of it. What's more, I know someone who lives there. Or used to.'

'In *Whitstanton*?' Blake was amazed.

'Small world, you know, sir. We've got a Sergeant from your home town. I'm not having you on. You could check.'

'I certainly will. What's his name? Where can I find him? Which part of Whitstanton—have you any idea?'

Ten minutes later he was heading in the direction of a Field Station set up by the Royal Army Medical Corps. Anticipation gave his feet a light step and the pain in his arm seemed to have worn off completely.

Passing the main entrance to the Field Station, he came to the door for which he was looking only to find his way blocked by a German soldier. The man was squatting down half-asleep but he soon woke up when Blake's shadow fell across him. Leaping up at once, he saluted as if by reflex and stood rigidly to attention. He was short, fat, and rather comical in appearance with the kind of features that would have been a gift to any cartoonist back in Britain. Hiding his amusement, Blake nodded ahead of him.

'The Den?' he asked.

'Bitte?'

'Is this the Den?' Blake repeated in a louder voice.

'Ja! Ja! The Den!' The soldier reached out and opened the door with great ceremony before stepping back and beaming stupidly. 'Victory! Churchill!' he added, giving the famous V sign.

'Carry on,' muttered Blake, ignoring the gesture.

He went straight into the room and saw a man in the uniform of a sergeant sitting on an upturned ammunition box, reading a letter. The man scrambled to his feet.

'Mark Warrington?'

'Yes, sir. . . .'

'Blake Hayward,' announced the other, glancing around the bare room. 'One of your blokes has just been seeing to my arm. Said that his sergeant came from Whitstanton.'

'Do you know it, sir?'

'My home town. . . .'

'Ah. . . .'

Sergeant Mark Warrington smiled and showed a perfect set of teeth. He was a well-built, clean-cut young man with an open face and an accent that did not seem to go with his three stripes. Blake took all this in, aware at the same time that he was being scrutinized by the other's sharp, friendly eyes. He felt that there was something vaguely familiar about Mark.

'Do you still live in Whitstanton?'

'My mother still lives there,' said Mark. 'An old farmhouse off the coast road. Used to belong to some people called Penworthy. Distant relatives of my father.'

'I know the house.'

'Better than I do, probably. I've only been there a couple of times. Mum moved in just before I was posted, three years ago.' He paused, shrugged and then supplied a post script. 'My parents are . . . sort of separated.'

'I've been away from there for four years. Never expected to meet someone else from the place in Germany.'

'Nor me.' He gazed at Blake's injured arm. 'Is it serious?' He smiled when the other shook his head. 'It certainly teaches you a bit of geography, doesn't it?'

'What does?'

'War. All those places I used to mark on a map in my school exercise book. I've been to many of them. All those rivers I used to draw with a blue pencil—the Seine, the Somme, the Rhine. I've actually crossed them. And now here we are within spitting distance of the Elbe. Fascinating in its own way.'

'Never cared much for geography,' came the blunt reply. Blake strolled around the room then peered through the cracked pane of glass in the window. 'Who's that character outside?'

'Mm? Oh that's Fritz.'

'Who's Fritz when he's at home?'

'He *is* at home, that's his one useful quality. We use him as a rough and ready interpreter.'

'Obsequious little sod, isn't he?'

'Oh, Fritz is not too bad,' said Mark, defensively. 'Got himself left behind somehow when the last batch of prisoners was moved out. We sort of . . . adopted him.'

Blake nodded in a non-committal way and there was the briefest moment of uneasiness between them. Mark then remembered something and brightened immediately.

'Would you like a beer?'

'Beer!' Blake sounded as pleased as he was surprised.

'In the truck outside.'

'Lead the way.'

Mark went quickly out through the door with Blake at his heels. Fritz jumped to attention and welcomed them with a salute, speaking with the happy intensity of someone who believes every word that he is saying.

'English and Germans . . . friends now. Ja? Sehr gut. Now we fight the Russians. Together. Ja?'

They strolled on past him without replying, exchanging a glance as they did so. The sun was shining boldly out of a cloudless sky now and it gave the whole camp a slightly unreal glow. Mark touched on the subject which was uppermost in every soldier's mind.

'They say it'll be over any day now. . . .'

'Back to Civvy Street!' said Blake with enthusiasm.

'Looking forward to it?'

'Can't wait. But it'll be a bit of an ordeal. Especially in Whitstanton.'

'Ordeal? You mean, the problem of re-adjusting after all that time away from the place?'

Blake wondered how many other sergeants would have phrased it quite so elegantly or have spoken with such educated assurance. Mark was clearly not typical of his rank.

'Most of the blokes I know are in reserved occupations,' noted Blake, with a hint of sourness. 'The ironworks, the mine and so on. . . . It's going to be another world to people like you and me till we get used to it again.' The sourness returned. 'If we ever do.'

They had reached the truck now and Mark was pulling a large wooden case towards him. He took out a couple of cans and passed one across to Blake. The latter examined it with the interest of a prospector who has just stumbled on a first gold nugget.

'The Yanks went through,' explained Mark.

'God bless America!'

They opened the cans and took their first long swigs of beer. Blake stared appreciatively at the can once again and then grinned his thanks. He was glad that someone from the R.A.M.C. came from Whitstanton. The coincidence was turning out to have all kinds of fringe benefits.

'It's not going to be all that easy for us,' he said, resuming his theme. 'Some of the men back home resent the uniform I'm told. Something to do with us getting all the girls.'

'*How*?' asked Mark with a laugh.

'Exactly. Fat chance, I've had, four years away.' He took another swig of beer and savoured it for a moment or two. 'Like Tawney said about managers . . . "The odium of capitalism with none of its rewards" . . . that's us. We do the dirty work and get no profit out of it. . . .'

'I wouldn't put it quite like that,' said Mark, reasonably. He finished his beer and reached into the box again. 'Another?'

'Please!'

He emptied the first can and put it down so that his hand was free to take the second. The beer was a shade warmer than he liked it and it had an unusual tang but it still tasted delicious to a man who had not leaned on the counter of his local pub for almost four years. Mark disposed of the two empty cans into a large brown litter bag standing nearby and he came back to find himself being watched rather carefully.

'What did you do before the war?' asked Blake.

'I was at university. This gave me a good excuse to leave. . . . What about you?'

'Mechanic at the ironworks. . . .' He was suddenly struck by a thought that had been hovering at the back of his mind ever since he had met Mark. 'You're not one of *Them*?'

'Them?'

'As opposed to Us?'

'You've lost me, old chap.'

'Sorry. Family thing. Dad's secretary of Whitstanton Labour Party, you see. Lives for it. I think that's why he wanted us to join up —Macdonald having been a pacifist and that. Dad never forgave old Ramsay.'

'I'm still rather baffled.'

'Conversation at home was littered with phrases like "Them and Us". . . . "Them" were the Warringtons.'

'Ah, I'm with you now.' There was a long pause and then Mark hunched his shoulders apologetically. 'Why deny it? Dad's chairman of the ironworks. He's been in America for most of the war, doing some job for the Ministry of Supply. I'm afraid that . . . yes, I am one of Them.'

'Don't be afraid.'

'But if you're one of Us. . . .'

'That's the point. I'm not any longer.' He did not know why he was able to confide in Mark but he felt better for doing so and let the words tumble out. 'I defected. Sold out. Betrayed my class. . . . That's what Dad will say, anyway. Won't be any fun facing him with the news. I'll be a second Macdonald to him. Committing high treason.' He sucked his teeth as he thought about the confrontation that was to come. 'How do you tell your father that you're not on his side any more?'

'I wish I knew,' confessed Mark.

'Why?'

'Because I'm in the same boat myself.'

'Are you?'

'Does happen sometimes. Even to Them. . . .'

Blake Hayward stared at him for a long while and then burst into laughter at the irony of it all. The war really had managed to stand everything on its head.

'I'll lose my rank and go back to being a political misfit in the iron-works, and you'll don your bowler and preach socialism down among the flesh-pots! Almost as if we've changed places but stayed where we are.'

Mark agreed and admitted that he was not relishing the battle he knew he was going to have with his father. By the same token, he was not going to pretend to be the same son who had left home three years ago to serve his country in the Armed Forces. For him the time in the ranks had been his real university and it had taught him things he could never unlearn. When he had finished speaking, he noticed that he had seen off the second can of beer.

'Must go,' decided Blake. 'Thanks for the booze.'

'Pleasure.'

'Might bump into you back home one day. I'll stand *you* a drink then. God knows when it'll be, though.'

'I'm going on leave in two weeks' time.'

'Lucky beggar!' said Blake with feeling. 'Look, you wouldn't do me a favour, would you?'

'What is it?'

'Just call at home and tell Mum that you saw me. . . .'

'Of course,' said Mark in his easy, affable way.

'You know what mothers are. . . . I'll give you the address.' Blake used his free hand to take out a pencil and a piece of paper. While he was writing, he talked about the house with a brisk fondness. 'It's a big old ruin. Stands on its own by the sea. It was falling apart when I left. Might even be a heap of rubble by now. Mum's old man left it to her—empty. My parents couldn't afford furniture so they filled it with us kids. Six of us. Here. . . .'

Mark took the paper, glanced at it, then slipped it into his pocket. Something told him that he was going to enjoy meeting the Hayward family. Blake's mind returned to the war.

'I still say it's a pity!'

'Pity?'

'Hitler. Doing himself in like that. I'd hoped we'd get that little bastard alive!' The venom in his voice disappeared at once. 'Be seeing you.'

'Cheerio.'

As Mark watched the tall, upright figure of Captain Blake Hayward marching away, he found it difficult to imagine that the latter would one day be exchanging his uniform for a set of overalls. Mark Warrington could no more see him going back to being a mechanic at the ironworks than he could see himself picking up the threads of his university career. War had transformed both men and not everyone at home would approve of that transformation.

The day had got off to an unpromising start with heavy rain falling out of a dark sky and a keen wind coming in off a choppy sea. Without warning, and in its own capricious way, the weather had then improved dramatically. Clouds had scudded away, rain had stopped, the wind had dropped to a soft whisper and the waves had become placid once more. Brilliant sunshine now lit up the whole of Whitstanton beach, making the wet sand and rocks glisten in sheer gratitude, and bringing out the gulls in profusion to wheel and swoop and call.

A large, solitary house stood on the beach and basked in the warmth of the morning sun. It was a solid building but it had a somewhat neglected air about it, as if its occupants could not quite afford to keep it in a constant state of repair; at the same time it had a defiant, almost indomitable quality about it, a place that had weathered countless storms within and without and which was proud of its isolation. Though it would not have been everyone's taste, it was undeniably a house of character.

Like the home in which he had brought up his family, George Hayward was big, well-built and purposeful though showing the effects of time in his face. He stood in the garden a short distance from the air raid shelter and jabbed his spade down into the soil before helping it on its way with the bottom of his boot. Middle age had given George a real interest in gardening and the wartime shortages had served to direct that interest to practical ends. In order to feed his family properly, he had found that a degree of self-sufficiency was more or less essential and he had turned the sandy soil of his land into one large vegetable patch. It was now time to plant his main crop of potatoes and he was setting about the task with his usual vigour.

Suddenly he paused and leaned on his spade. Above the cry of the gulls and the steady plash of the incoming tide, he had heard another sound. At that moment his wife, Helen, came out of the house: a handsome, bustling but drawn-looking woman in a dress that had seen better days. She, too, had heard the noise. The distant hum of an approaching car became first a drone and then developed into a positive roar as the vehicle raced along the pitted road towards them. Reaching the house, it screeched to a halt and a well-spoken man in his late twenties leaped out and waved happily.

'Great day, Hayward!'

'Aye—it's that all right,' returned George.

'Great day, Mrs Hayward!'

'Wonderful. . . .'

The man jumped back into the car which had an ARP insignia on it and pressed his foot down hard on the accelerator. George waited until he had gone out of sight and then spoke good-humouredly to his wife.

'He only did that job for the petrol.'

'Young Ainscough, wasn't it?'

'Aye, love. Last smile I'll get out of him, I reckon.'

'Why do you say that, George?'

'I've heard he's been short-listed as Tory Party candidate. Pawson's retiring before the election.'

'Election?'

'Any day now. Don't you read the papers, woman?'

'Can't get near them with you and your father about,' she chided pleasantly, then she sighed. 'It does seem a shame, though.'

'A shame?'

'That we can't depend on a smile any more now that the war's finally over. That we can't all be civilized.'

'Nay, young Ainscough'll be civilized enough. Those middle class types always are. He'll just not crack his face when I'm around, that's all. One war's over but t'other's still on.'

Helen Hayward had heard his political views far too often to want to listen to them again. Given his head, George could turn a casual conversation into an earnest discussion of the class structure and the ways in which a Socialist Government would alter it to the good. Trying to change the subject, Helen put her hand into the pocket of her dress and took out an envelope.

'We had a letter this morning. Someone's coming to see us.'

'Who's that, then?'

'Someone local who met Blake in Germany. He's on leave. Blake asked him to call in and see us.'

'Fine!' said George, pleased.

'He's coming today.'

'Today? He's putting himself out, isn't he? Coming here on V.E.-Day. Very kind of the lad. What's his name?'

'He's a Warrington.'

As soon as she spoke the name she realized that she had not managed to change the subject at all. Instead she was actually inviting her husband to display all his political prejudices. His face darkened with suspicion at once.

'Warrington? Ironworks Warrington?'

'Son of the chairman.'

'What's he want with us, then?' he sneered.

'Now don't be like that, George,' she warned. 'As you said yourself just now, he's putting himself to some trouble to visit us. We must give him a welcome.'

'A welcome! For a Warrington!'

'Yes! We'll not be like the Ainscoughs of this world. A smile costs nothing.'

'But a Warrington!' George was quite shocked. 'Does he know that I'm one of his father's wages clerks?'

'I daresay Blake told him. And why shouldn't he? Nothing to be ashamed of. It's an honest job.'

'It's not paid as an honest job should be paid. . . .'

'George—'

'It's not, Helen,' he interrupted, fully roused now. 'Where would we be without you giving music lessons? If we'd to rely on my pay packet we'd be struggling and no mistake. We've Lovett still at school. Peg doing that part-time job at library for some pocket money. Keir and Blake fighting for their country in return for a pittance. And Owen. . . .'

His voice tailed off and his anger became a soulful stare at the ground. Helen moved closer to him and took his arm.

'Blake's stopped asking if we've had news,' she said. 'He's not mentioned Owen in his letters for a year or more. . . .'

'He knows what we know then, doesn't he?'

'Yes, he's faced the truth . . . as we've had to. Though it's been hard, so hard to believe.' She shook her head slowly from side to side. 'I see now why we go through that ritual of a funeral. It sort of marks it, helps you to cope . . . not in Owen's case. If there'd only been a grave we could visit . . . to be *sure*. . . .'

'I *am* sure, love. In my heart. I'll tell you something, though. I kept on hoping long after I said we shouldn't.'

'Think I didn't know that, George Hayward?'

He put an arm around her shoulders and gave her an affectionate squeeze, then he tried to shake off his sad thoughts by looking to the future.

'Victory in Europe, eh!'

'V.E.-Day at last!'

'Difficult to believe it's all over, isn't it?'

'What comes next, that's the question? The Promised Land?'

Before he could answer she put a hand gently to his lips and then headed back towards the house. George spat on his hands and reached for his spade again.

Like the shabby exterior of the house, the kitchen needed a number of small repairs and a lick of paint. But it was clean enough and Jean Hayward, sitting at the table with a cloth in her hand, was determined to make the brassware in it gleam like new. She was still polishing for all her worth as her mother-in-law came in from the garden and put the dustpan back under the sink.

'You did that yesterday,' noted Helen.

'Did I? Oh yes. I'd forgotten.'

'You do far too much, on top of a job.'

'I like to do my share, that's all. You should charge me rent then I'd not feel so beholden.'

'Charge my daughter rent!' Helen was scandalized.

'Daughter-in-law,' corrected the other.

'No difference in my book, Jean, as you well know.'

Jean Hayward nodded and put down the cloth. She studied her reflection in the shining surface of a brass pot and thought that she could see worry lines that had not been there before. After a minute or so, she looked back at Helen.

'I'm sorry . . . since we were certain about it, I've tried to . . . what you said just now reminded me.'

'Owen?'

'I've had to put him out of my mind. Remembering my husband only makes me feel . . . guilty. . . .'

'Because of Ernst.' She sat down beside the younger woman whose pretty face was now furrowed with anxiety. 'We understand.'

'You might but the rest of Whitstanton won't.'

'It's none of their business, Jean! Who else knows, anyway? Only those people where you work—the Galways.'

'When I walk down the street in't town, I feel as if everyone knows and that they're all talking about it behind my back. It's bound to get round sooner or later, anyway. You know what this place is like. Yes, and Mum and Dad will be the worst.'

'It doesn't matter to us what they think. Owen was *our* son, not theirs.'

Jean Hayward had never regretted the fact that she had told Helen about her friendship with Ernst Sevcenko almost from the start. It was not, as she had explained, that she had stopped loving Owen because there was a sense in which she could never do that; but she had found someone who had taken away the pain of her suffering and who had enabled her to feel like a young woman again. George Hayward had been upset at first to hear that his son's widow had formed an attachment with another man, but he had come to accept the relationship for what it was, thanks largely to his wife's reasoning. Helen had been a great support to Jean in every way and had never shown the merest hint of any disapproval or resentment.

'They shouldn't have said "missing believed killed", should they?' argued Jean, polishing once more. 'It's not enough, is it? You can't start your life again with that.' There was a long pause as she took a deep breath. 'Can you take Colin to the street party with you?'

Jean nodded. 'Are you going to see Ernst?'

'Yes. It's Victory day for him, too. Even if he did fight for the Germans. He had a bad time in the war. Worse for him than for us, really.'

Helen was about to agree when her daughter, Peg, came rushing in excitedly to tell them that they had forgotten the King's broadcast on the wireless.

'My God—how long?' asked Helen.

'A minute if that clock is right, Mum,' said Peg.

'I'll turn it on,' decided Jean, going swiftly into the living room. 'Give the others a shout!'

There was a flurry of activity as Peg went out to the garden to call her father and Helen went after her to tell George to pass on the message to his father. Jean fiddled with the knobs on the wireless set with her ten-year-old son, Colin, bobbing about in front of her trying to get her attention.

'The King!' The boy's eyes were huge. When Helen and Peg came running in, he halted them with a wave. 'Sh! It's the King.'

George Hayward, meanwhile, had abandoned his potatoes and hurried in through the front door of the house so that he could go to the door of his father's room. Outside this door, on a small cardboard notice, was the name 'H. Hayward Senior' and beside that was a ship's bell. Hammering on the door, George yelled out that it was time for the King's broadcast. No answer came from beyond the stout wood and so he tried the handle. The door was firmly bolted on the inside.

'Dad! Dad! I know you're in there!'

Silence greeted this and George was about to repeat the words when his eye spotted the bell. Amongst other irritating habits, Harry Hayward liked to be summoned by the ringing of the ship's bell. George obliged.

'Dad!'

'Who is it?' came the voice from inside.

'You know damn well who it is. The King's broadcast. Now, Dad! The King!'

'I don't need telling that. I have him in here on my set.'

'But we should listen together. It's history!'

'Aye!' came the cynical reply. 'If we listened together it *would* be history! Now go away, you hypocrite! Anti-monarchist! . . . Anti-Christ!'

George stifled an answer to this and swore under his breath instead before stamping off down the passage. Inside his room, Harry Hayward allowed himself a smirk of triumph and continued to fiddle with the knob of his ancient wireless.

'That wasn't very nice, Grandad,' protested the boy who was creaking to and fro in the rocking chair. 'What you called Dad just now—it wasn't very nice.'

'Happen it wasn't, Lovett, but it was true. You ask him. Listening to His Royal Highness when he'd abolish the monarchy given half a chance—that's hypocrisy, son . . . and when did he last go to church?'

'When did *you*, Grandad?'

Harry Hayward ignored this question and concentrated on trying to find the Home Service. A tall, thin, angular man, Harry had an almost cadaverous face with a lantern jaw, a long, sharp nose and two piercing and mobile eyes that made him look like a ferret trying to find its way out of a cage. Lovett was the member of the family with whom he felt most at home and with whom he wanted to share this very special moment. The boy, for his part, liked his grandfather enormously and enjoyed the indulgence shown towards him by a man that so many people found difficult and irascible.

'Got it!' said the old man as he tuned in to the right wavelength. He consulted his pocket watch. 'Just in time, too.'

He settled back in his battered armchair and felt for once at ease with the world. The small, cluttered, comfortable room was his haven and there was nowhere he would rather be at this time.

Along with millions of other people at home and abroad, and along with the rest of the Hayward family in the living room, he heard King George VI address the famous words and felt a tearful pride stirring inside him.

'Today we give thanks to God for a great deliverance. . . . Speaking from our Empire's oldest capital city, war-battered but never for one moment daunted or dismayed . . . speaking from London, I ask you to join me in that act of thanksgiving. . . .'

Around the wireless in the living room, Helen, Jean, Peg and Colin sat motionless. George was even starting to forget his heated exchange with his father.

'Germany, the enemy who drove all Europe into war, has been finally overcome. In the Far East we have yet to deal with the Japanese, a determined and cruel foe. To this we shall return with the utmost resolve and with all our resources. . . .'

Harry Hayward, blinking to conceal the watering of his eyes, pointed to a photograph in the newspaper that lay on the table beside him. Lovett picked the paper up and studied the picture of the King as his voice continued to reach out across the nation.

'But at this hour when the dreadful shadow of war has passed from our hearts and homes in these islands, we may at last make one pause for thanksgiving, and then turn our thoughts to the task all over the world which peace in Europe brings with it. . . .'

The next words brought a pang to all members of the Hayward family and made George turn involuntarily to his wife.

'Let us remember those who will not come back; their constancy and courage in battle, their sacrifice and endurance. . . .'

At the very moment that Owen Hayward was in the minds of everyone, when parents were remembering a son, when a wife was grieving for her husband, when a son was missing his father, and when grandfather, sister and brother were feeling the weight of their loss, the doorbell rang with an almost sacrilegious clarity. Peg Hayward was the first one to move.

'I'll get it,' she volunteered, racing to the door and inwardly cursing the caller. When she flung the front door open she was met by a well-set young man with a ready smile. 'Oh. . . .'

'My name is Warrington.'

'We're listening to the King!' she gabbled.

'Ah, well, look . . . in that case. . . .'

'You'd better come in,' she decided, tugging at his wrist. 'Quick. We don't want to miss it.'

'Er, no. . . .'

Mark Warrington crept into the living room as quietly and apologetically as he could and nodded at the four puzzled and upturned faces that greeted him. Quite by accident, his arm caught the edge of a tray that was standing on the table and he sent it clattering to the floor. Colin had a fit of the giggles and the others turned on him with one voice and silenced him as if he had been responsible for the outrage.

Seeing one empty upright chair, Mark edged towards it as the King's voice continued to speak its message. Before anyone could stop him, the newcomer lowered himself rather too heavily on to the

rickety chair and it promptly collapsed. Colin again responded with
a giggle and Mark himself, along with the others, had to make a
superhuman effort to control his own laughter as the King came to
the end of his speech.

'Let us thank Him for His mercies and in this hour of victory com-
mit ourselves and our new task to the guidance of that same strong
hand. . . .'

It was a fine garden, set out with Germanic precision, and its abun-
dant shrubs and bushes gave the woman a choice of hiding places
from which she could watch the house. A figure appeared at a ground
floor window and she ducked down even lower to avoid being seen.
The figure soon vanished only to reappear again almost at once in
the doorway that led to the garden. Unaware that he was the object
of such rapt attention, the man in the uniform of an English captain
strolled along the gravel path and hummed a tune to himself.

He seemed alert, happy, buoyant even, like someone who has just
bought a house that he cannot afford and who is still intoxicated by
his own daring. Compared to most of the places he had stayed at
recently, this place in the prosperous suburbs of a north German
town was nothing short of luxurious and he was determined to make
the most of the fact while he could. Ownership, however temporary,
was going to be enjoyed.

The man grinned as he noticed the goldfish in the pond and he
watched them for some while before continuing his search of the
garden. He took the path off to the left and the woman was seized
with alarm when she realized that he was heading in her direction.
In jerking herself back deeper into the bushes, she made a lot of noise
and felt sure that he must have heard it, but instead of coming on
towards her, he stopped and gazed back at the house from which a
voice was now hailing him.

'Blake! Blake, where are you!'

'Coming!'

When Blake Hayward entered the spacious living room, Waters,
another captain in the same unit, was looking around. He was duti-
fully impressed and rolled his eyes in satisfaction.

'Roberts found the billet for us,' explained Blake. 'Six bedrooms.
Just the two of us. I've chosen the one with the Wagnerian paintings
on the walls. I'm looking forward to some pleasantly erotic dreams.'

'You know what Churchill said, old chap. Facts are better than
dreams.'

'In the absence of facts, I mean.'

'They're not so absent any more,' said Waters with a chuckle.

'Hundreds of them, refugees, streaming down the road out there in flight from Ivan. Some magnificent Brunhilda types, all pure Aryan blood . . . cream of German society.' He sat in an armchair and shrugged. 'From what I hear that's all that's left.'

'Don't believe every rumour about the Ruskies.'

'I don't but this little piece of gossip comes from a pretty impeccable source. Ivan is no gentleman, you see. He has no respect for the ladies. . . .'

Blake wandered round the room until he came to the piano. Without sitting on the stool, he played a few bars of a popular song and then saw that Waters was treating him to the vacuous grin he reserved for most situations.

'You couldn't anyway, could you?' asked Blake. 'Not with your pure upbringing. Eton, was it—or Harrow—or both?'

'Couldn't do what?'

'Pretend to save some innocent victim from rape by the Russian bear and then enjoy the spoils of war yourself.'

'I bet *you* wouldn't bloody hesitate!'

'It's my peasant upbringing,' taunted the other.

Waters had known and liked Blake for a long time but he did not begin to understand him. One minute the man was boasting about his working class background yet the next he was playing the piano or quoting poetry. It was as if Blake was trying to ape the manners and the surface culture of the people he claimed to despise. Waters had thus been both the butt of his humour and the object of sneaking admiration.

'What will you do after the war, Blake?' he said.

'Take over from you lot. You remind me of a character I met the other day, from home. . . . What do you upper crust left wingers *want*? You're like Orwell. . . . You're after expiation for the mess that your class have made of it in the last twenty years.'

'That's part of it, maybe,' admitted Waters, candidly.

'Come the end of the war, mate, and *I* take over the reins. . . . Hey, but it *has* ended,' he said, as if he had realized it for the first time. 'It has. All over. No more battles. We survived.' He crossed to the window and stared out. 'So quiet out there—there's a kind of death out there. A stillness.'

He tried to jolt himself out of this mood by thinking of the celebrations that must be going on at home. He talked wistfully about all the girls in search of a last fling with a uniform.

'And here we are stuck in this bloody monastery!'

'There's always Brunhilda,' reminded Waters.

'Sod Brunhilda! Strictly verboten, anyway. She'll have to

learn to love Jerry in his socks by the light of burning jackboots.'

Waters asked which bedroom was his and Blake offered to show him around upstairs so that he could choose. As soon as they had gone off upstairs, the woman came in silently from the garden. She looked around apprehensively and then crossed the living room with easy familiarity before straightening the ornaments on the mantelpiece. Tired and dishevelled, she looked a lot older than her twenty-five years, though her fatigue had not entirely drained her face of its beauty.

She stood in front of the fireplace as if not quite knowing what to do and then her attention was caught by something on the table. It was a gun. On a suicidal impulse she moved forward to take the revolver from the holster but a sound disturbed her and she froze in her tracks. Unable either to grab the weapon or make a run for it, she could only stand there as Blake Hayward came back into the room for his things.

He stopped short when he saw her and their eyes met.

## CHAPTER TWO

Staying in the shadow of the massive sea wall, they walked slowly up the beach, their footprints clear and regular in the wet sand. The tide was going out now and it had left a small selection of driftwood, seaweed, crabs, bottles and soggy cardboard along the shoreline. Peg turned back and called out to the boy who was still splashing about happily in the water.

'We'll have to go back soon, Col! We're going to Uncle Don's street party!'

Colin Hayward was enjoying himself far too much to pay any attention to this. Hitching up the thick, grey swimming trunks that had been knitted for him by his grandmother, he ran straight at an oncoming wave and dived into it.

'He loves it out there,' said Peg, stepping out into the bright sunlight. 'Goes deaf when I tell him it's time to leave. Col is awkward— just like Grandad.'

Mark Warrington was still fascinated by the sea wall, thousands of enormous concrete blocks, put there a hundred years before to protect Whitstanton's iron mines.

'Yes. They built it to keep the sea out.' Peg recalled the incident with the broken chair and wanted to laugh at him. Instead, she said, 'I thought you lived around here.'

'My mother has lived up the coast for a while. . . . I've only been there a couple of times. When I was much younger. . . .'

'So this has all got novelty value?' she teased.

'I just never realized it was like this. Almost as if you had your own private beach. Lovely here. . . .'

'Oh yes! Especially when the blast furnaces get going across the bay in Barrow there. Not to mention the noise from the ironworks itself, and the muck, and the stink, and the stuff they dump in the sea . . . it's lovely!'

Mark liked the pleasant sarcasm of her tone and the cheerful rancour that seemed to lie behind many of her remarks. She reminded him of Blake Hayward and as he stole a look now at her attractive, round face he could see distinct points of resemblance, not least in the hard line of her mouth. He was very grateful to Peg for the way that she had come to his rescue. When he had arrived in Whitstanton that morning he had been annoyed to learn that his mother had in fact gone to London, and so he had pressed on to the Hayward house. It was Peg who had invited him in, and helped him up when the chair had collapsed, and made him a cup of weak tea, and generally taken responsibility for him; and it was she who had asked him to join her for a stroll along the beach while she was looking after Colin.

'It was good of you to come,' she said. 'Meant a lot to Mum. Blake is her favourite—not that she'd admit it. But he is.'

'There are six of you altogether, aren't there?'

'There were. Me and five brothers. Blake you've met, of course. Ramsey died years ago—scarlet fever. Keir's in the R.A.F. Lovett, whom you'll meet later, is the baby of the family. Just twelve. We pull his leg because he's Col's uncle yet he's only two years older than him.' A frown creased her forehead as she looked at the boy who was playing among the waves. 'Col is Owen's son, you see.'

'Owen?'

'He was in the Regular Army. At Singapore. . . .'

'Oh. Was he taken prisoner?'

'Supposed to have been—and that was bad enough. We've heard some of the stories about the Japs. . . . Then they said he was presumed dead. We kept hoping for a long time but . . . well, there's a limit. Jean took it very hard. . . . Owen was great! He was . . . just great!'

'*Your* favourite?'

'Maybe,' she conceded. 'He wasn't a bit like you. Owen was big, full of life, always talking, joking. . . .' Peg smiled at him. 'You're a shy one, aren't you?'

'Am I?'

George Hayward was cleaning his shoes with a cloth when his wife came into the kitchen and asked where the visitor had gone.

'Sergeant!' he muttered. 'A Warrington. I expected a major at least. He must be the black sheep of the family.'

'I'm sure he isn't,' she said, defensively.

'I meant it as a compliment, woman.'

Helen moved to the sink and ran some water into the enamel bowl. Mark's visit had nudged her thoughts.

'They'd have been married now, probably, if it'd not been for the war. . . . Blake, Keir. . . . We've all that to come.'

'Don't expect it all at once, love. Life won't get better overnight, you know.'

'My sons'll come home. I can wait for the rest.'

She turned off the tap and then looked up as Harry Hayward came wandering in. George carried on as if he had not noticed his father.

'Might take time. The war in the Far East's still to win. Said so on the wireless. The R.A.F. won't let Keir go till that's over and done with.'

'Blake should get his discharge soon, though.'

'Happen.'

'June Kelly's daughter's back already—the one that went into the Nursing Reserve.'

'Yes, they'll want the nurses back in the hospitals to get this Beveridge Plan working.' He nodded towards his father. 'The one *he's* waiting for.'

'Me?' Harry sounded offended.

'Hanging on to your teeth like grim death you are. If they fell out you'd stick 'em back in with glue—pending Beveridge.'

'Country can't afford it!' moaned the old man.

'You'll be first in the queue, you know damn well you will. But the Tories only pay lip service to Beveridge. Doubt if we shall have it if they get in.'

'As they will!' predicted Harry with unassailable confidence. 'The country would never turn its back on Churchill after what he's brought us through!'

'He's not brought us through it to end up back where we come from—riches for the few and idleness and poverty for the many! Churchill's got the same old gang round him. Same hard faces. Remind me of yours, some of 'em!'

'George!' reprimanded his wife.

'I'd sooner have this clock of mine than look like that Stafford Cripps,' said Harry, his temper up now. 'Do you know what Churchill said of *him*?'

'Lads'll not have it! Lads that've fought'll not have it!'

'Don't shout, George.'

'They won't, Helen. Not them that went to war like so much skin and bone from years of deprivation . . . fetched off the scrap heap to fight for the country that put 'em there.'

'Aye, and what's the first thing they'll want?' asked Harry, waving a skeletal finger in the air. 'To be free. It's what we all want. We put our freedom in pawn while we fought for it. Now we want it redeemed. . . . We'll not be kept in chains by the likes of you.'

'And you call yourself a working man!' sneered his son.

'I worked free—not in chains!'

'You were chained to poverty for most of your working life!'

'I worked *free*!' insisted Harry with great dignity, and then he went out of the door. 'Free . . . free I worked. . . .'

George Hayward sat down heavily in the chair and ran a hand through his hair. He was annoyed both with his father and with himself and the expression on his wife's face told him that she understood this only too well.

'Take that bottle to him now,' she counselled.

'Nay. . . .'

'You'll have no peace with yourself if you don't. . . .'

George spoke softly but there was a wealth of bitterness behind his words. Helen listened in silence, trying not to take sides. That would be fatal.

'I can remember when I was a lad like our Lovett, seeing him come home worn out from working for a pittance . . . and he damns *me* for giving myself to socialism! I did it for him. I did it for him and yet it's come between us. . . . *Why?*'

'Go to him, George. It's the only way.'

He sat there quietly for a moment and then got up and crossed to the cupboard. Reaching inside he took out a bottle of whisky and stared at it blankly. He became aware that Helen was still watching him and he went quickly out, almost colliding with Jean who came bustling in. Jean had brushed her hair, done her make-up and put on her smartest dress.

'I thought you'd gone,' said Helen.

'They're just bringing Colin back. Saw them through the window. I'll get him ready before I go.'

'You could always take him with you.'

'To meet Ernst?' She was surprised that Helen should suggest such a thing. 'Well. . . .'

'They've got to meet some time.'

'You wouldn't mind?'

There was something very endearing in the tentative way that Jean asked this and Helen felt an upsurge of affection for her. If her daughter-in-law had a chance of happiness with another man, she wanted to do everything she could to help her.

'Why should I mind?' she said, briskly. 'Let's make this a good day, shall we? A new start. . . .'

Harry Hayward sat at the table in his room and pored over a navigation chart, ignoring the polite knock on his door and not even glancing up when, in deference to his own request, the knock was followed by the ringing of the ship's bell. His eyes remained fixed on the chart as George came up behind him and he was clearly not going to make it easy for his son.

'We've got to learn to live together, Dad. . . .'

Harry Hayward made a curious derisory noise through his teeth and began to search for a compass on the table. George tried to find the words that would get through to the old man and he decided to use some of those employed in the King's speech.

'Like he said . . . we must do nothing unworthy of them that died for us . . . to make a world as they would have wanted for their kids and ours.' When his father replied with the same noise again, George stiffened. 'I didn't catch that. . . .'

'I said I'm over seventy and I know more about life than you young 'uns though you live to be a hundred. . . . Now, south-west to where ironworks chimney comes in line with shipyard towards. . . .'

'Eh?'

'I'm plotting a course to Silport.'

'You can't take the boat out!'

'War's over, isn't it?'

'Estuary'll not be free to us for months. A year or more, even.'

'It'll never be free if your lot get in. . . . Why the hold up? There's been no mines laid on this coast. Beaches is clear apart from them towards t'range.'

'Not officially clear.'

'I don't recognize officials. Canutes!'

'Now, Dad. . . .'

'They're Canutes! They stand there telling the tide to go back would officials, and prove that it had been done on paper. With their trouser legs rolled right up!'

He turned to face George for the first time and saw the bottle of whiskey. He slipped on his spectacles and then looked at the label over the top of them. A whistle of admiration followed and he moved the back of his hand across his lips.

'Had it put by for months,' explained George.

'Liquid gold!' Harry chuckled, enjoying his joke before he had even told it. 'Heard about the chap that got a bottle of whisky from under the counter at the Club? On his way home he had a nasty fall. Puts his hand down, feels his leg—wet! Gets his torch out to have a proper look and says: "Thank God––it's blood".'

'It's for you,' said George, offering him the bottle. 'To celebrate. It's a great day, Dad . . . let's not sour it.'

Harry Hayward took the bottle from him and inspected it more carefully. He teased his son for taking advantage of a black market that the latter had always spoken about with contempt, though he knew that George would never really have done that. What amazed him was how George had restrained himself from drinking the bottle himself.

'What did you swap for it?'

'Half my clothing coupons. Never make full use of 'em, anyway. . . . This damn house takes any spare cash we've got. Falling to pieces. Gutters rotting, window bottoms, perished brickwork . . . as for paint, *this* stuff's easier to get.'

'When do you think they'll bring petrol ration back?' asked Harry, eagerly.

'Forget about the boat, Dad.'

'It were all I looked forward to when I retired, that boat. Could have made myself useful if they'd let me. I'd have gone to Dunkirk if I'd had the petrol.'

'You'd have just about made it for D Day in that. . . .'

The joke gave them both an excuse to laugh and a tacit truce was declared. Lovett came in to tell his grandfather that they were all ready to go off to the town but Harry was in no mood to watch the celebrations. He announced that he would polish the engine on his boat instead and Lovett asked if he could help him. Pleased that he was at least back on speaking terms with his father, George Hayward took his leave before this fragile situation was put to any real test. Lovett, a lively and interested boy, stared at the navigation chart and scratched his head.

'Pity we can't actually start the engine up, Grandad.'

'Of course, you've never been out there, have you? I'd forgotten that, lad. . . . Oh, it's a different world out there, away from the rubbish in life. We shall be off, you and me, when petrol comes back. . . .'

He looked down at the bottle of whisky that was still in his hand and a glint came into his eye.

Blake Hayward was doodling at the piano in the lounge when Waters came in with a wooden box that was packed to capacity.

'Where've you been? Looting?'

'Negotiating with Roberts. . . . Don't seem to be any official celebrations so I thought we'd have our own little party here. Got plenty of goodies, and a few bottles.' He put the box down on the polished surface of the oak table. 'Where is she?'

'In my room.'

'My God! You don't hang around, do you!'

'She's in—I'm out. Seems that room belonged to her, anyway. I had no right to pick that one so I moved out. Like the perfect English gentleman I am.' He laughed then added, 'I've not only adopted your accent: I've adopted your tactics as well. Before the attack, appear to drop your defences.'

'Has she been any more forthcoming—conversationally?'

'The only words she seems to use are Ja and Nein. With an eye on the future, I pretended not to notice the difference.' He ran his finger up the scale and grinned wickedly. 'What's the German for "Thanks very much, love"?'

'Why did she come back, that's what I can't understand? Maybe there's someone hidden in the attic. A husband, possibly . . . Colonel in the S.S.'

'It'd go with the house,' agreed Blake. 'I mean, you'd have to be one of the party faithful to hang on to a place like this. I'm surprised there isn't a shrine to the Fuhrer. As for some high-ranking Jerry crouched high in the rafters. . . .'

'Shall we take a look?'

'Yes. Never relax, that's the secret. Had an uneasy feeling round about the middle of my back ever since we were told it was over. It's always that last stray shot across no-man's-land that gets you.' He lifted his fingers from the keys and looked at them carefully. 'Did you know that Ramsden lost both his eyes in that last tank battle?'

Waters nodded and Blake brought his hands down on to the keys in anger. Ramsden had been a friend of his and yet another of the thousands of incidental casualties of the last days of a long war. He tried to cheer himself up by congratulating himself on having found such a luxurious house for them but Waters told him they might not be staying there for long. The 11th Armoured Division, it appeared, were on the Russian side of the Yalta line and might soon have to pull back to make way for their Allies from the East. Neither man was impressed by what they had heard about the Russian treatment of prisoners and German civilians.

Herta Wenkel appeared at the door, looking much smarter and

more composed now: there was a kind of subdued arrogance in her gaze. When she turned it on Blake he felt quite guilty and closed the lid of the piano.

'I'm sorry. I should have asked permission.'

'Why?' she shrugged. 'You have won the war. Everything we have is yours to grab now.'

'It's not quite like that,' reassured Waters with bland smoothness. 'Not really.'

'It will be the same as after the last war. After Versailles. You took seven million people from us. And billions of pounds in reparations.'

'That was to stop another war,' reminded Blake.

'It gave us inflation and unemployment . . . out of that, to save us, came the Fuhrer . . . with him came the war you wanted to stop. . . .' There was a firm, accusatory note in her voice now. 'So much for your gift to us from Versailles.'

'And what about the concentration camps?' demanded Blake, getting up from the piano stool. 'Or maybe you haven't heard about those yet. Gas chambers to destroy people, ovens to burn them . . . factories for mass murder! Were *they* our gift from Versailles?'

'I know of no such places,' she murmured, avoiding his eyes.

'For your sake, I hope that's true,' he said. Then he relaxed and beckoned her into the room. 'We're all a bit tense at the moment . . . thanks to your Fuhrer I've been away from home for over four years . . . so has Waters here. One day we shall have to talk about these things. Not now.'

'Better to play the piano, you think?' she asked. 'You play well for an English gentleman. I heard.' Blake started to laugh. 'I have said something funny?'

'It's just that I'm not what I appear. They ran out of officer class, you see. That's how I came to be in this uniform. It's not part of my birthright as it is for old Waters here. . . .'

'Oh crap, Blake!'

'Now he's the genuine article; a pukka English gentleman educated at Eton. That's where the war was won: on the jolly old playing fields of Eton.'

'Crap!' Waters sat on the arm of a chair and grew nostalgic. 'I'd love to be back in England now. They'll be hanging on the lamp posts outside Buckingham Palace.'

Fearing that she had just heard of some dreadful war atrocity, Herta started forward in disbelief.

'They are hanging people outside Buckingham Palace?'

Both men tried to hold in their laughter but it would not be controlled and they were soon screaming hysterically. Hurt and insulted,

Herta turned on her heel and stalked out of the room. The men were sorry they had upset her but it did not stop them laughing their fill and releasing some of the tensions that had built up during the earlier argument with her. When their mirth had completely subsided they looked up to see that she was standing in the doorway, her anger gone, her manner polite, almost ingratiating. She glanced down at the food and drink in the wooden box.

'For our little party,' said Waters. 'We thought . . . Blake and I . . . in the circumstances. . . .'

'If there is anything I have in the house, please use it. There is not much left in the kitchen but . . . it is yours.' She was quite cowed now, all trace of her earlier tired aggression having gone. 'I am sorry for what I say about Versailles.'

'Forget it,' suggested Blake.

Herta Wenkel did not even hear him. There was a note of desperation in her voice now and the words tumbled out of her, apologizing, explaining, justifying, almost as if she felt she were on trial for the crimes of her country.

'It is not for me to sneer at you about Versailles. You have won: we have lost. Everything is yours. . . . Three weeks ago I went to Berlin because I had had no news from my father. . . . The destruction was terrible. Street after street, not as here. . . . In Potsdamer Platz the tanks and trucks were driving over dead people. German people. . . . My father's flat had been destroyed . . . he is probably dead. No old person could live through that horror. Many times in the queue for bread, women . . . children . . . next to me were shot by planes or by snipers . . . and other people took their places in the queue! Over the bodies . . . we queued to get bread . . . I was wrong about the Führer . . . he did *not* save us. I spit on him . . . see, I spit. . . .' She spat at the floor and then shook as she realized the enormity of what she had done. Still trembling, she continued her story. 'Women and children sheltered in the subway tunnels . . . engineers flooded the tunnels because they thought the Russians would come in through them . . . the women and children were drowned . . . you could see them through the shell holes in the street . . . layers deep . . . floating.' She put her hands to her eyes as if to block out the vision, then she became ingratiating again and scuttled to the fireplace. 'I have a few things. I hid them. You shall have. . . .' She reached up the chimney and brought out a bundle wrapped in cloth and covered in soot. 'It is yours . . . take it, please. . . .'

'But we have some,' said Waters.

'Look, Frau Wenkel. . . .' began Blake.

'Please!' she begged. 'You listen . . . you understand. . . .' She sank wearily down to the carpet. 'My husband died over a year ago in Russia . . . at the end his letters were unbearable . . . without any hope. . . .' She lifted up the bundle. 'This was his . . . and this watch I wear. . . .' Her eyes filmed over and she started to tremble again. 'In Berlin . . . we went on queueing over dead bodies . . . queueing for bread. . . . I have not eaten food for three days. . . . Why do I not want food? . . . Food is life. . . . I should want life? Please . . . tell me . . . why should *I* want life?'

It was a cry of pain and neither man was able to answer it.

Whitstanton, in common with everywhere else in Great Britain, was determined to erase the memory of six long, lean years in one glorious day of eating, drinking, singing, dancing, shouting, laughing and general abandon. The drab face of the iron town had been brightened out of all recognition by flags and bunting and posters and banners. Down streets that were a riot of colour, a raucous brass band led a happy crowd of people and blared out the message of victory with its stirring music. The sense of joy and release and celebration was overwhelming. Children played games and wore party hats, wives and mothers talked proudly of absent husbands and sons who would soon return, civic dignitaries made speeches, old heroes of the Great War looked out tattered medals to pin on the lapels of their Sunday suits, and even the cats and dogs shared in the explosion of fun and good humour.

The war in Europe was triumphantly over and the town of Whitstanton was able to remind itself, in the best possible way, that it was also a close-knit and warm-hearted community.

'Come on, Peg. Dance. . . .'

'Love to. . . .'

'This way, then. . . .'

Peg Hayward and her partner, a young mineworker whose job had helped him to miss the call-up, were soon dancing a kind of improvised jig with the other couples to some scratchy music from an old gramophone. As Mark Warrington watched her leaping about between the trestle tables that ran down the street, he wished that he had had the courage to ask her to dance or the simple ability to let himself go in the way that everyone else was managing to do. Fascinated by all that was going on and moved by the sight of so much collective enjoyment, he could not somehow become part of it and settled instead for being a sort of privileged spectator.

'When I came back home after the last lot in 1918, I couldn't settle at all. . . .' George Hayward had joined him on the fringe of the celebrations. 'I'd changed more than people I came back to had. There was a gap between me and those who hadn't been. . . .'

'Like a class difference, you mean?'

'Aye, you could say that, I suppose,' replied George, after giving him a shrewd look. 'Be the same with Blake, I daresay. A big change. His letters don't tell us much. Only writes to keep his mother happy. I've missed him. We were just beginning to understand one another, I think. . . .'

'I didn't see much of my parents before the war. I went to boarding school. I do hope we've seen the last of that pre-war world.'

'What do you want—a land fit for heroes?'

'I'll settle for a land fit for ordinary, decent people,' said Mark with emphasis, 'and damn the old order!'

'You'd not get ideas like that at boarding school,' noted George, warming to the other for the first time.

'Nor at home. They won't take me seriously, of course. They'll put it down to the war, I daresay . . . delayed adolescence . . . one of the stages to pass through before coming round to seeing it their way. . . . Well, you know the saying, Mr Hayward: "Breathes there a man with soul so dead, who wasn't in the Thirties, Red".'

'They'll be fond of you, though, your parents. . . . Maybe it's better to agree to disagree than live in a house where the doors are slamming all the time . . . not to mention bells ringing!' He broke off to watch the street party which was still in full swing, then turned back. 'What's it like in Europe?'

'Terrible, in Germany . . . waste, devastation, suffering . . . millions of people with nowhere to go to. They brought it on themselves, mark you.'

'Yes,' agreed George. 'They let it happen. It's the few that does it but the many that lets it happen. . . . We've never known that here. Defeat . . . occupation . . . hope to God we never do!'

Mark Warrington looked at all the people who were still so totally absorbed in the celebrations and nodded a silent endorsement.

Sitting in the bows of the small dinghy, Lovett Hayward enjoyed the feel of the spray on his face as the craft moved steadily towards the horizon. Harry Hayward sat at the tiller and followed a course that he had plotted a hundred times in his room back at the house. The sense of freedom that he now had was quite exhilarating and he was delighted to be able to share it with his grandson. This great, open world of the sea was his world and he had been separated from it for far too long.

'What do you reckon to it, then, Lovett?'

'Bang on, Grandad!'

'Bang on!' snorted the old man. 'Bang on! What the hell kind of language is that?'

It's what Keir kept saying when he joined the R.A.F.'

'I know what he said, lad, but I've not a damn clue what he meant by it.'

'He meant . . . well, bang on! Wizard!' Lovett put a hand over the side and let it trail through the salt water. Then he sat up again as if he had come to an important decision. 'I should have liked to have gone into the R.A.F.'

'Thank God you've been spared.'

'You believe in God, don't you, Grandad?' asked the boy, almost chirpily.

'Aye, I do that. And Satan, and Hell Fire, and Damnation . . . angels and archangels . . . Sodom and Gomorrah . . . the ten commandments and the King's Own Yorkshire Light Infantry!'

Carried away by the sheer sound of the words, Harry Hayward had missed hearing another sound. While he had been speaking, the inboard engine had faltered and died.

'The engine's stopped, Grandad.'

'Aye . . . so it has, Lovett.'

He looked back towards the shore but it now seemed to be a very long way off.

The oval mahogany dining table was set for three and a single candle burned in a holder in the middle of it. Blake and Herta were already seated when Waters, in chatty mood, brought in a tray of food and put it down in front of them with mock servility. His casual reference to a family cook was seized upon by Blake who teased him once more about his moneyed background. The banter was interrupted by the sound of shots being fired quite close to the house and both men rushed to the window. When the shooting stopped and they could see nothing outside, they relaxed and decided there was no cause for alarm. Their celebratory meal could continue.

What they now saw shocked them. Herta Wenkel, racked by hunger, had fallen on the food and started to devour it like some ravenous animal. She became aware that they were watching her and she paused while they sat down at the table; but her needs were too strong and she immediately grabbed more food, thrusting it into her mouth with a desperate greed.

Water lapped at the sides of the dinghy as it drifted helplessly out to sea, its occupants all too aware of the fact that it would soon be dark. Harry Hayward was pleased that his grandson had shown no signs of fear and he made sure that he concealed his own worries.

'Your Dad'll give me some stick for bringing you out here. . . .'

'I'll tell him I stowed away,' said the boy with a grin of loyalty. 'You and Dad argue a lot, don't you?'

'Can't deny it, Lovett. . . . He's an idealist, is your Dad. Believes in a better world. . . .'

'Don't you, Grandad?'

'Aye, but it's far removed from this vale o' tears. Heaven on earth? Not in my lifetime. . . . Only heaven I know's up there. In't sky.'

'What's that over there?' asked the boy, pointing back towards the now distant shore. 'Are them flames?'

'They've lit a bonfire in Whitstanton . . . to burn Adolf Hitler on. . . . Best place for him, too!'

'I wish I was there,' confessed Lovett.

'Shame on you, lad! What's wrong with out here?'

The boy was now openly afraid and looked small and vulnerable as he gazed at the expanse of water all around them.

'I don't want to go to heaven just yet, Grandad. . . .'

'We shall not go just yet,' promised Harry with a gruff defiance. 'I'm not in what you might call a state of readiness myself. Any rate, I'm not sure it'll be heaven . . . a stoker in t'other place more like . . . that's what I'm trained for. . . .'

Lovett took some comfort from this and stayed huddled up in the bows, searching the horizon in the falling dusk for the sign of another craft. Harry's eyes were alert, too, and he watched and hoped until the darkness began to black out everything.

'Shall we light the lamp now, Grandad?' asked Lovett.

'Aye . . . aye, I shall light it now, lad. . . .'


While Harry Hayward and his grandson put their faith in the dim glow of an acetylene lamp, the people of Whitstanton threw cardboard and timber on to a fire that was lighting up the sky for a mile or more. A crude effigy of Hitler, complete with manic stare and toothbrush moustache, was thrown into the heart of the blaze, its arm raised stiffly in the notorious Nazi salute, its thin uniform of sacking covered in swastikas yielding at once to the lick of the flames. The crowd danced and cheered loudly, then broke into a song that was set to the tune of 'Run, Rabbit, Run, Rabbit, Run, Run, Run. . . .'

'Burn, Adolf, burn, Adolf, burn, burn, burn. . . .

Burn, Adolf, burn, Adolf, burn, burn, burn. . . .

We'll get by without your evil eye

So—burn, Adolf, burn, Adolf, burn, burn, burn. . . .'

Mark Warrington found himself mouthing the words and he joined in the redoubled cheers when the effigy suddenly lurched backwards and vanished into the fire. Peg Hayward came and stood beside him watching the blaze. It triggered off some memories for her and she talked with real feeling.

'Remember when the Nazis burned the books before the war? . . . I'd just left school then and started at the library. . . . Dad was a Pacifist in those days. . . . I thought we were going to have an awful row about it but he wouldn't even talk about it. . . . I think that's when he changed, Dad. . . . I had a row with my brother, Keir, instead. Keir didn't change until the Germans ratted on Stalin. The Russians were on our side then. It was all right after that. War against Hitler fitted the party line. . . .'

'Your mother asked me to see you home,' he said.

'Charming! I'm to have a military escort now!'

Mark felt that he had been put in an embarrassing position but there was no help for that. While Peg was dancing earlier on in the day, he had overheard her parents talking about her and could appreciate their concern.

'They've told you, obviously,' said Peg with a slight edge. 'I'm supposed to be "delicate".'

'Your father mentioned some . . . heart complaint.'

'I had scarlet fever when my brother did. Ramsey died of it and I was left with this.' She waved an arm dismissively. 'Mum and Dad make far too much of it.'

'They care for you,' he reminded her.

'I bet that your parents don't coddle you.'

'No, they don't as a matter of fact. They never have. They just dumped me at school and left me to survive. . . . I was ready for the army . . . those iron beds . . . the life you live in your head when the talking stops after the lights go out . . . the dark. . . .'

Peg was surprised that he said this without any trace of bitterness or reproach.

The meal was over now and Herta Wenkel was sitting calm and upright in her chair. Blake and Waters had drunk enough to grow lazily argumentative.

'You're quite wrong, Waters, old chap!'

'I'm right, Blake. You know I am!'

'Okay, you're right, you're right,' he conceded, mimicking the other's accent. 'Who am I to argue with a public school education?'

'We don't have to bring that in, surely? The war's put an end to all that.'

'Like hell it has!' retorted Blake, reaching for the bottle.

'Don't you think you've had enough wine as it is?'

'Now that's one thing *I* can decide for myself, mate. . . . The Ruskies are not here yet.'

An awkward pause followed as he remembered that Herta was still with them and he glanced across at her guiltily. She shrugged her shoulders with a philosophical resignation and then gazed down at the remains of the meal quite wistfully.

'He came on leave, my husband, in the good times . . . when the Russians were retreating and it seemed nothing could stop us from reaching Moscow . . . we sat here often, with friends, dining . . . good times. . . .'

There was a loud knock on the door and Waters went out to see who it was, excusing himself as he got up from the table. Herta continued as if she was not aware of the interruption.

'It was very civilized . . . here with friends . . . but how strange it must have seemed to my husband . . . he had seen what I now have seen . . . worse. . . . He spoke of whole Russian villages left to starve in the advance . . . and of other things. . . . He was ashamed. . . . They shot Russian partisans out of hand . . . no prisoners were taken. . . . Then one day they came to where the Russians had caught our own troops . . . had stripped them naked in the snow except for their helmets . . . had poured water over them until they froze in a solid block of ice. . . .' She looked up at Blake. 'Hate breeds hate, is that not so . . . it gets worse and worse . . . is that not so?' She got up as Waters came back into the room. 'I am glad that my husband was ashamed. . . .'

Herta Wenkel stood there erect for a moment then, looking softly at Blake, mumbled her thanks for the food and went off to bed. Blake now got to his feet and stifled a yawn.

'I think I'll get my head down, too.'

'Good luck!' grinned Waters.

'With *her*? Good God—what do you take me for man? She's not the type, anyway.'

'Smitten?' wondered the other, with surprise.

'I don't propose to behave like our glorious Allies, that's all. She's perfectly safe with me.'

'Not for long, Blake.'

'What?'

'That was Roberts at the door. We're pulling back to a new line, eventually, to let the Ruskies in.'

Blake swallowed hard and looked involuntarily upwards, thinking of what the future might hold for their dinner guest. Waters had no difficulty reading his mind.

'I'm sorry but it's a face now . . . not just a fear. . . .'

Harry Hayward was singing his way through all his favourite hymns in order to keep up his spirits and those of the boy who was now fast asleep at his feet. The lamp was burning low, the night was chill and the darkness began to seem menacing. Harry reached out to touch the boy's head.

'We'll be okay when dawn comes, Lovett. Don't worry, lad. . . . He'll see us right. . . . He's up there, watching over us. . . . He won't let us down. . . .'

He started to sing another hymn but his voice was cracked and his throat sore. Making himself more comfortable, therefore, he offered up a silent prayer and then closed his heavy-lidded eyes, dozing off almost at once.

'Where d'you think tha's bound, Harry, lad?' called a voice, strangely amplified in the dark.

'Is it thee, Lord?' asked Harry, waking up.

'Nay, it's Bill Withers, coastguard, here. . . . Don't you know there's a bloody war on!'

## CHAPTER THREE

Mark Warrington slept soundly that night and awoke shortly after dawn to find himself in an unfamiliar bedroom that was in need of decorating. He lay there for a while studying the patch on the ceiling discoloured by damp and taking his bearings. Then he heard flapping noises and a sustained burst of clucking. When he got out of bed and crossed to the window, he saw something that made him dress quickly and go straight down to the garden, though he did not yet understand the impulse behind it all.

Peg Hayward was still scattering the hen feed about as he came out of the house buttoning up his shirt cuffs. For someone who was supposed to be delicate, she looked remarkably healthy and spry and she treated him to a broad, wide-awake grin.

'Do you always get up this early?' he asked.

'Someone has to feed this lot and collect the eggs.' She finished sprinkling the grain about and crossed over to him. 'Longest day of the year very soon. Did you know that?'

'June's my favourite month,' he announced.

Peg had the feeling that if it had been darkest December, he would have described that as his favourite month as well. For some reason, Mark was as shy and nervous with her as ever.

'I hope they didn't mind me dropping in yesterday,' he continued. 'I didn't expect to stay here, you know. I meant to spend the night at mother's place.'

'That was your own fault,' she scolded, smiling.

'Why?'

'Telling Mum that your family was away. She wouldn't let you stay in that house on your own. That's why she made a bed up for you here. She looks upon you as one of us now.'

'Does she?' He sounded honoured.

'Yes, you can do no wrong here, Sergeant Warrington. You went out of your way to call in at our humble abode and bring her news of her son in Germany. Even if you did roll up bang in the middle of the King's speech.'

'I've never forgiven myself for that.'

'It had its compensations. . . .'

'Yes,' he agreed, not realizing that she was laughing at him. 'I was able to stay and join in the celebrations at Whitstanton. That was a marvellous day for me. Not just because it was V.E.-Day, I mean but because . . . well, I just loved all that.'

'Good. . . .' The urge to tease him was irresistible. 'And it was so kind of you to find the time to pop in here to see Mum yet again on your way back off leave. . . .'

'Well, to be perfectly frank. . . .'

'Go on.'

'It wasn't exactly on the way.'

'Now that you mention it, I couldn't quite work out how we came to be situated between Euston and Victoria Station. I've always believed we were somewhere in Cumberland.'

'You are, Peg,' he said, experiencing a slight thrill at simply using her name.

'Yet your mother was in London. . . .'

'Yes, well . . . I mean, I just wanted to see you all again . . . if you understand me. . . .'

'See us all?' she repeated, raising an eyebrow.

'That's right.' He became conscious of the fact that he had not washed or shaved and ran a hand across his chin. 'See you . . . all.'

Peg resisted the temptation to tease him again and instead looked over his shoulder towards the beach. In the distance she saw a figure moving steadily in the direction of the house.

'I'm supposed to have very good eyesight,' she boasted. 'Better than yours, I daresay. See that man on the beach?'

Mark turned around and scanned the horizon but there was not a soul in sight now. The man had gone behind the sea wall, but he refused to believe her.

'You're pulling my leg, aren't you?'

'I'm not, Mark, but I could . . . easily. You're so shy sometimes.'

'The first time I came here you said that.'

'It's true. When you're with me, anyway. . . . You shouldn't be, you know.' She touched his arm lightly. 'Life's very short. . . .'

Hidden from view by the bulk of the sea wall, Ernst Sevcenko walked happily along over the sand, enjoying the early morning sounds and taking in deep draughts of air to fill his lungs. Ernst was a swarthy, thick-set man with dark eyes and a strong, lined face. Suffering and anxiety had added ten years to his appearance and he looked almost middle-aged, but his gait was sprightly and a safer guide to his age. As he headed up the beach he thought he heard something approaching and his cheerful expression vanished at once to be replaced by a taut, frightened look. He flattened himself against the sea wall and did not dare to breathe as the sound came closer and closer and identified itself as an aircraft flying low over the bay.

Ernst watched and waited until it had gone past and then he lifted his arm slowly and began to beat it hard against the wall. Then he started to relax and relief brought an almost manic laugh out of him.

'Fool!' he yelled. 'Idiot! Fool! The war is over! Is finished now! The war is over!' He began to repeat it all over again in his native Ukrainian tongue as if that gave it an added authority. 'War is over . . . is over. . . .'

He felt tears of joy trickling down his cheeks.

'You were right,' said Mark, hearing the yells. 'There is someone there. Shouting his head off.'

'They're like that, Ukrainians. Excitable. It's how they express themselves.'

'Ukrainians? You couldn't possibly tell that he was talking in Ukrainian at this distance.'

'Didn't I tell you? I have very good hearing as well. Not to mention an intuitive grasp of languages.' She laughed at his bafflement and explained. 'I was cheating. I know who he is.'

'Ah. . . .'

'He walks five miles here every morning from the P.O.W. Camp down the coast. Just to meet a lady. There's devotion for you.'

Mark's mouth went dry when she told him this and jaw sagged. He had jumped to a conclusion that seemed self-evident to him. Peg rescued him from the mistake.

'It's not *me*, Mark. Heavens, no. All I manage to inspire is shyness, not devotion. . . . It's Jean, my brother's wife. They both work at a farm down the coast.'

'Brother's wife? I still get them mixed up. Is it Keir?'

'No—it's Owen.'

'Of course. Owen. Your favourite. He was in Singapore.'

Peg nodded, pleased that he had remembered now and no longer denying the fact that Owen Hayward had been her favourite of the five brothers. She missed him more than Jean did in some ways and he always returned to her thoughts sooner or later. After all this time, the sense of loss was like a physical pain.

'Yes. Owen was killed in the first year of the war. Dear Owen. . . . Dear Owen. . . .'

Mark felt awkward and in the way, as if intruding on some moment of private grief, but the feeling did not last long. The mood was shattered by another outburst in Ukrainian from the ebullient Ernst who was making his way up the beach and addressing his remarks to a passing bird. Mark and Peg looked down at him, then at each other, then both enjoyed the spontaneous relief of laughter.

They had been hacking their way through the jungle for days and the undergrowth seemed to be getting thicker. Intense heat added to their problems and their khaki shirts were sodden with sweat. Their progress was slow and their weapons heavy but they trudged on at the heels of their sergeant and kept their grumbles to themselves. The war in Europe might be over but the battle for the Far East was still very much in operation and a second's loss of concentration could be fatal.

At length they reached a river and waded across with their rifles held high above their heads. Along the bank on the other side, they found a clearing and it was here that they saw the first legacy of the fleeing Japanese. It was a scene that caused more than one stomach to turn. A small unit had been brutally murdered and left in various grotesque postures on the ground. The lucky ones had been shot dead, others had been run through with a bayonet, others again had had their throats cut. Some had undergone even worse before they had died.

The corpses were all dressed in faded British uniforms, nearly all of them stained with blood. They were the bodies of former prisoners-of-war, killed at random by vengeful captors forced on the retreat. The sergeant motioned his corporal to join him.

'Make sure the Japs aren't still around. . . . There's nothing we can do for these poor sods.'

The corporal rounded up his men and went off into the jungle to
check that the enemy were not still close by. Left alone with the
slaughtered prisoners, the sergeant shook his head in disbelief at the
horror and did his best to ignore the stench that was already hanging
over the clearing.

'Sergeant. . . .'

The voice was faint but it did not come from far away.

'Sergeant . . . over here. . . .'

He followed the sound to its source behind the twisted trunk of an
old tree and saw a soldier lying there, his right leg bent under him.
The man was filthy and haggard and perspiring freely, but his voice
fought off complete fatigue.

'It's my leg. . . . I lay doggo or they'd have finished me like all the
others. . . . Are they all—?'

'Yes,' confirmed the sergeant.

'There's a bloke back over here . . . R.A.F. type . . . was in the truck
with us . . . he made some noise just before you came. . . .'

'Where is he?'

'Over there . . . just there,' he said, pointing.

'Crosby,' called the Sergeant, 'come and take a look at this leg. . . .
You'll be all right, mate,' he added with a wink.

He walked across to the body in the R.A.F. uniform and saw that
the man was lying face down in the matted grass. Even at a cursory
glance, he could see several bad wounds and feared that the man was
dead. He turned the body over so that it lay on its back and he bent
over the face. No breath stirred and he saw the tell-tale hue of death
around the sunken eyes. And then, miraculously, those eyes opened,
briefly and falteringly maybe, but the Sergeant did stare into them.
There was a faint memory of life there, after all.


The Hayward kitchen had too many people in it trying to do too
many different things at the same time. Peg was handing Mark a plate
with a fried egg and toast on it, Helen was at the stove cooking the
other breakfasts, George was standing by the sink trying to peer
into the tiny mirror as he tied his tie, Colin was searching on the floor
for some marbles he claimed he had lost under the table, Harry was
wandering in and out to see if his food was ready yet and Jean
Hayward, dressed for work, was worried about being late.

'I'll forget about breakfast for today,' she said.

'You can't go to the farm without food inside you, Jean. You must
eat something, girl.' Helen was firm. 'Now sit down.'

'I can't.' Jean looked at her son to make sure that he was not
listening. 'It's Ernst. He'll think I've gone.'

'No, he won't,' reassured Peg. We saw him coming just now, didn't we, Mark?'

'What? Oh yes. Him.'

'He'll only just have got there, Jean. I'll go and ask him to wait ... or even bring him here if you like.'

'Ernst won't come here, Peg. He's shy.'

'Another one!' came the reply and Mark knew it was aimed at him. Peg threaded her way past various members of her family to get to the door and then turned back.

'I'll keep him company till you come, Jean. I don't have to be at the library until eleven.' She looked at Mark. 'What time's your train?'

'I've hours yet.'

'Of course! You've only got to get from Euston to Victoria, haven't you?' said Peg with a giggle and then she went out.

George Hayward, who had been pretending to hear none of all this but who had not missed a single word, now sat at the table beside Mark and nudged him gently with his elbow.

'What did Peg mean by that?'

'I think she was pulling my leg, Mr Hayward.'

Colin had extended his search to the other room now where he could be heard encountering irritable questions from Harry, who had pottered off yet again. Jean felt that she could speak freely.

'You told her about Ernst, then?'

'Yes,' said Helen, 'we told her.'

'She loved Owen.'

Mark wanted to say that he was the favourite among the brothers but he felt it was not his place to contribute to this particular family discussion and so he carried on eating.

'We all loved Owen,' reminded George, gravely, 'but Owen's dead. Peg blames the Japanese not you, that someone's taken his place. Life goes on. It must. How could it be otherwise?'

'And the war's over,' added Helen, putting eggs on to a plate.

'Except for people like Keir, and it'll be over for them before long,' said George.

'We hope,' smiled his wife, sadly.

'The Japs can't hold out much longer, Helen. Question of time that's all. Meanwhile, we must get stuck into the peace. There's an election in two weeks.'

'That'll solve everything, will it?' she asked with a trace of cynicism in her tone.

'It'll shape the future. It'll do that for better or for worse. . . . We can't expect the fruits of victory overnight, love. Facts are facts.'

'Like those on your plate, you mean?'

She put the plate in front of him and he looked at the small, shrivelled fried egg and the half-slice of fried bread. It was hardly a full breakfast for a grown man. George took a philosophical view.

'There's plenty worse off than us, Helen. I'll bet there's many a German'd be glad of this.'

'They started it,' came the blunt reply.

'They didn't all love Hitler,' he countered. 'When the dam breaks, you get carried along in the flood. . . . The innocent and the guilty. Right, Warrington?'

'Well . . . er . . . yes,' mumbled Mark, not wishing to be drawn into the argument.

'There you are,' said George. 'He knows. He was there. He's seen it all, like Blake. Now let me get on with my grub. . . .'

While George Hayward was tucking into a small breakfast in Whitstanton, another member of the family was making an early morning pot of tea in Germany. Wearing only his pyjama trousers, Blake padded around the kitchen in search of a tray. When Waters breezed in and saw what was happening, he smirked and took the opportunity to mock Blake for a change.

'She gets tea in bed now, does she?'

'Where's the sugar?' asked the other, opening cupboards.

'Your Frau has got you well-trained, old chap. It'll be lunch and dinner up there next. Room service.'

'Ah, here we are.' Blake took out a crumpled bag.

'Does she tip handsomely?'

'You're only jealous, Waters.'

'I'm not, actually. I'm a great one for counting my blessings, you see.' He pulled up a chair and sat down, crossing his legs. 'Best billet we've ever had, this. Just think of some of the stink-holes we've had to put up with. Not to mention those tents in the desert.'

'Yes,' agreed Blake, checking that everything was now on the tray, 'this place has certainly got the lot.'

'We've turned into quite a jolly little family in the weeks we've been together. You, me and Frau Wenkel . . . or rather, you, Frau Wenkel and me. . . . Incidentally, I do wish she wouldn't keep calling me "Waters". It makes me feel like the butler. I do have a Christian name. Three, to be exact. She could take her pick.' He leaned across to Blake and lowered his voice. 'What does she call you when the two of you are alone? Lieb-something-or-other, I daresay. Is that who you are up there, Captain Hayward—Mein Liebling?'

'Mind your own damn business!' said the other with a grin.

'Entschuldigen Sie bitte! One thing, anyway. All this fraternizing in the master bedroom must have done a power of good to your command of the German language. At least you can say "Thanks very much" now.'

'I'll take this up.'

'Quite a reversal, really, when you think about it. . . .'

'Reversal?' Blake paused in the doorway.

'I've watched it with interest. "To hell with the Fraus and the Fräuleins", he used to say, biting on his enforced celibacy. "Let them learn to love Jerry in his socks by the light of burning jackboots." Remember that line?'

'Dry up!'

The force with which he said this surprised them both and led to a long pause.

'You're always going to Brigade H.Q.,' said Blake, changing the subject. 'Every morning as soon as they open. Can't wait to get home, can you?'

'Neither could you until you started to fraternize.'

'Stop using that word! It's dirty.'

'That's why they chose it, Blake. They wanted a dirty word for it.' He glanced up then looked back at his friend. *I* don't begrudge you but you must know you're playing with fire. The skies would open if they ever found out about you and her. . . . I'd hate to see you in trouble, old chap.'

'I'll survive.'

'Of course!' reassured Waters. In any case, we'll be moving on before long. The Ruskies will be using this kitchen. Now there's an odd thought, isn't it?'

'They've not set a date?' asked Blake, anxiously. 'Brigade?'

'Not that anyone's told me. . . . She doesn't know it's going to happen, does she?'

'I'll tell her when the time comes. . . .'

'Don't envy you that chore. I hate to think of her being left to the tender mercies of Joe Stalin's boys. I've grown quite fond of the lady —in a purely platonic way, of course. . . .'

'This tea is getting cold,' said Blake, turning to go.

'You're the one I'm really worried about, though. . . .' The remark stopped Blake in his tracks. 'At least, I would worry if I didn't know that you had the sense to make sure it won't get too serious. . . . You *are* keeping it under control, aren't you?'

'You think I should?' he asked without turning back to look at Waters. 'Is that your considered opinion, Captain?'

'Well . . . oh hell, Blake! There's no future in it, is there?'

Blake Hayward stayed long enough to adjust the cups on the tray and then he went off upstairs at speed.

Ernst Sevcenko was sitting on a rock and throwing stones at the sea wall for amusement. Used to being kept waiting after years as a prisoner-of-war, he had developed a kind of patient resignation to cover all situations. When Peg Hayward joined him on the beach, therefore, she found him relaxed and unworried, though rather wary of her at first. She introduced herself and told him that Jean would not be long, showing by the openness of her manner that she had no reservations about his friendship with her sister-in-law. Ernst was pathetically grateful for this and he talked about Jean with enthusiasm, saying what a difference she had made to his whole life. Peg asked a question that had been on her mind ever since she had first heard about him.

'If you're from the Ukraine, how did you come to be fighting for the Germans?'

'We're not an island like you,' he explained, bitterness deepening the lines in his face. 'We live with the Germans on one side, the Russians on the other. . . . The Russians, they took our country. . . . They started to—what is your word for it—collectivize us . . . to change us from Ukrainians into Russians . . . even our language. . . . They took my family from the house where they lived.' He stopped for a moment and looked down at the sand. 'Then came the Germans . . . they broke their pact with the Russians . . . so we change masters, do you see? . . . They promised us we should only fight the Russians, but some of us they sent to France . . . I was taken prisoner there. . . . You understand?'

Peg knew that she could never understand how awful it must have been because she had not lived through the experience herself. Compared with what people had suffered in Europe, the war had been an easy time for those left in England. She admitted that she had no conception of what it was like to have her country overrun by an enemy power and she felt almost guilty about this. Suddenly, she put a hand on his shoulder and told him she was glad that he and Jean were happy.

'I wanted you to know, that's all . . . just wanted you to know. . . .'

Herta Wenkel put her empty teacup back on the tray and lay back naked in the bed. Blake was beside her, hands behind the back of his head, at once content and apprehensive, enjoying to the full the pleasure of their togetherness at the same time as he feared its early disappearance. When Waters had told him there was no future in it, the words had cut him like a knife but he was realist enough to accept the truth of them.

Herta rolled over to look at him, her hair falling down over her pale shoulders, her face puckered with worry.

'Do they starve in England as here?'

'No ... but the rations are small ... less so now that the war's over, I'm told ... but still nowhere near enough. ...'

He brushed the hair back softly from her shoulders and then leaned over to kiss her gently between the breasts. Then he lay on his back and put her head on his chest, stroking it as they talked and happily at ease in the warmth of their closeness.

'What is it like ... where you live?'

'Whitstanton? Oh, it's a small, ugly little town in the North. Mucky old place because of the industry ... dirty streets. ... But tidy people. Very clean and tidy ... friendly, too. We live just outside near the sea ... a big house that we can't really afford. But I loved it when I was a boy ... down by the sea.'

'You want to go home. I can hear it in your voice. ...'

'No! I mean. ...'

'Is only natural. ... This is my home ... when you go, I will be alone in it again. All alone.'

'Do you want to stay here, Herta?'

'Is my home,' she repeated, simply. 'There will be ghosts ... all over Germany there were ghosts. ... My husband ... my father ... and you, Blake ... you also will be a ghost. ...'

'Will I? Is that what you want?'

'Is what I have,' she said, with a sad acceptance of her fate.

'Suppose you were asked to leave here?'

'For what reason?'

'For any reason. ...'

'But where would I go?'

'You said you had relatives to the West,' he reminded her.

'Why should I go to them?'

'Well ... because there might be fighting here. ...'

'Fighting? But no—the war is over—that is all done with. Why do you say such a thing?' She was leaning up on her arm now, the mood broken. 'Why, Blake?'

'I just wanted you to think about the possibility, that's all ... there might be a time when it would be wiser not to stay.'

'But I must stay. There is my father. ...'

'You talked about him as a ghost just now. I thought you had given up hope. ...' She nodded and looked so crestfallen that he began to reassure her. 'You never know, Herta. I got those prints of that photograph you gave me. They're in my valise downstairs. We can put up the picture of your father now. That may help.'

'All over Germany they are nailed up, those faces. ... On the doors of dead houses. ... "Has anyone seen this face? A name, an address ... dead faces. ... I have no hope any more. ...'

'There's always hope,' he insisted.

She bent over him and kissed him lightly on the lips, staying very close as she asked her next question and searching his eyes with great care.

'That day I first came here . . . with you and Waters . . . did you know then that I had given up completely?'

'Yes.'

'I had no hope at all.'

'That was pretty obvious. . . .'

'And it made you feel sorry for me? Pity?'

'Well . . . yes. It was bound to . . . I'm not heartless. . . .'

'Is that why you wanted to . . . give me hope?' She held his chin between her fingers. 'Was it something you would do for anyone?'

'Is that what you believe, Herta?'

'No,' she smiled, relaxing a little. 'No, funny man. . . .'

'Funny?' He was puzzled.

'When I ask *you* a question, you answer by asking *me* a question . . . oh you funny man!'

'Funny ha-ha, or funny peculiar?' he wondered, then saw from her frown that she did not understand him. 'One day I'll explain. It's a saying.'

'You will explain . . . one day before you go?'

'Yes, yes . . . one day before I go. . . .'

Blake caught sight of the time on his watch and realized that he had to get up. She stopped him as he swung his legs out of the bed and gripped his hand tightly.

'When the time comes . . . for you to go home . . . you will tell me?' He nodded but she wanted a definite promise. 'You swear?'

'I swear. . . . Cross my heart and hope to die.' He grinned as she looked bewildered. 'It's something my mother used to say. She's funny, too. . . .'


Unaware that she was being talked about by her son in this way, Helen Hayward dipped the last of the plates into the hot washing-up water and started to rub it vigorously with the dishcloth. Eight breakfasts had meant a lot of preparation and clearing away but Helen did not complain, having been used to a ceaseless round of domestic chores for most of her marriage. She found herself taking great pleasure from Jean's happiness and she hoped that nothing would happen to blight the romance that had lifted her daughter-in-law out of her depression. When George came in to take his leave before going to work, she asked him something which she had not dared to before.

'Will they be able to marry?'

'Marry?' He did not seem shocked at the suggestion.

'Will they, George?'

'Don't see why not. Happened after the last war. . . .'

'They will let him stay in this country, then?'

'Probably. It's not as if he's a real P.O.W. More of a refugee. We've always opened our doors to refugees.'

Helen took her hands out of the bowl and dried them on a tea towel, trying to find the words to break some news to him and slightly worried as to what his response would be.

'It's his birthday next week . . . Ernst . . . I wondered if . . . I thought it might be nice if. . . .' She decided to grasp the nettle and came straight out with it. 'I've told Jean to ask him here.'

'Fine.'

'You don't mind?'

'Why should I mind? Good idea. We should get to know the man. All in favour.'

Lovett Hayward now came in to ask if his grandfather's breakfast was ready yet. Harry Hayward did not eat with the rest of the family and usually came through himself to spirit away his plate and mug of tea to the privacy of his own room. Annoyed that he had been kept waiting while others, in his view, had been given preference over him, Harry had taken himself off to sulk. George resented the way that he had now sent Lovett as an emissary.

'Why can't he eat with us?' he demanded.

'After the election, he says, Dad. . . . Saves argument, he says. . . .'

'He's right,' agreed Helen.

'Who argues?' George blustered. '*I* don't. Waste of time. He'd vote for a blooming pig if it had a blue ribbon round its neck.'

'With bacon ration cut to three ounces, he'd be showing some sense,' opined Helen. 'Pigs are more use than politicians. You can eat pigs.'

'What do you say to that, Dad?' asked Lovett.

'Ah, women aren't interested in politics, son. . . .'

'Aren't they?' she retorted, taking a plate out of the oven. 'It's the women's vote that puts the Conservatives in, according to you.'

'Oh, yes, they'll vote all right but they won't study what they're voting for.' He consulted his pocket watch. 'Time to go.'

'I'll tell Grandad the coast is clear, then,' said Lovett, taking the tray which his mother now handed him and going out.

'So I don't know what I'm voting for?' challenged Helen.

'How many do, woman? One in five'd be putting it high in my opinion . . . on our side of the fence, that is. On t'other side they know better—they want to keep what they've got.'

'I only want one thing.'

'Aye? And what's that?'

'The old life back again,' she said, wistfully.

'The Depression? The dole?' George was horrified.

'You kept your job through it, anyway. It was a lot better here than some places.'

'By heck, you've forgotten already! You've forgotten what it was like to wait and wonder if it was your turn to be laid off next. And you want to go back to *that*!'

Helen shook her head but he was in no mood to listen to her explanations. She turned to a topic which had started to prey on her mind over the last month or so.

'I do wish Keir would write.'

'Don't fret about him, woman.'

'I can't help it, George.'

'Know him for what he is—a lousy letter-writer. They take a fair while to get here, anyway . . . letters from the Far East.'

'Why don't the Japanese give in?' she said with exasperation. 'They must know they have no chance.'

'They're fanatics are the Japs, love. We used to think they'd swamp the world, them and the chinky, chinky Chinamen. . . . The Yellow Peril we used to call 'em. They put the fear of death into me. . . .'

Something in his voice suggested that that fear had not entirely abated.


The Field Hospital was a ramshackle affair, thrown up at speed to cope with the steady flow of appalling casualties that were being brought in. Supplies were low and conditions primitive but there was no shortage of care and dedication from the medical staff. They worked the most punishing hours and drew on all their resources of strength and compassion.

A man in the tattered remnants of an R.A.F. uniform was being brought in on a stretcher by two orderlies. They were lifting him carefully on to the bed under the watchful gaze of the hospital Sister when, for no apparent reason, the man suddenly let out such a cry of anguish that they both jumped back.

'Don't worry,' said the sister, bending over him. 'It was nothing you did . . . came from somewhere inside his head.'

The orderlies went out with the stretcher and she sat beside the new patient, mopping his brow with a damp cloth. From a bed further down the room, a soldier with his leg in a splint sat up and called out to her.

'He's not one of our lot. . . . There were half a dozen of them in the truck when the Japs picked us up. They were moving prisoners back before the camps were overrun . . . this one looked in a bad way even then. . . .'

'No identity tag,' she observed.

'Japs like to strip you of those sometimes . . . it makes you somebody . . . if you're taken prisoners, you're dishonoured, in their eyes . . . less than nobody . . . worse than dead. . . .'

'Calendula officinalis!'

The newcomer had let out another cry but neither the sister nor the soldier with the broken leg could understand what he had said. It had not sounded like English. With a great convulsion the man yelled out once more, this time in real agony.

'Calendula officinalis!'

# CHAPTER FOUR

In the weeks that he had been staying at the Wenkel house, Blake Hayward had worked his way through the sheet music in the piano stool several times. He played every day without fail, usually in the evenings, sometimes for sheer enjoyment, sometimes by way of relaxation or escape, and sometimes as an antidote to occasional bouts of homesickness. Tonight he was playing by request and the strains of a Beethoven sonata were echoing around the room. Herta, smiling in gratitude for this favourite piece of music, stood beside the piano and watched his hands move up and down the keys. Waters, only half-listening, was slumped in a chair reading a British newspaper that was a week out of date.

Blake came to the end of the sonata and gave Herta a mock bow, like a concert pianist acknowledging the applause of a vast audience. She responded by clapping her hands softly a few times.

'Tell me about England, Blake.'

'Ah, England!' he cried and immediately began to play the opening bars of 'Land of Hope and Glory'.

'Give it a rest, old chap!' said Waters. 'Now answer the lady's question. She wants to know about England.'

Blake stopped pounding the keys and got up from the stool.

'Which England? *Your* England, Waters? . . . My England? . . . *Real* England? . . . Or the soldier's dream of home?'

'Your England?' decided Herta.

'You appreciate there's a difference between them, then?'

'Of course. . . .'

'Well, to be honest, I'm not sure I have an England. . . . I've a place in my head . . . and a gallery of faces. . . . Hang on!'

He crossed to his jacket which was lying on a chair and he took out a snapshot of the entire Hayward family before handing it to Herta. She studied it with interest.

'You'll find some of those faces on there. . . . I'm the one in the middle, next to the dog. . . .'

'This is *you* . . . before the war?' she asked with almost girlish excitement. 'I can keep it?'

'I'll swap you, for something similar.'

'Swap?' she did not know the word.

'Exchange.'

'Ah yes.' She went straight out. 'I will get it. . . .'

Blake wheeled on Waters who had been mocking him silently and making gestures with his hands.

'Like a pair of teenage lovers, is that what you're trying to say! Go on—out with it. Tell me it's the kind of thing I should have got over when I was a pimply youth!'

He walked past the piano, thumped the keys and then carried on until he reached the window. Waters joined him, folding the newspaper before offering it to him. Blake shook his head.

'What are you going to do?' asked the other.

'Take her with me.'

'They won't let you do that.'

'I don't mean now, you idiot! Herta has relatives in the West. She'd have to stay there till the climate was right . . . till we stop hating the Jerries. . . . How long does it usually take?'

'You've got it all worked out, obviously. . . .'

'More or less.'

'Don't you think you should tell her? The facts.'

'I've started to break it to her—gently.'

'Gently! Heavens, Blake, is there time for *that*?'

Before he could answer, Blake saw her coming back into the room with a photograph of herself in younger days in her hand. With a mixture of pride, coyness and tenderness, she gave it to him and he forgot completely what Waters had been saying.

Ernst Sevcenko was an excellent worker and he redoubled his efforts when he had Jean alongside him. They were helping with the hay harvest at the Galway farm, Ernst pitching the bales on to the back of the wagon and Jean stacking them as best she could. It was tiring work but they felt strangely exhilarated at the end of the day

and walked briskly back in the direction of Whitstanton beach.
When Jean told him that she would bring her son to meet him soon,
he was surprised and asked if the boy's grandparents had no objection. Jean assured him that they did not.

'But I am an enemy. I fought for the Germans.'

'Only because they made you, Ernst.'

'No one can "make" you. I chose to fight for them rather than die
in a concentration camp. And I chose to fight against Russia.'

'We call that Hobson's Choice.'

'Hobson's Choice?' The expression was new to him.

'No choice at all. . . .'

When they reached the point near the sea wall where they had to
part, they kissed and hugged for a moment, Jean assuring him that
it would not always be a case of having to go separate ways.

'They will allow us to marry?'

'I told you, Ernst. They're happy for me . . . they understand.'

'And the people who rule—do they understand? Will they know
about Hobson's Choice?'

'Wait for me!' It was Peg, running towards them. 'Wait!'

When she caught up with them, she was panting for breath and
her cheeks were red with excitement. She simply wanted to remind
Ernst that he was going to tea with them on the next day and having
done so she raced off again.

'Her mother'd have a pink fit if she saw Peg charging about like
that.'

'Why?'

'She had scarlet fever as a child. It left her with a bad heart. . . .
She could go tomorrow but she lives as if there's nothing wrong
with her.'

'Maybe it is not so serious. . . .'

'The doctor thinks it is,' sighed Jean, looking after the figure
moving up the beach towards the house. 'Very serious.'

'And Peg hopes it is not. . . . Hope is what you have when you have
nothing. . . . Hope is everything then . . . I know.'


They had made love in the darkness and now lay entwined in each
other's arms. She talked, as always, about the way that he had
brought her back from the very edge of despair and given her the
desire to live. Then she told him that she had put her father's photograph up on a door in the town in the vague, almost forlorn hope
that someone might just know of his whereabouts. Blake let her tell
him about her family once again and waited for the moment when he
could break to her gently some news that she had to be told.

'We shall be going soon,' he said. 'The Russians will come.'

'How could that be?' she asked in alarm.

'It's something that's been agreed with them. At Yalta . . . we're inside the Russian sector, you see . . . we must pull back.'

'*You* would do that to us?' she hissed, tense and hurt, disengaging herself from his arms.

'Look, it wasn't something I arranged personally, Herta. I don't like the idea very much myself but it's the kind of thing that happens when you lose a war.'

'You hate us, don't you? As a people?'

'How can you hate a whole people?' Blake reached out a hand to touch her. 'I want you to come with me, Herta.'

There was a long silence in which only their breathing could be heard. Blake began to wonder if she was ever going to give him an answer.

'It would not be permitted,' she said, at length.

'You've friends in our sector, haven't you? Relatives? Go to them for the time being . . . then one day, eventually, we can be together. In England.'

There was another long silence as she realized what he was asking her and tried to come to terms with it. He felt her tears trickling on to his arm but could find no words to stop them for her.

'It is not necessary that you do this, Blake . . . I am with you because I wanted to be. It is not necessary that you do this for me.'

'It's necessary for me. Like my Dad always says: "What you care is what you do". . . . Understand now?'


The soldier with the broken leg felt much better after a week in the Field Hospital and he had developed a real friendship with the Sister and some of the nurses. He was a little sad, therefore, when told that he would soon be moved out and sent back to England by sea. Because of what he had been through, he felt no urge at all to go back home to face his family. In their savage and unrelenting treatment of him, the Japanese had somehow made him stop liking people or caring about them in any way. When he looked at the empty bed further down the room and asked if a certain person had died, the Sister shook her head.

'They're doing their best for him in the operating theatre. Some of us do still care. . . .'


From her position in the window of her father-in-law's room, Helen Hayward could see them clearly. Far below her on the beach, George stepped forward and shook Ernst Sevcenko by the hand before leading him back towards the house. Pleased that her husband was giving their guest such a warm welcome, Helen came away from the window to confront someone who had very different ideas on the subject. Harry Hayward, quite unrepentant, sat at the table with his charts all over it. Lovett, standing beside him, scrutinized the three-masted schooner in the empty rum bottle and tried to work out how it had got in there in one piece. Helen did not pull her punches.

'If that really is your attitude, you'll not eat with us at all. . . . It's disgraceful! . . . You understand, don't you, Lovett?'

'Yes, Mum. . . .'

'If George and I can accept it, so can you.'

'But I can't,' said Harry, curling his lip. 'We've been through a war . . . millions have died . . . your own lad among 'em. Blake's been away four years, Keir's still out in Far East . . . and you ask *me* to sit at table with a man that fought for the Germans!'

'That's where you'll sit or you'll get no food here! Yes, and if you do eat with us, you'll hold your peace!'

'Well I'll be damned!' Harry was on his feet now. 'Are you listening, Lovett? You'll know who to blame when the next lot starts, won't you!'

'He'll know who to blame. He's more understanding than you, it seems!'

'You go along with this, Lovett?' demanded the old man.

'War's over, Grandad. . . .'

'Who's won?'

'We have. . . .'

'And what have we won, lad?'

'Freedom,' said the boy, unhappy about being questioned.

'Freedom, is it? I could have sworn we had that when we started.'

'Hitler wouldn't have let you keep it, though, Grandad.'

'Answer that!' challenged Helen.

'Aye, you've got a point there, Lovett . . . he'd have no more let me keep my freedom than your mother would.'

'Me?' she said, nettled.

'They're all the same, these dictators. You've to think as they want you to think not as the mind dictates.' He stared at Helen with defiance. 'You've to keep your mouth shut at table, else you get nowt to eat.'

'You've got the choice. It's up to you!'

Helen Hayward swept out of the room and slammed the door after her in her anger. Her father-in-law scratched his head and looked quite baffled.

'How did we win the war, Lovett? It's quite beyond me.'

'English teacher at school says Errol Flynn won it, in Burma. . . .'

'We've spent up, lad, and what have we got to show for it? Eh?'

'What I said, Grandad—freedom. Except from at table, that is. . . .'

'Taking her side, are you?' Harry sounded quite betrayed.

'I don't take sides, Grandad,' said Lovett, firmly. 'I don't like sides. I don't, honest.'

As soon as he came into the room, Blake realized that she had been told. He turned accusingly to Waters who was setting out the dinner things but Herta came to his defence.

'It was not his fault. I ask him.'

'I wanted to tell you myself. Later. . . . Bit of a shock. Going tomorrow. . . . I thought you might be upset about leaving home. . . .'

'But I cannot leave now, Blake. I cannot come with you.'

'Why not?' he asked, hurt.

'I learned today that my father is still alive. Someone knew him. He is in Dusberg, a village not far from here. I do not understand why he has not come to me here. . . .'

'I do,' said Waters. 'Dusberg's in the Russian sector. They probably won't let him out.'

Herta's expression altered at once and her shoulders sagged. She soon rallied and decided that the situation was not so bad. Her father was at least alive and she did not believe all the stories about the Russians' maltreatment of German civilians. Blake reminded her of her husband and the atrocities about which he had written shortly before his death in Russia.

'That was different . . . at the Front . . . the real war. . . .'

'*Real*?' echoed Blake. 'Wasn't what you saw in Berlin real? The dead . . . the women and children drowned . . . you still think war only happens at the Front?'

'War is over, Blake! Over! My father is an old man. They would not hurt him, would they?'

'Maybe not, if he plays his cards right, doesn't say too much, doesn't eat too much.'

'When the Russians come here, he will be able to come with them. If not, I go to them.'

Blake exchanged a meaningful look with Waters and then took her by the shoulders to make sure that she listened.

'Herta, you're a woman. Do you know what they do to women? They do what your soldiers did to their women. They do it very efficiently. To the death sometimes. They have no compassion at all because that was burned out of their souls.'

'Such stories are always told in war,' she replied. 'As for compassion. . . . Dresden? Hamburg? Was that compassion? Who are you English that you should condemn.' She pushed his hands away. 'Your shame makes you speak so of others. And tell stories!'

'Were there ever stories about the concentration camps?' he asked, levelly. 'Were there?' She shrugged, moved away. 'They were all true. In fact, the truth was worse . . . if the stories had been closer to that truth, they would have been unbelievable.' Herta was unconvinced and Blake appealed to Waters. 'For God's sake, tell her, man! Don't just stand there!'

Waters cleared his throat and then assured her that the stories were true. She refused to believe him and start ranting against the English and what they had done to Germany. Waters could find no reply to it all but Blake cut her short.

'Whatever else we might be, we're not practising barbarians!'

'Not even after Dresden? What are you, then? A romantic people, perhaps, you get what you want by pretending to be gentlemen . . . by telling us how much better you are, how superior!'

'Coming from one of the master race that takes a bit of swallowing, by God it does!'

Blake was fuming now and he faced her for a second as if about to explode. Then he swung around and stormed off out through the door. Herta's temper was roused as well and she ran to grab a vase that was full of flowers picked only that day by Waters in an effort to brighten the place up. Before he could stop her, she had hurled the vase and its contents straight through one of the windows.

'War is over! Is done!'

She collapsed to the floor and leaned against the arm of a chair as she wept. Waters, not quite knowing what to do, stood there in his embarrassment until her tears were over and then knelt down beside her to comfort her.

'Blake will be back, Herta, don't worry. He's a funny man. . . .'

'Ha ha funny or ha ha peculiar?' she whispered.

Eight people sat around the long wooden table in the Hayward kitchen and munched their tiny pieces of birthday cake. Ernst was so moved by the trouble that had been taken on his behalf and by the goodwill being shown towards him that he said very little. Lovett and Colin competed for attention from the adults, Jean spent most of the time gazing at Ernst, George and Helen kept the conversation on a pleasant and uncontroversial level and Harry maintained a wounded silence. It was left to Peg Hayward to stir things up, albeit unwittingly.

'What do you think of Mr Attlee, Grandad?' she asked.

'Peg. . . .' warned her mother, shooting her a look.

'I know what he thinks of the Labour Party, Mum, but what about Mr Attlee?'

'Can your Dad stand to hear it?' said Harry, mischievously.

'I don't have to agree with all that's said. . . .' began George.

'But he'll defend to the death your right to say it,' Peg and Lovett sang in unison, all too familiar with one of their father's most hackneyed quotations.

'Aye, but he's not master here,' noted Harry, without daring to turn to Helen. 'I shall not get me pudding if I open me mouth.'

'You'll not get it in if you don't, Grandad,' giggled Lovett and even his mother laughed.

'Making fun of me, Lovett?' said Harry. 'I thought you were a friend of mine. . . .'

Helen asked Ernst if he would like something else to eat but the latter declined. He had had more than enough and had particularly enjoyed the token birthday cake which had been baked with improvised ingredients by Jean. But Peg once again pushed the conversation towards a possible flashpoint.

'Tell us about the Russians, Ernst.'

'I'm sure Ernst doesn't want to talk about that,' announced Helen firmly.

'I think he does. I think he wants to warn us about the Reds but he's trying to be English—and polite!'

'Nothing wrong with politeness!' argued her mother.

'Well what *can* we talk about in this house?' complained Peg.

'Your mother's hero—Churchill,' said George. 'You'll be on safe ground there, Peg. And I'm prepared to keep my gob shut in the interests of peace.'

He winked across the table at Ernst who was rather bemused by what was going on but who returned an obliging grin nevertheless. Harry Hayward chuckled and seized on the mention of Churchill.

'Shall I tell you what he said about Clem Attlee? Churchill said— "An empty cab drew up and Mr Attlee got out". . . .'

'That's cruel, Grandad!' said Peg, as Lovett sniggered.

'That's politics, my lass. . . .' He goaded George who was biting back a rejoinder. 'Having trouble with your mouth, are you?'

'Ernst hates the Russians,' Jean blurted out. 'The Germans, too.'

'He fought for the buggers, didn't he?' sneered Harry.

'It was Hobson's Choice, Grandad. They made him.'

Helen directed a withering look at Peg, blaming her for getting the row started in the first place. Harry was in his element now.

'Is it right what she says?' he asked Ernst.

'Perhaps it is better not to talk of such things,' Ernst replied, anxious not to upset anyone.

'They don't send folks to Siberia in this country for speaking their minds—they just give 'em nowt to eat. Bloody shame!'

'Watch your language!' scolded Helen.

'What did the Russians do to you, then, Ernst?' prodded Harry.

'He doesn't like discussing it,' said Jean.

'So don't embarrass our guest,' added George.

'Embarrass him? Should we not know what'll be coming to us if we don't stand fast? Happen you'd sooner we didn't know—eh?'

'You are right,' Ernst agreed. 'I should tell.'

'Don't feel obliged to talk about what you'd sooner forget, Ernst,' said George.

'No, no, Mr Hayward. I never forget.'

'It's the others who want to forget,' chided Harry, aiming this at George. 'Or don't want to know in the first place!'

There was a long silence as everyone watched Ernst, who was rubbing his big hands together as if washing them. Staring down at the table cloth he told his story with straightforward dignity.

'When the war came we first had the Germans . . . they took our neighbours, who were Jews, but us they left . . . then came the Russians . . . the NKVD called at our house . . . said we were boyars—"nobles"—though we were only a small estate of little farms . . . they call my mother a bladiuha—a "tart"—and beat my father when he came between them . . . then they took me to another room and beat me also . . . then, before I was unconscious, I heard my mother screaming. It was the last thing I heard . . . when I open my eyes they have all gone . . . I do not see them again . . . I join others who have suffered also, worse sometimes . . . we try to survive. . . . Perhaps if my family live they think I am dead. . . . Sometimes I believe I am dead. . . .' He paused and his hands now gripped each other tightly. 'We sit in the firelight of the family. Outside it is dark . . . the night cold . . . we talk to make sound . . . so that we will not hear the wolves coming down from the hills . . . we pretend not to hear . . . we are afraid . . . we do nothing . . . but we talk . . . we talk. . . .'

Ernst lowered his head and took deep breaths through his nose. Jean put a sympathetic hand on his arm. Harry used the story as a weapon against his son.

'You hear, George?'

'What's your point, Dad?'

'You that wants to make friends with the Russians . . . like that Laski and your other mates . . . now you know what sort of scum they really are!'

'We have to be at peace with the Russians, Dad. We want no more war! . . . I'm a Labour Party man, anyway, not a communist . . . but they do exist, communists. They're there. We've got to live with 'em.'

'Oh aye, they're there all right. In your own fold. . . .'

'We don't have communists in the Party. The constitution forbids it.'

'You've got 'em nonetheless. What's Laski, then? And them other fellow-travellers? Wolves in sheep's bloody clothing! That's what they are.'

'Your language, Dad!' snapped Helen, eyes blazing.

Harry Hayward relaxed, feeling that he had won the argument and interested to see what it had cost him. He raised his eyebrows and ran his tongue around his lips.

'Er . . . do I get any more pudding, then?'


Herta Wenkel had cried herself to sleep and the pillow was still damp beneath her head. The door of the bedroom opened quietly and then closed without a sound, a figure then moving across to her to crouch beside the bed. As soon as the hand touched her, she awoke and cried out in fear but Blake's voice calmed her.

'It's me . . . I'm sorry . . . I'm sorry. . . .'

'I thought it was—'

'Oh I'm a fool!' he said, angry with himself. 'I didn't think.'

She sat up in bed and took his hand, apologizing profusely for the vicious argument they had had earlier in the evening.

'I said things to hurt you, Blake. . . .'

'I know. . . .'

'I wanted to . . . get back at you somehow. And *hurt*!'

Blake explained where he had been and how he had returned to the house earlier and gone to sleep in another bedroom. But he had woken almost at once, tormented by the thought of what would happen to her if she stayed in the house after the British army had pulled out of the district.

'Don't stay, Herta. *Please*. Listen to what I say. . . .'

'But it is because of what you say that I cannot leave.'

'What?'

'Have you forgotten so soon? You taught it to me: "What you care is what you do". He is my *father*, Blake. Suppose he were to come here and there was no one?'

'Herta, he is an old man. His life is nearly over. . . . He wouldn't want you to risk yours for his.'

'Is there no place in this world for old people any more? . . . Your father . . . your mother . . . what would you do if it was them?' She began to stroke his hair as if trying to comfort him. 'What would you do? . . . As I do? Yes?'

'We used to say that the only good German's a dead German. . . .'

'We say that, too, about others. We sometimes say things we do not mean because we do not think. . . .'

She let him lie on the bed beside her and put his arms around her. A long kiss reminded both of them of how much they had missed each other during the short period of a few hours. The pressure of the situation suddenly seemed unbearable and they clung to each other for support. Then Blake tried again to persuade her against her decision.

'I've imagined a life for us in England. . . .'

'Blake. . . .'

'No, listen! After four rotten years of living from day to day, I thought at last I had some glimmer of hope for the future!'

'It was . . . illusion. . . .'

'It wasn't, Herta!'

'You think that only because we share this bed together for a few weeks . . . in a house . . . living together as normal people . . . almost as if it was like before the war. . . . But I am not really special to you. I am just the first woman you meet as a new life starts.'

'You *are* special!'

'No, I am the beginning of your peace, that is all. . . .'

'Maybe that's how it started . . . but it's not like that now. . . .'

He kissed her again and she did not resist, lying back in the bed and he pressed himself against her. At length, she broke gently away and put a hand on his lips to stop him kissing her again.

'Don't make it hard for me. . . .'

'I have to, Herta. I want to be sure you don't give up. . . .'

'Oh, I will never give up. I promise. . . .'

He hugged her to him, his head buried in the pillow behind her. When she rolled over on top of him and looked down in an almost forlorn way, Blake knew that it had been no illusion for him.

'Do you remember that thing that was missing?' he asked.

'Missing?'

'A certain word . . . when we lay together here, you always said that a certain word was missing. . . .'

'Oh yes . . . that. . . .'

'You said that I could not say it because I did not feel it. But I do feel it, Herta. And I can say it to you now.'

'Please, no—not now,' she pleaded. 'Save it. Save the word. Save it for when I come to you. . . .'

Helen Hayward cleared away the tea things and listened to the babble of voices from the next room. Despite her warnings, arguments had developed and she was very annoyed both with her husband and with her father-in-law. She felt guilty on Ernst's behalf and wished that she had been able to protect him more effectively from what had happened. Her one consolation was that Ernst had seemed to recover from the anguish he had so clearly experienced when recounting his story about the Russians. As she cocked an ear now, she could even pick out his throaty laughter. Perhaps the birthday party had not been such a disaster, after all.

'He's sweet, isn't he?' said Peg, bringing out more dishes. 'You can see why Jean's fallen for him.'

'I'm surprised at you, Peg Hayward!'

'No, you're not, Mum,' came the tart reply.

'Why ever did you stir it up like that?'

'I didn't mean to. But what's all the fuss about? It needed saying. Sort of cleared the air.'

'The air was still thick when I came out,' noted Helen.

She filled the kettle from the tap and set it on the stove to boil. It would take at least three kettles of boiling water to wash all the dishes that had been piled on the enamel draining-board. Still clicking her tongue at her daughter, Helen took out the bowl and the washing-up powder in readiness.

Jean now came in with Colin who had one hand up to his ear and held his head over at an angle.

'He has an earache and he wants Gran to fix it,' said Jean.

'Will you, Gran?' asked the boy. '*Please*?'

'Of course, love. . . . Bring him over here, Jean. . . .'

Helen went over to a cupboard and searched among a pile of bottles and boxes, at last finding what she wanted. She showed Colin the medicine and shook it up violently.

'Your father used to think this cured everything, Colin.'

'Owen?' Jean was interested.

'Yes. He asked for it whenever he was hurt . . . Marigold oil . . . only I was a bit of a show-off in those days and called things by their Latin names. "I'm poorly, Mum," Owen would say, "can I have some Calendula Officinalis". . . .'

He lay on the makeshift bed and twitched violently in his sleep from time to time. Every so often he muttered something and it had an almost childish quality to it. The Sister came to see how he was and bent over him as his lips moved once again.

'What did he say, Sister?' asked another patient.

'I don't know ... it sounded a bit like Latin. ...'

Herta Wenkel arranged freshly-picked flowers in the vase and put it in the middle of the table. She was all alone now and determined to keep herself busy so that she would have time to dwell on Blake's absence. An ominous sound in the street outside made her stop what she was doing and remain perfectly still. The tank stopped outside, there were raised voices and commands, and then there was a hammering on her front door. Before she could move to open it, the door was forced back on its hinges and a Russian officer burst in.

## CHAPTER FIVE

The troop ship steamed through calm waters with a full cargo of pain, regret and disillusion. Men who were wounded, fatigued or rescued from their humiliation at the hands of their Japanese captors now had time to begin a slow recovery as they sailed between one life and another. It was July, 1945, and the war in the Far East was still being fought, but for these soldiers and airmen of the British forces the hostilities at last were over.

Like many others aboard, Barstow, confined to the sick bay by his injuries, kept up an almost constant flow of chatter to hide the dull ache of his memories. His chirpy sense of humour raised many laughs in the small, four-berth cabin and the two men in the upper bunks were grateful for his company. When they fell asleep, however, Barstow had to take refuge in reading or in doodling aimlessly with a pencil and paper because the fourth patient seemed to be in some sort of coma and spent most of his time on his back gazing sightlessly at the springs of the bunk above him.

It was a great moment for Barstow, therefore, when the head rolled over and the eyes stared at him with something approaching curiosity. He laughed and put down his magazine.

'Come back from the dead, have you? I was wondering when you'd join us.'

'Where am I?' asked the voice, slurred and confused.

'Heading for Blighty, mate. Two weeks out of Singapore and all the better for that! I've tried to tell you before many a time but you didn't seem to be able to take it in.'

'Singapore,' murmured the other. 'Singapore. . . .'

'Feeling better, are we?'

The man gave a weary smile and then tried to take in his surroundings, still quite bewildered.

'What's your name?' said Barstow.

'Name?'

'You didn't have a tag on you when they picked you up, they said. What happened? Japs take it off you?'

'Name? . . .'

'We all have one of those, mate. Name, rank and number!'

'Hayward. 627544.'

'That's a start, anyway. I'm Barstow. Les, to my pals . . . hey, pity you didn't make it earlier. You missed your B2626.'

'My what?'

'B2626—your voting form. Postal ballot. They reckon the servicemen's vote'll decide it. Two million of us.'

'I don't follow. . . .'

'Election in two days' time back home. Hell of a battle, it'll be. Churchill versus Attlee and no holds barred. They've to wait best part of three weeks for the result because of us . . . our votes come in from all over the world.' He grabbed something that was tucked under his pillow. 'They've sent out masses of bumph. This lot's from the candidates in my home town. . . . Don't reckon much to either of 'em. Civvies! They look like Hobson's Choice to me!'

Optimism had put a real spring into George Hayward's step and his daughter was having a job to keep up with him and they walked back towards the Committee Rooms of the Whitstanton Labour Party. Another busy evening of canvassing had rewarded them with a whole forest of ticks against their lists of names, though Peg was very sceptical about some of the promises they had been given, fearing that they were simply a means of shifting two unwanted callers from a doorstep. George, however, was supremely confident and he paid no heed to her warning that a large number of their declared supporters might not even turn out to vote on Polling Day.

'We're going to win, Peg! It's in the air! People are thinking. Do you know, Party Political broadcasts are getting more listeners than Tommy Handley.'

'Only because there's twice as many laughs!'

While her husband and daughter had been knocking doors up and down the streets of Whitstanton, Helen Hayward had been lending a hand at the Committee Rooms, addressing envelopes and making tea. Jean had been with her and had worked hard though her mind was clearly on something other than the fortunes of the Labour Party. On their way back home, she talked only about Ernst and the plans that they had made for the future. They arrived back at the house to find Harry lurking outside the door of his room as if waiting to speak to someone.

'Where've you been all this time?' he asked.

'Down at the Committee Rooms, Dad.'

'I'm surprised at you helping that lot!' He snorted.

'I'll just pop upstairs,' said Jean, keen to escape yet another row about politics with the old man. 'Excuse me. . . .'

'You don't agree with the Socialists, woman, I know you don't,' continued Harry.

'Do you?'

'Be on t'losing side if you did!' he insisted, keeping one eye on Jean as she went up the stairs. 'They're shouting for Winnie from the roof-tops. . . . "A triumphal progress" the papers call it. . . . Country'd never stand for it if Labour won!' Helen laughed and his voice changed to a hushed whisper. 'Never mind laughing. You come in here for a minute. . . .'

'Give me a chance, Dad. I've only just got in. . . . I'll put my other shoes on first. . . .'

She went off to the kitchen and he came to an instant decision. Slipping back into his room, he picked up the telegram that was on the table and then took it through to the kitchen where Helen was now taking off her best shoes and rubbing her feet. Harry stood behind her so that she could not see what he was holding and wondered how she was going to cope with what he had to say.

'Kettle's not long boiled,' he said.

'Good. I took my share of the tea ration with me. You need plenty of tea down at those Committee Rooms to keep you going. . . . Not all the others did, of course. That Mrs Harrison and Mrs Curtis from Bessemer Street never bring any. . . . "Oh, would you believe it! We forgot!". . . . War's only been over two months but they're getting back to their mean old habits, some of 'em. . . .'

She had put on her comfy working shoes now and sat back in the chair, looking round to see why he had gone silent.

'Can you stand to hear some news, Helen?'

'News?'

'I knew you'd want me to open it. . . .'

'Telegram?' she asked, feeling a stab of fear.

'Aye. . . .' He handed it over.

Helen began to look at it and then changed her mind, preferring to hear it direct from her father-in-law. His solemn expression made her prepare herself for the worst and put a name to it.

'Keir?'

'Nay, nay. . . . Good news . . . your other lad. . . .'

'Blake?'

'Nay, lass . . . Owen. . . .'

Helen was struck dumb. Fumbling with the envelope, she took out the telegram, unfolded it and ran her eye over the words without really seeing or understanding them.

'*Owen*?'

'Aye. . . .'

'Alive?'

'Aye . . . alive . . . I wanted to tell you first. Before Jean. . . .'

'But Ernst has asked her to marry him and she's agreed. We talked of nothing else all the way back. They love each other. She and Ernst want to wed.'

'Jean's already married. To your lad. . . .'

'To Owen. . . .'

'And he's alive.'

Helen buried her face in her hands, trying to cope with it all, with the miracle of her son's survival, with the upsurge of joy she was now feeling, with the knowledge of some of the harsher consequences of the news. When Jean walked into the room, she saw at once that something had happened.

'What is it?'

Mark Warrington thanked the woman with a smile and then walked along to the door of the next house. The fact that they were terraced dwellings made canvassing much easier, though he could have wished that more of the doors possessed either a knocker or a bell. His knuckles were sore from having rapped on so much wood. Mark could also have wished that there were less children about to peer at him so insolently, and less dogs to sniff at his trouser legs or bark at his advance.

He came to a door with a fine brass knocker on it and he used it gratefully to summon the householder. Within seconds the door was opened by an elderly man with grey, wispy hair and loose, bagged skin. Mark automatically began his set speech.

'Good evening, sir, I'm canvassing on behalf of the—'

'Mr Warrington, isn't it, sir?' interrupted the other with a note of deference. 'Young Mr Mark. It's Moxon, sir. I was in service with your father at Lake House before the war. . . .'

'Oh yes. Moxon . . . I didn't recognize you. . . . How are you?'

'Oh well enough, sir. I get by . . . and your father? Is he still in America?'

'Yes. Yes, he is. . . .'

'And your mother lives down the coast now, they tell me.' Moxon was quite delighted by the chance meeting, though Mark was rather unnerved by the man's reflex servility. 'And your sister—young Miss Rosalynde?'

'She's somewhere in Scotland still.'

'You do look well, sir, and no mistake. Yes, you're John Warrington's son all right . . . you'll be out of the army now, then?'

'Not yet, actually . . . soon, I hope.'

'Using your leave to help with the election, eh? Typical, if I may say so. . . . Great tradition of service in your family. . . .'

Mark peeled a leaflet off the pile in his hand and passed it to the old man who took it with an ingratiating grin. After glancing at the leaflet, however, and seeing the slogan, 'Let Us Face The Future', Moxon's tone and manner changed.

'This is for *Labour*, isn't it?'

'Of course. I'm canvassing for the Whitstanton Labour Party.'

'But. . . .' He was shaking his head in disbelief. 'Your father was Chairman of the Conservative Party in this constituency.'

'Yes, well, Dad always was a grotesque old Tory but I saw the light. . . . What I want to know is whether we can count on your support at the polls.'

'I'll give this leaflet back to you, if you don't mind,' said the other with dignity, 'because I think I know where my loyalty lies. . . . Good evening to you.'

Mark Warrington found himself staring at a closed door and then he felt the inquisitive nibble of a dog around his ankles.

The ship lay peacefully at anchor about a hundred yards from the nearest shore, the sunshine giving it a dull glow and the setting lending it a kind of makeshift glamour. Both shorelines were richly wooded and the mountains that towered behind them added a friendly solidity to the skyline. Almost everyone was on deck relaxing, even those who had to be carried there on stretchers. After years in the steaming heat of the jungles of Malaya and Burma, or in the moist stench of Singapore's Changi Jail, the men found the fresh breeze of the British climate invigorating and the rugged grandeur of the loch a solace.

'We dock tomorrow, then,' said Barstow, always the first with the latest news. 'Not before time, too. I thought they'd keep us here till Christmas. Pleased?'

'Yes,' muttered his companion, non-committally.

'You've put on weight, Owen,' noted Barstow, looking at him.

'Have I?'

'We all have, mate. That was why they brought us home by sea instead of the quick way. So that they could build us up a bit. Put back some of the weight those little yellow bastards sweated off us!' He spat with contempt over the rail. 'Seven bleeding thousand of us they had crammed together in Changi! Not one of us ever had a square meal. . . .' He scratched his bare chest and looked forward to the next day. 'It'll be great to be home again. . . . Will your missus be there?'

'I expect so. If they've been told. . . .'

'Any kids?'

'One. A boy. Colin. He was a toddler when I left . . . he'll not know who I am. . . .'

'Daresay Dad'll be waiting for me. Mum died while I was in Changi. . . . Wish I'd wed before I joined up, in a way. Gives you someone to come back to. . . . The Civvies'll have had the pick of the women while we've been away. . . . I hope they've left one for me. . . .'

'I've been four years dead to Jean,' mused Owen Hayward, trying to understand how his wife must feel. 'Four years. . . . "Missing believed dead", they were told. . . .'

'Like starting all over again for you, then,'

Owen spread his hands out and leaned on the rail gazing out across the loch to a point where birds were swooping for their food. He sounded lost.

'Are we all right?'

'All right? We're back on our feet, if that's what you mean.'

'I know they *say* we're all right, that we've come through it and that we're "normal" again—whatever that is . . . but I'm not so sure.' His voice went flat. 'The doctor asked me all about it, you see.'

'And me. Talking about it's supposed to get it out of your system. Like hell!'

'I told him the best I could but . . . it didn't sound real somehow . . . not like it happened. . . . Somehow, I just didn't want to tell him the truth . . . to talk about the Japs. . . .'

Barlow spat into the wind again.

'I never want to see a Jap again unless they put one in a cage in the zoo!' he said. 'I'd get a bloody season ticket, then. . . .'

When the result of the General Election was known for certain, ecstatic joy and sour gloom swept through the town of Whitstanton. Labour Party members and their supporters went wild with glee at the size of their overall majority in Parliament, a hundred and forty-five seats: Conservatives, like the beaten candidate, Ainscough, were shattered by what had happened and simply could not see where they had gone wrong. The mood of the town, like the mood of the country at large, was favourable to the socialist policies of reform and rebuilding. People who had never tasted power now sang with full voice—'We Are the Masters Now. . . .'

Harry Hayward, a life-long supporter of the Conservatives and a man who was convinced that they were the natural party of government, suffered an enormous blow to his pride and to his principles on that fateful day at the end of July, 1945. When he left the Conservative Club with his friend, Bert Moxon, he looked betrayed and utterly defeated. He certainly did not want anyone to make matters worse by jeering at him and so he ignored George Hayward's comments as he and Moxon hurried past the Whitstanton Working Men's Club.

'Been celebrating with champagne, have you?' asked George, enjoying his hour of revenge over his father.

'It's syrup of figs we'll need after that lot have finished with us!' complained Moxon when they were out of earshot. 'And John Warrington's son on their side, too!'

'That'll teach Churchill to sneer,' said George, swaying with the effects of the beer he had drunk. 'Now he can say that an empty taxi drew up and *Prime Minister* Attlee got out!'

'Did you really think we'd sweep the board like this, Dad?'

'Of course!'

'I didn't,' said Keir, resplendent in his uniform. 'It's been a marvellous night. Thank God I'm home to enjoy it!'

'Labour—398 seats; Tories—213. I'll have those figures inscribed on that bloody bell of his and ring it all day long!'

A cheer went up from inside the club and many voices called Keir back in so that they could buy him another drink. He shouted that he would be in soon when he had had some air.

'Bit of a hero in your uniform, Keir.'

'I'd sooner be another kind of hero in another kind of war. . . . We won, Dad! I can't get over it—we won!'

'Aye, what a night! We're broke, we're tired, we're both as near pissed as damn it . . . but we're on the way, son. . . . It's grand you got leave just now. Blake's back tomorrow and then there'll be Owen. Your mother's dream come true. . . .'

'She seems quiet about Owen. Is he well?'

'They tell us he is.'

'But after all that time, Dad. . . .'

'He's fine now, they reckon. Have you not talked to your mother about it yet?'

'Not had time, really.'

'She'll have a good long natter with you when we get back. We're up to Glasgow tomorrow to meet Owen's ship. . . . By heck, what years they've been, eh! What years! And all over! We've put the lights on at last! Come on—let's go back in.'

'One for the road?'

'Yes, Keir, the road to tomorrow.'

Father and son were soon submerged in a sea of laughter and celebration as the working men of Whitstanton savoured their moment of victory.


Arriving home during the relative quiet of the next day, Blake Hayward was glad to have missed the hysteria of Election night. He wanted nothing more than to see the old house again, to admire the way that Colin and Lovett had grown in the time he had been away, and to take a first walk down to the edge of the sea. It was still morning when he went back to his room, changed and came down for a late breakfast cooked for him by Peg. When she saw that he was wearing his Tropical Issue uniform of khaki shorts and shirt, she giggled.

'You're not at El Alamein now!'

'This is the only stuff I'll feel comfy in. That demob suit is death.' He sat at the table. 'How's the romance going, anyway?'

'Mind your own business!'

'You wouldn't have met the lad but for me,' he pointed out.

'True—and thanks. Mark's home today, as a matter of fact. Only stationed at Catterick. He thinks he'll be out before Christmas, with luck.'

'All smooth sailing, is it?' Peg looked fuller in the face than he remembered her and she had a bloom that he found touching. 'Any problems?'

'It threw Dad a bit when he discovered that Mark was one of *the* Warringtons, then he learned that he had a political soul-mate. . . .'

'One of Them becoming one of Us!'

'Dad still only half-believes it. A Warrington on the Left!'

'Sign of the times, Peg,' said Blake, sardonically. 'We've had the reality, now we want the dream!'

'Cynic!'

'Been called worse. . . .'

'So what's *your* dream?'

'To join the club. You'll never beat them—except in the odd election now and then.'

'Defeatist!'

'You feel the same as me but you won't admit it. Not in this house. I can't do not—not even for Dad's sake. After four years of doing as I'm told, I've had a bellyful of State control!'

Jean put his breakfast in front of him and he started to eat. She sipped at her tea and thought about a third returning brother.

'They'll be meeting Owen's boat this morning. . . .'

'He'll not be the same man, you know. You must have read what the Japs have done to the lads.'

'Why did they never let him write home? Other prisoners did. But not Owen.'

'It was because he held out, if I know him. Refused to behave as abjectly in front of them as a soldier of a defeated nation should. Owen always did have more guts than the rest of us.' He munched some more toast. 'Does he know about Jean and that chap?'

'We're all trying to pretend it didn't happen. I liked Ernst. . . . He'd had a rotten time. . . . She was his future.'

'Poor devil!' he said with feeling. 'What will happen to him?'

'There's a rumour he'll be sent back to the Russians.'

'God help him!'

'You say that as if you know what's in store for him.'

'I've had a taste of it . . . of someone I care for disappearing into that . . . silence.'

'Someone in Germany?' she pressed. 'Fraternizing?'

'That's a stupid word, Peg.'.

'Sorry, but it's the word they use over here.'

'Over here they know nothing—nothing!' he exploded.

During the pause that followed, Lovett wandered in to have his breakfast and the tension was broken. Harry Hayward, taking advantage of the fact that George was out of the house, now rolled up to eat with them. He was pleased to hear that Blake was thinking of spending his demob pay on a boat but critical of his grandson's 'posh' accent. Colin was the next in, talking excitedly about the return of his father. When Keir joined them all for his breakfast, the talk immediately swung to politics and argument buzzed all round the room.

Blake was in the middle of his family once more and it was exactly as he had remembered it. He winked at Peg and then threw some stray remarks in to keep the debate happily acrimonious.

Rosalynde Warrington snipped away in the garden of her mother's house until she had enough flowers to fill the large cut-glass vase. When she took them back into the house, her brother, still in uniform, was fastening the straps on his pack.

'Sorry we can't give you a decent breakfast, Mark,' she apologized, putting the flowers down on a newspaper. 'Mum's got her coupons but we haven't had time to go shopping yet.'

'I'm not staying.'

'But you have a week's leave.'

'They're expecting me at Peg's house.' He continued quickly as his sister arched an eyebrow. 'It was arranged long before I knew that you and Mum were going to be in Whitstanton.'

'So last night was a duty call.'

'Don't be an idiot! I wanted to see you . . . and Mum, of course. I've only seen her once in the last four years—and not so damned often before that.' He put down his pack and perched on the arm of the settee. 'When I was at home from school, she always seemed to be in the garden reading.'

'That was one of Dad's complaints, when she went down to London after the war started to do her bit in the A.T.S.'

'Not the reason they separated, though. . . .'

Ros went into the kitchen with the vase and came back with water in it. She was a neat, shapely woman with brisk but feminine movements and she had Mark's colouring and open countenance. As she selected flowers and put them into the vase, she asked him if either of their parents had ever told him why they had parted.

'Mum did. Very briefly. . . . I wasn't surprised she broke loose, to be honest. It happened to a lot of women. She must have had a damned boring life playing the lady of the manor for the benefit of Dad's county friends.'

Almost on cue, Beth Warrington, a handsome and elegant woman in a stylish blue dress, sailed in and admired the flowers. She sensed the atmosphere at once.

'Should my ears be burning?' she wondered.

'No, of course not,' lied Rosalynde. 'By the way, Mark's not staying. He's arranged to visit someone else around here.'

'Found himself a new family, has he?' Beth said, with a look in his direction. 'We can hardly blame him. We've not been much of a family to him over the years.'

'Rubbish!' protested Rosalynde.

'I notice that you don't deny it, Mark?'

Mark was so unused to being with his mother that he could not tell if she was mocking him or showing her disapproval. Beth

Warrington had a surface sophistication that he had never managed to penetrate or understand. When she asked him the name of his new family, he told her and explained that George Hayward was the secretary of the Whitstanton Labour Party.

'Oh . . . that's interesting,' she said, without any scorn.

'I find him fascinating to talk to. He knows all the phrases. I've learned a lot from Mr Hayward.' Seeing that his mother's attention was starting to wander, he told her about his meeting with Moxon. 'He used to work at Lake House.'

'I could never forget Moxon, dear. . . . I daresay he bowed from the waist. He was always so correct.' Her eyes were roving as if she were searching for something. 'Where did you bump into him?'

'On his doorstep. I rather shocked him, I'm afraid.'

'Have you seen my reading glasses anywhere, Ros?'

'I was canvassing for the Labour Party!'

Mark blurted this out as if fearing, and at the same time inviting, some kind of rebuke. Instead, his mother simply looked at him with an amused curiosity then went out.

'Good God! I thought she'd be as rattled as old Moxon.'

'I told you that she'd changed, Mark.'

'Don't tell you both voted Labour, too?'

'My beliefs aren't political. I just know where my loyalty lies, that's all.'

'Funny! That's exactly what Moxon said.'

'Good for him!' she replied. 'It won't last, you know. It's only a superficial wartime conversion. Yours is like a lot of Labour votes.'

'You mean, one day I'll come to my senses?' he teased.

'Of course,' she said, seriously. 'It's the same with Mum. Her conversion is only skin-deep. The man she went off was some kind of socialist who fought in the Spanish Civil War. Last time I saw her he'd just been killed in France.'

'You could be right, Ros—about her, not me. With her passion for books, she probably stumbled on Shaw by mistake and had a freak conversion that way.'

'I hope it doesn't last. It'd ruin any chance of her coming back to Dad.'

'Would she ever do that?' he asked with surprise.

'I don't know. We've all changed, haven't we?'

'You as well?'

'Oh yes, Mark,' she said, firmly. 'I had my war, too, you know.'

The war which had made Blake Hayward turn against the values of his father had only served to make his brother, Keir, hold to them more strongly. There were times when he even sounded like George Hayward and Peg was finding that out now. Keir was questioning her about her friendship with Mark.

'He's one of the landed gentry, I hear. One of the Ironmasters.'

'Mark is not like that.'

'Isn't he? . . . Have you met his parents yet?'

'No. His father's still in America and his mother's away a lot. . . .'

'They're going to find this hard to take—you and him, I mean. Even in our new People's democracy! All this stuff about class going out with the war is pure eyewash. It's not as if the Warringtons are *nouveau riche* either. They're your traditional county types.'

'If you're trying to put me off you're wasting your time,' she said, armoured against any criticism of Mark.

'All I'm saying is "Beware".'

Peg crossed to the ironing board and started on one of the other chores she had inherited in her mother's absence. As she ran the flat-iron over the sleeve of a grey shirt, she asked Keir what his plans were. He confessed that he was not looking forward to being demobbed at all because he had somehow, against all odds, really enjoyed the war and thrived on its danger and excitement. Being at home a mere three days had made him restless and bored and he said that he felt only half-alive.

'Yet you were always the brains of the family, Keir. The studious one of us kids. We all used to have to keep quiet while you did your homework. You slaved away hour after hour, as if your life depended on it.'

'And where did it get me? Do you know, I had a pal in the R.A.F. who was a brilliant bloke. First class honours at Oxford, The lot. . . . A Jerry cannon shell smeared him over the runway like jam!'

Peg went on with her ironing for a moment then told him of her mother's wishes that he would resume his studies by taking a government grant for ex-servicemen. Keir's disenchantment, however, was complete.

'Not a chance!'

'You'll have to do something, Keir.'

'That's what worries me.'

'If the war hadn't happened, you'd be teaching by now.'

'Can you see me in a classroom, Peg? The very thought of it gives me the heeby-jeebies.'

'I wish I could help,' she offered.

He was touched by the simple affection of her remark and ruffled her hair playfully before putting an arm around her shoulder and whispering in her ear.

'Don't let those people take you over and make you one of them. Promise?'

'There's no danger of that, Keir,' she asserted.

'No,' he laughed. 'They couldn't do that to you if they tried. You have a mind of your own. Always did have. Does this Mark character know that?'

Helen Hayward sat on the edge of the bed in the hotel bedroom as Jean paced up and down like a caged animal. They had decided that it was best not to go to the dockside to meet the boat and were instead condemned to a long wait in a strange room. Jean did not know how she could face a man she had put out of her mind and she was certain she could never tell him about Ernst. When Helen reminded her that her husband would need her, she gave a shrug of despair. There was a knock on the door and George came in with Owen, who looked pale, strained, apprehensive. Tension made all four of them stand quite still for a long while, then Jean and Owen embraced each other in a formal and joyless way, because it was expected of them.

Whitstanton beach was deserted as the two women trudged across it with full carrier bags. It was Beth Warrington who suggested that they take a rest and she sat on a rock with a sigh of relief.

'I told you we should have had a taxi. We haven't been able to carry half the things we need.'

'So? We go again tomorrow. I like shopping in Whitstanton.'

'It's so shabby!' said Rosalynde, wrinkling her nose.

'Shabby with the wear and tear of keeping the Warringtons in the manner to which they've been accustomed!'

'You sound like Mark.'

'Is that a compliment?' she asked, then continued quickly, 'and before you say it, I *know* I'm not a true Warrington at heart. Nor by birth. I'm a Hardrow. My father was a self-made man. I'm not even a Northerner. I'm from the soft south. When I gave up my Faith— such as it was—to marry your father, it didn't make me a member of the other club—the Kennel Club, as I call it. You can't acquire pedigree. You're either born with it or you're not.'

Rosalynde Warrington gazed along the beach in the direction of the sea wall until she spotted a building which, from her brother's description, had to be the Hayward house. Even at that great distance it looked lonely and dilapidated.

'I wonder if she'll be able to go through with it?'

'Through with what?'

'Everything. Becoming one of us. . . . I've a feeling that Mark hasn't told her yet that we're Catholics. That blow is yet to come. Along with many others. . . .'


## CHAPTER SIX

Under any other circumstances, a night in a comfortable Glasgow hotel would have been a real treat for Helen Hayward, if only because it would have rescued her from her daily round of cooking, washing, mending, and accommodating the needs and temperaments of a wilful family. But the night she spent there with Jean and Owen was nothing short of an ordeal for everyone concerned. When she had watched the couple go off to their room, two strangers with nothing in common apart from an instinct to do what had to be done, Helen had found her heart missing a beat. She felt for both of them, for her own son who had come back in a daze to a world he did not recognize and a role he did not know how to play, and also for Jean, who had sacrificed a chance of happiness with one man in order to do her duty by another she had long since buried in her mind.

There had been little sleep for any of the Hayward family in the hotel that night and it made Helen irritable the next morning.

'Where've you been?' she snapped, as George entered.

'Downstairs . . . with Owen. . . .'

'Give me a hand with this case. The catch is stuck again—I don't know why I always have to do the packing!'

'Maybe it's because you're so much better at it, love,' soothed her husband, putting his full weight down on the lid so that the catch slipped easily into place. 'There . . . okay?'

'I'm not really cross with *you*, George,' she apologized.

'I know, love.'

'But seeing him eat that breakfast this morning, not even the tiniest spot of egg stain left on the plate. You'd think he'd not had food for a month.'

'That's what kept me so long down there. The waiter brought more toast, so he ate it. So the waiter brought some more again, so he polished that off as well. It would have gone on forever if I'd not said something.'

'What have they *done* to him out there, George?'

'Thousands of 'em died of starvation. Owen was one of the lucky ones.'

'Lucky!'

She had been shocked to see him. He had looked vaguely like the son that she had known but he had seemed so different, so vacant, so unfocussed. Her guilt stirred.

'Have we done right?'

'What way?'

'Expecting Jean to give up Ernst ... to go back to things as they were. Because she can never do that, George. You've seen them together. There's ... nothing ... a huge gap. They've lived different lives for the last five years.'

'She's his wife,' said George, as if that settled matters.

'Would you have expected it of *me*?'

'I can't answer for him like that, love. All I know is that. ... Jean is making the effort. We can't ask for more.'

'Owen will never know about Ernst.'

'I hope to God he doesn't!' said George. 'Seeing him like that, I doubt if he could live with it!'


Breakfast at the Hayward house that morning was a hectic affair with Colin gobbling his food down so that he could get changed to go to the station, Harry complaining about the request that he should wear his best Sunday suit to meet Owen, Lovett disputing Blake's right to the largest piece of fried bread, and Keir asking out loud why Peg and Mark were such an interminable time feeding the hens. At length the two boys went off to get ready for the trip to the station and the three men were left alone. Keir's immediate concern was for Colin.

'Has someone prepared him?'

'How do you explain what goes on in a Jap P.O.W. camp to a lad like Col?' asked Blake.

'His generation needs to know,' insisted his brother. 'And about Buchenwald, Dachau, Belsen. ...'

'Yes, and what the Russians are now doing in Europe,' added Harry.

'By God, yes!' agreed Blake. 'Everyone needs to be told about what they're doing there. In Poland, Germany. ...'

'You've been reading the Tory press,' said Keir with scorn.

'The Tory press doesn't print what I *know*, Keir. And it's to their shame. Their honeymoon with Ivan isn't over yet. They're afraid to upset our glorious allies.'

'You've changed, Blake! Has Grandad been working on you?'

'No, he hasn't!'

'He needs nowt from me,' said Harry, pointing a long finger at Blake. 'He was there. He saw it.'

'Oh yes. I saw it all right!' recalled Blake, then he noticed the twinkle behind his Grandfather's glasses. 'What's the joke?'

'Way you've done an about turn, lad. You were t'other way around in your views before the war. What changed you?'

'Five years submission to authority.'

'You'd rather have submitted to Hitler, would you?' yelled Keir, thumping the table.

'That's a cheap simplification!' retorted Blake.

The argument became a slanging match between the two of them and it was left to Harry Hayward to end it by standing up angrily and speaking with querulous intensity.

'The war's over! Your brother's coming home, that's had more stick than either of you, so bear that in mind. He'll need what we all need. Peace!' He waved a fist at them. 'Bloody peace!''

The others looked shamefaced but said nothing. Peg entered.

'This letter just came for you, Blake.' She handed it over. 'Can I have the German stamp when you've done?'

'Yes, yes. . . .' muttered Blake and went out.

'Well, well,' said Keir, raising his eyebrows. 'Letters from Germany, is it? Well, well. . . .'

Fearing exactly this reaction, Blake went down to the beach to read his letter in private. Unfolding the flimsy airmail paper, he read Herta's neat, rounded handwriting. It seemed oddly inappropriate for the expression of so much despair.

'. . . a friend will post this to you, should he be able to leave the Russian sector. For most here it is impossible. I cannot give you an address to which to write. I move from camp to camp, looking for my father. He was not at Dusberg. There are many like me, searching, looking for the lost. I think of you often, free in your England. I did not dream much in the past. Often now I dream. In the cold, dirty places in which we have to live because it is all there is, I close my eyes and dream to escape.'

Blake read the letter again and he could hear Herta's voice speaking some of the words—'There are many like me, searching, looking for the lost. . . .'

The train was travelling at speed along the track, listing gently and leaving a long trail of steam in its wake to autograph its passing. It had crossed the border now and was heading for Carlisle through open countryside. Owen Hayward stared through the window of the compartment like a boy on his first train ride, trying to take in the wonder of it. He became aware that his father was watching him and turned to face him.

'England!' he said, with a smile.

'Aye, son. . . .'

Jean seemed to be in some discomfort and excused herself. After she had disappeared down the narrow corridor, Owen furrowed his brow as if working something out in his mind.

'She's different, Jean . . . from how I remembered.'

'Aren't we all?' said Helen.

'She's quiet, Mum. Never used to stop talking.'

'She's a bit overcome by it all.'

'Aye, that'll be it,' said Owen, as if the problem had been solved. 'It's a big day, after all, a big day.'

He turned back to the window and watched the English country-side rolling by.


Blake Hayward had his grandfather's love of the sea and he liked nothing more than to sail across the bay in a small boat. He had been quite pleased when Keir had asked to go along with him because it meant they could talk more freely away from the house, and because he felt the need of some company. As they cut through the water in the direction of Barrow, it was Mark Warrington who became the chief topic of conversation. Blake explained how he had first met Mark in Germany and asked him to call in at the house when he was on leave in Whitstanton.

'He's got his eye on our Peg, that's for certain,' said Keir.

'If you ask me, it's the other way round.'

'Why did she have to fall for one of Them? Dad's played Bob Cratchit to the corporate Scrooge of the Warrington family for the best part of his life. Underpaid, undervalued in some petty little job for those screwing sods!'

'I worked for them myself before the war, Keir.'

'Would you do it again?' challenged the other.

'May have to.'

'Back to being a mechanic? You'll find that a bit painful.'

'It's not the rank, I'll miss. It's the company, that's what the Army gave me. I've more in common with any private who served in the same campaigns as I did than with anybody who stayed back here. Family excluded, of course.'

'Camaraderie of war? Sorry, Blake, but there'll be precious little of that in the peace. We'll be back to the same old political strife, mark my words.'

'Not me, Keir. Not on your side, anyway. We've had five years of not being able to call your soul your own. Remember that famous National Savings poster—"Lend to defend the right to be free"? Yes, well I lent five years of my life. I'm back to collect.'

'That shouldn't be difficult with the kind of half-hëarted socialism we'll get from this lot. Dad thinks they're great, of course. He'll learn.'

'I prefer a Labour Government to the state of bondage you'd have us in, brother!'

Blake relieved the tension by bringing the boat around in a graceful arc and setting a course for Whitstanton again. Keir talked about the possibility of his own discharge soon and admitted that he faced the future with misgivings. Nothing that was on offer seemed to have any appeal for him. He lay back in the boat and enjoyed the tug of the wind for a few minutes. Then he asked the question he had been saving up all morning.

'Are you going to marry this Fräulein?'

'She's a Frau, actually. Who told you about her? Peg?'

'Eventually.'

'When the barriers come down, yes ... I shall marry her. But don't you dare say anything to Mum.'

'Because she's German, you mean?' said Keir, sitting up. His tone became sardonic. 'I wouldn't worry about that, Blake. We've cut out own bread ration to feed them, after all! When we've rebuilt their factories and re-armed them, they'll be ready for another go at us. About a decade on my reckoning. . . . We'll never learn not to trust. . . .'

Keir now lapsed into a brooding silence and his brother did nothing to break it on the journey back to the shore.


When they got back from their second shopping expedition to Whitstanton, she saw something that needed instant attention. A keen gardener who liked to keep everything tidily under control, Rosalynde Warrington went straight across to some roses that needed tying back, telling her mother to go on into the house with the carrier bags. While her daughter was searching for some twine and her old gloves in the shed outside, Beth let herself in through the front door and dumped her cargo down. The sound of footsteps above her head made her stiffen but her fear changed to amazement as she recognized the figure descending the stairs in a characteristically smart suit.

'John!'

'Hello, Beth,' said her husband.ᶻ

'I thought you were still in Washington.'

'The Ministry wanted me back here for a few days. I fly off again next week.' He appraised her from under thick brows. 'You look well.'

'So do you.'

John Warrington was a big, distinguished-looking man with wavy hair that was greying discreetly at the temples. Time had been kind to him and he was exactly as she had remembered him. He, however, noticed an immediate difference in her.

'Your hair's shorter.'

'Is it?'

'I like it that way.' He led her into the living room as he talked about wanting to be released from Ministry work so that he could come back to Whitstanton. Then he shrugged. 'Well? Aren't you going to ask me how I got in?'

'I assumed it was with a key.'

'Why should I have a key, Beth?'

'The house is yours,' she reminded him. 'You own it.'

He ignored the sharpness that lay behind this and told her that he had climbed in through a window and been quite impressed with his skill as a burglar. He had come back to the house for some papers but had been unable to find them. Earlier in the day, he had been to search at Lake House as well but the papers had not been there either. Beth wondered what Lake House was like now.

'Like a barracks. The army hasn't moved out yet. The furniture's crammed in the stables. . . . I wouldn't mind preserving some of the ditties on the wall. Vulgar but very entertaining.'

'That doesn't sound like you, John. Has America coarsened you?'

'It's made me want to come home, I know that.'

'Home?'

'England. Still green . . . a bit battered, maybe, but it's not changed all that much. . . . I walked through London yesterday, through the City, down by the docks. Like being with a dear old friend again. I also went to Uncle's house—or where it used to be, anyway. Just a bomb site now. I hope they don't spoil it when they put it all back together again.'

'That funny old world we lived in together . . . all that time ago.' Feeling the pull of memories she had tried to subdue, she turned the talk to the Election result and found her husband surprisingly resigned to the prospect of a Labour government. 'I'd forgotten how philosophical you can be about some things.'

'If not about others. . . .' He could see she did not want to pick this up and announced that he was off to Scotland soon. 'I simply must see Ros.'

'Then step out into the garden.'

'She's here!' he was thrilled. 'What about Mark?'

'Oh he's with his new family.'

'Family?'

Before she could explain, there was a call from the garden. Rosalynde Warrington was asking her mother to take out the scissors so that she could cut the twine.

'She seemed unhappy, reading between the lines of her letters. Is she?'

'I'm afraid so. She's been involved with a man up there.'

'Is he married?'

'Yes, but he's a Catholic, too.'

'Poor Ros! It's so much worse when it's one of us.'

At that moment Rosalynde herself came into the room to ask what was keeping her mother. She halted in the doorway.

'Dad!'

'Hello, my love.'

She ran to his arms and the reunion was warm and very touching. Beth Warrington looked away and began to wish that her husband had not come.

The train was late and they stood on the platform of the tiny station at Whitstanton with growing impatience. Harry Hayward, unused to wearing his best suit on a weekday, grumbled about the state of the railways under a Labour government that had not yet taken office. Keir wandered restlessly up and down. Blake studied the time-tables pasted up outside the ticket office. Peg tried to contain her excitement and told Mark over and over again about her favourite brother. Lovett and Colin played games together, dodging in and out of the red fire buckets that stood along the platform, and paying no heed to the constant orders from other members of the family not to get themselves dirty.

At length the train announced itself with its clank and hiss before coming into view around a bend in the distance. A sense of nervous anticipation united everyone waiting and they lined up together in a tight bunch. As the carriages pulled up to a juddering halt, a door opened and George Hayward stepped out and helped his wife after him. The welcoming party hurried along to the door and were in time to see Owen, bemused but happy, getting out with Jean. There was a babble of voices as everyone tried to cover the great gap of a five-year absence with inane chatter, then Owen spoke himself for the first time.

'Col. . . . Where's Col?'

A space was cleared for the youngest member of the family, whose size and diffidence had got him pushed to the back. Blake eased him forward towards his father. Colin said nothing.

'Cat got your tongue?' asked Harry, nudging him.

'Col. . . .' Owen went up to his son, took him by the shoulders, and looked searchingly at his face. 'Hello, Col. . . .'

He suddenly put his arms around the boy and embraced him with an almost frightening intensity, like a drowning man clinging to a spar of timber that is the only thing that might save him. Colin was hurt and afraid and the others watched with evident concern. Jean felt yet another spasm of fear, Helen grasped her husband's arm by instinct and Peg's cheeks were drained of all colour. Lovett was as embarrassed as the adults and shifted his feet.

Owen now let go of Colin and stepped right back as if afraid of the awareness that the moment had created inside him. He looked around the strained faces of the others, then saw that Colin had drifted over to his mother to stand slightly behind her. Owen could find no words to break the tense atmosphere and it was left to the oldest member of the family to do it for him.

'I said the cat had got his tongue. . . .'

'Let's all go home,' suggested George Hayward.

The group moved slowly towards the exit and a laboured conversation started up. Colin, holding his mother's hand, kept a distance between himself and his father.


Herta Wenkel got out of the back of the truck and thanked the driver for the lift. She groped in her pocket for a few coins but he waved his hand dismissively and drove off. Picking up her small bundle of belongings, she set off towards the buildings that stood a few hundred yards away. Like all the other camps she had visited, this one was large, sprawling, filthy, unwelcoming and full with the miseries that only a defeated people can suffer. A bunch of Russian soldiers saw her coming and she immediately became the butt of some coarse jokes. She kept trudging on towards them, however, sustained by the urge to find her father no matter how long it took her and by the fleeting memory of a captain in the British Army.

'Papers!' demanded one of the Russian guards.

Herta handed over her documents and withstood the now familiar interrogation and abuse. When she was allowed into the camp, she was met by the knowing stares of other German civilians who had felt the cold aggression of their captors.

The other brothers were fine. Blake had come back pining for a lost love and Keir had developed a kind of obsessive restlessness, but otherwise they seemed fine. Jean thought this as she watched them chatting and laughing in the living room that evening, two healthy young men who had come through the war relatively unscathed. This was not the case with her husband. Jean found herself wishing that she had married either Keir or Blake. It was a cruel thought but it gave her a momentary comfort. When she left them all, the brothers were arguing happily about politics again with their father. Only duty took her away from them.

Owen was at the window when she entered the bedroom. He seemed to be miles away and did not notice she was there for minutes. They had made no contact yet in any way. The night at the hotel in Glasgow had been one of quiet torment for both of them as they had lain, side by side and wide awake, in a bed that they had forgotten how to share. Jean was not looking forward to this first night at home.

'It's the same wallpaper,' he said, softly.

'Yes, it's still the same. We've thought to brighten the room up but you can't get the paint.'

'I used to look at it . . . at the camp. . . .'

'The *wallpaper*?'

'At night, in the darkness of the hut. I used to look at it in my mind, like lerlum.'

'Lerlum?' She thought he was rambling.

'Col . . . when he was a baby . . . when you put him in his cot at night, he'd reach for the ribbon that bound the end . . . touch it . . . suck it. . . .'

'Yes, he did. I'd forgotten.'

'One of the first words he ever made up on his own was . . . lerlum. . . . Lerlum, he'd say.' Owen turned away from the window. 'Where is Col?'

'Gone down to the beach with Grandad. . . .'

'He seemed a bit . . . scared of me. His father.'

'It's all been a bit much for him, Owen. . . . You understand.'

'How old is he?' asked Owen, confused.

'You don't remember?'

'I remembered at first. Then I got it mixed up . . . and the wallpaper . . . it's the same except that the bit at the end curled the other way. . . . Daft, isn't it? How you forget.'

'I've forgotten things, too,' she admitted.

'Yes?'

He was offering her the chance to tell him what had happened while he was away and what her true feelings for him were now. But

Jean was not able to talk to him in this way, preferring to keep her thoughts to herself and simply to help Owen get through each day in as gentle and painless a way as possible.

'I've put the things they gave you in the top drawer,' she said, pointing. 'The tablets and that.'

Owen came and stood close to her, his expressionless face at last breaking into a brave smile.

'I think I'm all right, you know. They say I'm all right.'

When Jean looked at the sunken cheeks and the sad, haunted eyes and thought about the Owen Hayward that she had married, it was almost too much for her to bear and she had to bite her lip.

'You've only just missed them, actually. They've gone to Lake House. Mummy wanted to see it again.' Rosalynde bestowed a polite grin on the guest. 'You must be Peggy. . . .'

'Peg,' corrected Mark.

'Hello, Peg . . . I'm Ros.'

'Hello,' said Peg.

'It's short for "Rosalynde",' explained Mark. 'My mother's favourite character from Shakespeare.'

'Except that I've got the Olde Worlde spelling with a "y". I'm sure they thought it was quaint at the time but it means that everyone gets it wrong when they write to me.'

Peg was still staring at her rather intently, struck by the clear proof that she was Mark's sister. The resemblance was striking and yet it was more in her bearing and manner than in any physical details. Not wishing to appear rude, Peg now glanced around the room and admired the futniture.

'It's mostly from the Lake,' explained Rosalynde.

'Nicked while the old man was in Washington,' supplied Mark.

'Don't listen to him, Peg!'

'It's all right. I'm used to him.'

'That means you've seen through him already.'

'Let's just say that I know he puts on an act sometimes. Like pretending to be shy.'

'I haven't seen that one!'

'Oh shut up!' said Mark good-humouredly, as they both had a laugh at his expense. 'Peg wanted a look round, Ros.'

'Yes, I love houses. . . .'

'Help yourself,' invited Rosalynde. She waited until Peg had gone out. 'You're in deep, aren't you?'

'Yes. I am, as a matter of fact.'

Rosalynde waited for him to enlarge on this but he changed his mind and asked about their father instead. He was interested to hear that John Warrington had been talking about him the previous night and pressed for details.

'He wanted to know what you're going to do when you've been demobbed.'

'I haven't the faintest idea.'

'He thought you might like to start in the main works office at Silport, just until he gets back.'

'And perpetuate the Warrington name in the family business,' he said, verging on sarcasm.

'I told him I didn't think you'd be keen.'

'It'd keep me in the area.'

'Is that a good enough reason, Mark?'

'It's a good temporary reason. By the way, I'd rather not see him this time round. Rather glad we missed them. We'll slip off before they get back.'

'He'll be hurt,' she protested.

'I'm sure you can find some plausible excuse to protect him.'

'You weren't like this with mother.'

'Oh mother!' he said, smirking.

'Is it because they separated? Is that why you turned against them, Mark?' He shrugged and moved away. 'That's how it looks from here.'

'Ros, I hardly know them, do I? How can I be expected to have any real relationship with them? Away at school, and then the war years. I just want to . . . to go my own way, that's all. As I have been doing.' He tried to make the next question sound casual, though it was something that was very important to him. 'Getting together again, are they?'

'What makes you think that?'

'Separated couples don't often go off to look at the old homestead together.'

'I wouldn't know . . . as for them. . . .'

Rosalynde was not ready to speculate any further. Mark decided that he would like to leave soon and asked after his books. When he was told where they were, he went off to find some of them and Rosalynde was left alone to consider his ambiguous attitude to their parents, avoiding them and yet wanting to know what their plans were. Peg joined her.

'Mark says we're off. Is that true?'

'Apparently.'

'I like it here. Couldn't he be persuaded to stay longer?'

'I doubt it.'

'Is it some deep psychological reason?'

'Probably.' Rosalynde did not feel able to confide in her yet. Peg had found a lot out about Mark but there were some things that he had not even accepted about himself. 'You love him, don't you?'

'Well. . . .'

'Even with that hard streak he's got?'

'Mark? Hard? Never! He's as soft as butter, really.'

'Oh yes, he's that, too. Sometimes.'

The two women exchanged a laugh, each of them liking the other more than they had expected to and yet still having a few reservations. Peg now wandered around the living room itself, intrigued by everything she saw. She stopped beside the ornate crucifix on the wall and asked why it was there.

'I've never seen one like this outside a church before.'

'We're Catholics. Didn't Mark tell you?'

Peg Hayward was quite shocked, not by the information itself but by the fact that it had been kept from her all this time. Her gaze was almost resentful when he came back into the room.

Keir Hayward wandered aimlessly into the kitchen and started to examine his mother's small collection of Coronation mugs. The sight of a king and queen staring back at him from the glazed china soon put a stop to the exercise, as Keir's views on royalty were similar to those of his father. His eye now fell on the enamel bread bin and he lifted the lid tentatively, finding to his delight that there was still some bread in there. He now set off on a spirited search for something to have on the bread and the third cupboard he opened yielded him something that made him yell out with pleasure. He took the pot to the table, cut himself a slice from the batch and started to spread.

'You'll spoil your appetite,' said his mother, coming in behind him. 'Don't they feed you in the R.A.F.?'

'Not with luxuries like bread and dripping!'

'I hope you've brought your coupons. Especially for meat.'

'Of course!' He surveyed the sandwich he had made. 'This is what it's all about . . . home. Being able to drift in here when you've a mind to and pig yourself on this. It's what they mean by calling your soul your own.'

'That's what you missed most, is it?'

'You know what I missed most,' he said, through a mouthful of bread and dripping.

'Do I?' she asked, pleased that he meant her. 'Well, time I went and practised, I suppose.'

'Piano? You can play it with your eyes shut.'

'This is special. I'm singing in Chapel next Sunday with one of my prize pupils.'

It was heart-warming to have all four of her sons under her roof again and Helen had not yet got used to the idea. Lovett had helped to get her through the darker days of the war. She would now have to help Owen through his darker days, but this would be a labour of love. Blake had arrived home with his usual jauntiness and reminded her why he was her favourite; and Keir, unsettled as he obviously was, still talked to her sometimes as he had done when he was a boy, with a refreshing candour.

'Blake's going back to his old job,' observed Keir.

'He'll not be content with that for long. Blake's ambitious. Look how he got on in the Army.'

'Full captain, while I'm just a humble sergeant.'

'He's a bit strange since he came back. Moody. Goes walking along the shore a lot, for hours sometimes.'

'Dreaming of his Fräulein, I expect.'

'Fräulein?'

'Hey, have I said something I shouldn't?'

'Yes, and you did it on purpose. You never could keep a secret. Who is she?'

'Secret!' he grinned.

'A German girl?'

'You'd better ask Blake,' he said, eating the last of his sandwich and smacking his lips.

'Oh you!' Her curiosity was aroused now. It would certainly explain Blake's behaviour. 'Will she be allowed to come here?'

'Who?' He was pretending ignorance.

'This German girl.'

'*What* German girl?'

'The one you told me about.'

'But it's a secret!'

She grabbed the tea towel and flicked it at him in mock irritation, having played this sort of game with him so often when he was young. Keir grabbed the tea towel and grinned at her. George Hayward arrived in the doorway in time to witness the scene and it brought a chuckle out of him. Helen leaned against the table and ruffled Keir's hair.

'Oh, you're maddening, but it's good to have you back!'

Mark Warrington got to the halfway stage and stopped but Peg just carried on walking. She felt that she did not need a rest on the long walk back to her house and she was annoyed by his insistence on treating her as if she was some sort of invalid.

'Stop trying to wrap me up in cotton wool,' she called over her shoulder. I don't want to live like that.'

'It's just a sensible precaution,' he argued, catching her up and falling into step beside her.

'I know when to stop, Mark.'

'But you don't, that's the trouble. You just go blinding on as if . . . as if. . . .'

'As if I was normal?'

'I don't want to lose you, Peg,' he said.

'I don't want to lose you either.'

'Me?'

'To God—or whatever doubts and uncertainties kept you from telling me you were a Catholic.'

This time they both came to a halt. Mark was not sure if he felt annoyed or guilty. He knew at once who had told her.

'Ros?'

'I sensed that there was something holding you back. I'd have popped the question myself only I thought you'd turn me down.' She put a hand to his face. 'What is it? What's the problem?'

'I'm a bad Catholic,' he shrugged.

'You mean, you don't believe any more?'

'I don't know, Peg. It's all so difficult.'

'Well I can't wait forever while you sort it all out, Mark. It's not the way I cope with things, bottling them up.'

'I know.'

'So what *is* the problem?'

'Simply that . . . I don't want to believe. . . .' He shrugged his shoulders again. 'But somehow I can't let go . . . not completely. . . .'

'Where do I come into it? Would I have to join the Catholic Church?'

'Father Ross would say so. "Become a Catholic, or be damned", he'd say. Laughing, mind you.'

'I don't think I like Father Ross.'

'He's all right. You two would get on.'

'Mark, I'm not that stuck on marriage, you know,' she said, slipping her arms around his neck. 'Not desperate, I mean. I can wait for it. You're the only thing I can't wait for.'

He pulled her close and kissed her full on the lips for a long time. When he released her so that he could speak, he had forgotten Father Ross.

'You don't have to wait for me, Peg. God can wait. He's got more time than we have.'

They struck off to the right and headed straight up the beach towards the outcrop of rock and grass.

John Warrington had dined with his wife and daughter for the first time in ages and he had enjoyed the experience enormously, despite the raw nerves that were touched by occasional remarks. The wine made him lapse into a chauvinistic mood and he talked about the future that Britain would have if only they listened to the right people for advice about the running of the economy. Beth heard him out until she grew tired and then excused herself and went to bed. She did not seem disturbed that she would not see him in the morning because of his early departure.

John was glad of the time to talk alone with Ros. Her letters had been a lifeline while he had been in America and he told her so.

'Great to be back. We may be the biggest debtor nation in the world, but this is still the only place worth living in!'

'Mark doesn't think so.'

'I suppose he's become a socialist idealist?'

'It's the fashion. . . .'

'Goes with the times. . . . All right, we made a mess of it before the war. Better to put it right now than get involved in an unproductive class struggle, surely? It's going to take all of us, not just some of us. Especially the young who've got the energy.'

'I think he'd be glad of that job if you could arrange it.'

'Not averse to a spot of nepotism, then?' commented John, with a wry smile.

'Oh Mark is so confused! Doesn't really know what he wants.'

'I wish I could have seen him, Ros.'

'He'll be on his way back now,' she lied. 'He only had forty-eight hours.' She could see that he was not convinced. 'Mark would like what I'd like really. For us all to be a family again.'

'Again?'

'You know what I mean?'

'Yes, of course, and it's what I want, too. Only it isn't quite so easy, I'm afraid.'

'How was it today?'

'With your mother? We got through it . . . five years lost between us. That doesn't help. I kept thinking about that other chap—God knows what his name is, I've forgotten. But she must've seen something in him that I lack. *What*?'

'There doesn't have to be that kind of reason.'

'Mea Culpa,' he mused. 'Is there a name for people who become late converts to beliefs they're already supposed to hold? If there is—that's me.'

'She never talks about it, you know. Not even about the job she was doing. Coding work—that's all she'll admit.'

'*She* was in Intelligence!'

'You're amazed as well. And yet there's nothing to prove she wasn't. I do think she's capable.'

'You're right. The woman she's become may well be capable enough to have done that. I was thinking of the woman I'd lost, and perhaps she doesn't exist any more . . . and yet. . . .' He drained his glass of wine and sat back reflectively. 'And yet I did see her once, her face half-turned towards me, that same young girl I met all those years ago, putting on a bit of an act—charming me—I loved her more than all the world, as if the world were ever worth such loving.'

Rosalynde Warrington squeezed his hand and let her gaze travel upwards. He had never spoken so frankly to her before.

Owen was fast asleep but he was emitting a low moan. When it turned into a howl of pain, Jean put a hand over his mouth to quieten him and shook his arm. He awoke with difficulty.

'Did I do it again?'

'Yes. Were you dreaming?'

'I don't know . . . sorry . . . you'll get no sleep . . . is there another room I can go to?'

'Not till Mark goes off leave.' Owen began to sob and buried his face in the pillow. 'Don't worry, don't worry, Owen, it'll pass.'

'Will it?'

'Yes, it'll pass,' she said, looking away to a dark corner of the bedroom. 'Everything passes in time.'

## CHAPTER SEVEN

Owen Hayward put his shotgun down on the bank and waded a little way out into the river. The fish had got itself completely enmeshed in the trap and it could do no more than twitch its defiance as his strong hands closed on it. Before he could release it and return it once more to the freedom of the water, however, he heard a noise which sent him scrambling madly to the bank to retrieve his shotgun. The sound in fact was that of a car backfiring nearby but it had set off a whole array of phantoms inside his head.

Crouching, sweating, shivering and panting, he pointed his weapon at the woods from which the taunting cries of Japanese soldiers were now coming. As he waited for the first menacing, yellow face to appear, the tension built to bursting-point and he let out an almost animal howl before collapsing to the ground. It was almost a year since Owen had left the Far East but he was still trailed in his mind by his captors.

When he looked up and saw that nobody was there, his fear began to subside and he sat up with relief, taking out a handkerchief to wipe his face. A voice behind him made him swing round.

'Poachers, eh?' It was John Warrington.

'Yes, sir ... been out most of the night, but not a sign of 'em except their handiwork.' He was respectful but firm. 'You'll excuse me, sir, but these are private woods.'

'I know. On my way to see Major Roberts now, as a matter of fact, then I heard you shout.'

'Me?' Owen looked genuinely puzzled.

'Then it wasn't you?'

'No, sir.'

'In that case, you must have heard the shout.'

'No, sir.'

'There was a car backfiring on the road and then, a minute later....'

'I heard the firing, sir, but nothing else.'

'Oh well,' said John, tactfully. 'Sound does play funny tricks in these woods. New here?'

'Been working for Major Roberts since I was discharged, sir. Best part of a year, it would be.'

'Where were you stationed?'

'The Far East, when the war broke out.' He lowered his head. 'I was taken by the Japs early on.'

'That's a long time to be a P.O.W.,' observed John, with sympathy. 'Look, can I give you a lift or something?'

'Thanks all the same but I'm on my way to catch the bus from Silport. Only a step away on the road, sir. Drops me off near my home, you see.'

'In that case, I'll be off then. Well, cheerio.'

'Goodbye, sir.'

Owen waited until the figure of John Warrington, dressed in tweed jacket and flannels, had vanished into the trees. Then he went back to release the fish before picking up his gun and heading for the road.

No sooner had Helen Hayward finished making the breakfasts than it was time to start the preparations for lunch and she was beginning to feel that she would never get out of the kitchen at all that morning. Keir entered, yawning loudly. He had arrived home at five o'clock that day and been surprised to see one of his brothers up.

'Does Owen always work such ungodly hours?'

'They've been having a lot of poaching lately. Meat ration being what it is, I'm not surprised.'

'You seem to have filled him out a bit since I was last home, in spite of the rations. Young Col got used to his Dad yet?'

'No. Almost shrinks from him.'

'Takes time,' he said, sitting on the edge of the table.

'Owen still doesn't talk much, got his own private world—never a mention even of what those savages did to him.'

'We dropped the atomic bomb to those "savages", Mum. I wonder what they think of us over there?'

'Are you trying to excuse what they did to your brother?' she said, bridling.

'No, no, of course not. It's inexcusable. So is what we did.'

'Blake says it shortened the war.'

'Blake!'

Helen took the opportunity to ask him not to argue about politics at mealtimes now that he was back. She knew the provocation he would get from the other members of the family but hoped she could rely on him not to let her down.

'For you—even that,' he promised, gallantly.

'And there's something else I want to say, Keir.'

She told him about Jean's wartime romance and was a little put out that he already knew something of it. Her main concern was that Owen should never find out about it. Ernst Sevcenko had long since gone and there was no reason at all why his name should ever come to the ears of a man who already had enough to torment him.

The fine old shire horse had backed the haycart up until it was only a few feet from the door of the barn and the men had unloaded the bales with a steady rhythm. They had how gone over to enjoy a restorative swig of cider from a flagon that they kept in the cool of the dairy. Ernst Sevencko, still wearing the tell-tale P.O.W. patch, was left to stable the horse and reward it with a nosebag of oats. She came up behind him.

'Ernst. . . .' It was Jean Hayward. She sounded as nervous as he now felt. 'Mrs Galway told me you were here.'

'They needed help. Mr Galway asked the camp. He did not think they would send me. I go back after the holiday.' He looked carefully at her. 'I promised them I wouldn't talk to you.'

'Yes. I promised, too.'

Lunch at the Hayward house that day had been a noisy, lively, laughing affair until a stray remark by Keir about the white collar employees at the ironworks being 'lackeys' had upset his father so much that George had left the table earlier than was good for his digestion. Keir had to withstand a painted stare from his mother, a blunt reprimand from Blake, another from Peg, and a few muttered complaints from Harry.

It was Mark Warrington's car that helped to get the conversation back on to a light and uncontroversial level. Mark's vehicle had been the one backfiring in the woods and he had given Owen a ride home then stayed for lunch. He put up with the teasing about the unreliability of the car which he had bought on impulse with the last of his demob money, and then offered both Blake and Peg a lift back to their respective workplaces.

All three left and the house went quieter for a while. Lovett then returned from a fishing expedition with a jam jar of tiddlers and Colin immediately voiced his envy. When Owen volunteered to take him fishing that afternoon, however, the boy seemed reluctant, and it was left to Keir to suggest a compromise. After a long morning's stint on the estate, Owen needed a rest, he argued, and so he himself would take the boy fishing. Colin was delighted with the idea and his father concealed his hurt feelings behind a vacant grin. He went off with Colin to help to find his son's wellington boots, and Helen Hayward shook her head sadly.

'The way Col pulls back from his Dad all the time. . . .'

'It'll pass, Mum,' said Keir.

'When Owen used to come in this kitchen before the war, it was like a gust of fresh wind blowing in. He was so full of life. And now. . . .'

An experienced mechanic like Blake Hayward had been able to identify the problem with the engine of Mark's car at once. Five minutes under the bonnet had put everything right and the vehicle started without difficulty first time. They drove to Whitstanton first and dropped Peg off at the library where she faced an afternoon of cataloguing; then they left the town and headed towards the ironworks where Mark, more from habit than desire, still worked at his old job. Mark was thrilled with the contented hum of an engine that had caused him so much trouble.

'You're a magician, Blake!'

'Tell me something new.' He reached up and slid back the sunshine roof with a squeak, then jumped up and put his head and shoulders through. 'I am the Genie of the Lamp!'

'Steady!' warned Mark.

'Sieg Heil! Sieg Heil!' shouted Blake, giving a Nazi salute to some cows in a field. Mark started to brake and he was thrown forward. 'Go easy, mate. I don't want to be thrown out!'

The car came to a halt and Mark gazed with interest into the distance, raising a finger to point.

'There's smoke coming out of our house.'

'Where?' asked Blake with mild alarm.

'Just above Galway's Farm there. Smoke coming out of the chimney.'

'I thought you meant the place was on fire!' He cupped his hands like binoculars. 'Yes, I see it now. . . .' He turned the whole thing into a game. 'Get Division on the R/T . . . give them the bearing. . . .'

'They're supposed to be away for Whit,' said Mark.

'Division? Our chaps are away for Whit! That means Jerry could be holed up in there! Get me Carruthers at H.Q. This calls for action!'

He continued to sweep the landscape with his imaginary binoculars and did not hear what his companion was saying at all.

'I'd better go and check, I suppose. Just in case. Look, sit down again, Blake, and I'll run you to the works first.'

'Don't bother,' murmured the other, seeing something that took all the bounce out of him. 'Don't bother.'

'But you'll be late.'

'So? I'll be late.'

'Blake. . . .'

'If they want to fire me because they think they can get someone better for the job, let 'em!'

'What's made you suddenly take that attitude?'

'No offence, Mark, but I've always had that attitude. . . . Can't expect the boss's son to appreciate it. You're management: I'm one of the proletariat.'

'Rubbish! Now let me drive you over there.'

'Forget work! I've given five years of my life to this bloody country. Maybe I ought to find out what my credit is.' He sat down again and opened the door. 'Drop me here, I'll walk across to the farm, see if Jean's ready to come home.'

'If that's what you want, Blake.'

'Could you pick me up here on your way back?'

'Of course!'

'Thanks.' Blake got out of the car and shut the door.

'I won't be long.'

'Oh, you take all the time in the world. . . .'

Blake Hayward walked off towards the farm and Mark was quite non-plussed for a moment. Then he saw the smoke rising from the chimney again and started the car up. Blake paid no heed to the valedictory toot on the horn that he was given because his attention was fixed on someone ahead of him, a dark, stocky man who was closing a gate to a field and who seemed to be lost in thought. The man did not see Blake until the latter went right up to him.

'Ernst Sévcenko?'

'This is my first name . . . yes.'

'You don't know me. . . .'

'Well. . . .' The other's tone had already given him a clue.

'I'm Blake Hayward . . . Jean's brother-in-law.'

'Oh. I see.'

'Owen—her husband—is my brother.' The emphasis he put on the word 'husband' made the other nod sadly. 'We thought you weren't here any more.'

'I came again for the first time today. Mr Galway asked for someone at the camp and they send me. I plead with them not to, but they are hard with us these days, Mr Hayward. Not listen to me. Make me come here.'

'Make you?'

'I am a prisoner-of-war,' said Ernst, simply. 'But after tomorrow Mr Galway will send me back.'

'Why is that?'

'He will say that I am no good. I have asked him to say this.'

'Bit rough on you, isn't it?' asked Blake.

'That does not matter.'

'But I'm sure you'd much rather work out in the fields than be stuck in that camp down the coast. I've heard the conditions are pretty rotten.' He felt a sympathy for the man but at the same time he remembered the danger that Ernst Sevcenko represented. 'You say you'll stay till tomorrow.'

'Tomorrow is the holiday. Mr and Mrs Galway ask me to stay for that. They are friends.'

Blake looked behind him to the field that was still littered with wisps of hay. As the Ukrainian talked about the farm and the way it was run, Blake could see how much it meant to him to work there and how close he obviously was to the Galways. Once again, however, he reminded himself why he had felt he must speak to Ernst.

'So you'll be here tomorrow?'

'For the last time.'

'Jean will be at home with us.'

'She will come here also—for a short time. She has said.'

'I will ask her not to,' Blake replied.

'If you wish, Mr Hayward.'

'I do wish. It's the only way. Even you must see that.'

'Even *me*?' Ernst gave a hollow laugh at the irony of this remark. 'Look, I also ask Jean not to come. It is because of her that I get Mr Galway to send me back. I beg her not to come.'

'So why are you staying tomorrow?'

'Mr Hayward. . . .'

'Wouldn't the easiest thing be for you to go today?'

'She said that if I did not see her for a short time tomorrow she would kill herself.'

'You believed her?'

'Am I not to believe her? What am I to do? Wait until she is dead and then believe her?'

Blake was beginning to realize just how important Ernst Sevcenko had been, and still was, in the life of his sister-in-law. Though he knew only too well the threat that the man posed, he could nevertheless see what the latter was going through and he softened slightly towards him. Ernst talked very quietly.

'At the beginning it was understood that he was dead. If it had not been so, this would not have happened. I am from the Ukraine, Mr Hayward. I know about pain, about separation, about losing those that you love.'

'I'm sure,' murmured Blake, thinking for a second of Herta.

'I do not wish to hurt your brother in any way. You believe?'

'Yes,' said the other, after a pause. 'Yes, I believe it.'

'Believe also then that it will end between us.'

'I hoped that it already had ended. The day Owen came back home to his wife and child. . . .'

Ernst Sevcenko lifted his arms helplessly and repeated that he was not at the farm by choice. But he had promised that he would see Jean once more and he was ready to fulfil that promise.

'Even if I see her tomorrow, it will end.'

'I find that harder to believe,' confessed Blake.

'Yes,' agreed Ernst, a distant look coming into his eye. 'Some things are hard to believe. Very hard. . . .'

John Warrington crossed to the living room window when he heard the car pull up on the drive outside and he was delighted when he saw who the caller was.

'It's Mark!' A slight doubt nudged him. 'I think. . . .'

'Don't you know your own son?' asked Rosalynde.

'He seems to have changed.'

'It is four years,' she reminded him, then went to open the front door. 'Mark! Lovely to see you again!'

John Warrington waited while the civilities were exchanged between brother and sister, surprised at how nervous he felt about meeting his son after all this time. When Mark entered, his father stepped forward rather too anxiously and extended his hand.

'Hello, Mark.'

'Father!'

The handshake was brief but it was important to both of them. Rosalynde helped things along by looking out the bottle of sherry that her father had managed to get and she kept the conversation going with bright comment whenever it threatened to flag. Gradually, both John and Mark began to relax with each other and their wariness eased away. When they had all explained how they came to be at the house, Rosalynde suggested that they might adjourn to the garden, where she had already put in a stint that morning. They were soon sitting out on the terrace in the sun, the men trying to catch up on four years of missing time.

'How long were you in Germany?' asked John.

'For three months after they surrendered. When the Yanks came it was like Christmas.'

'They're a very generous people,' confirmed his father.

'They can afford to be generous!'

'But a lot of people who can afford to be generous, aren't, wouldn't you say?'

There was a polite edge to this remark that caused a moment of tension. It was relieved by Rosalynde's announcement that she had to see to the oven and she left them alone. John plunged straight into family matters.

'You got that letter about your mother and me?'

'A week or so after we landed in Italy, I think.'

'I couldn't quite tell from your own letters whether you'd actually received mine. I didn't want to go into the whys and wherefores, Mark. These things happen in marriages.'

'Yes. . . .'

'She's made it very cosy here, I must say. Your mother never really cared for Lake House, I don't know why. Except that I was there. . . .' He felt that Mark's stare had an element of accusation in it and he became defensive. 'I do still keep an eye on things. As far as I can.'

'I'm sure,' nodded Mark, glancing at his watch.

'Have you had all you can take of your father already?'

'No, of course not. It's just that I've left a friend down the road. I've got to get him back to work.'

'I see. Look, Mark, is there any chance you could come up to Lake House and spend the holiday with Ros and me? We'd love to have you.'

It was a direct appeal but Mark was unable to greet it with any enthusiasm, saying that he had promised to stay with friends.

'But I would like a chat some time, Father. About the job.'

'Not liking it?'

'No. Not really.'

'Well, it was only something to start you off with. Been a bit out of touch myself, I'm afraid, so I've not been able to watch over you. Still, I'm through with the Ministry at the end of the month so I'll soon be back in harness. If you want a natter, why not pop up to Lake House this afternoon?'

'I'm not sure if the people I'm. . . .' Mark was starting to mumble in his embarrassment. He tried to pull himself together. 'Could I give you a ring, maybe?'

'Heavens! There's no need for such formality between us. Just drop in as and when you're free.'

There was a bluff good humour in the way John said this but a deep sense of pain lay behind it. He could see that there was an unresolved tension between them and sensed that he was still being blamed by his son for so many things. Mark began to make departure noises and they went back into the house so that he could take his leave of his sister. John kept up a jovial front until his son had actually left and then he slumped in a chair in the living room. Beside him, on a coffee table, was a photograph of his wife, taken some years ago when her hair was longer. He picked it up and looked at it for a long time until he heard Rosalynde's footsteps in the hall. Then he put the photograph on the table face down.

When she walked into the room, he was lighting a cigarette and inhaling gratefully. She waited until he had thrown the match into the ashtray before she said anything.

'Sticky?'

'It seemed to get worse somehow.'

'It wasn't as bad as I feared it might be.'

'That's only when you were there, Ros.'

'Oh. I acted as a kind of buffer, did I? Keeping the pair of you apart.'

'There are all too many things doing that,' he sighed. 'I just don't understand him. You'd hardly think he was our own flesh and blood sometimes.'

'Why?'

'His letters, for instance. Not that there were many of those, either. But they never mentioned your mother and me. Doesn't that strike you as odd? Your letters were full of references to . . . well, you know. . . .'

'It could be that he was pretending that it had never happened. The separation.'

'Or that he somehow held me responsible, even though I explained to him that it was your mother who. . . .' He inhaled some more cigarette smoke and then blew it gently out. 'He's closer to her, isn't he?'

'I don't think so.'

'It sticks out a mile, Ros.'

'I don't think he's close to any of us. Besides, I've always thought that side of it was something of a myth.'

'A myth?'

'All this closeness that's expected of families. What's the virtue in it?'

'I should have thought your religion would have taught you that, Ros.'

'Oh, my religion—that old thing!' she exclaimed.

'Slipping?'

'All the time.'

'I thought you might be,' he said, sadly.

'What do you expect, Dad? All that accumulated guilt. "Forgive me, God, there's a war on, didn't you know". . . .'

'We're out of touch, aren't we?' he said, stung by the hardness that had come into her voice. 'First, you were away at school, then the war.'

'All those years at school you were paying for us, and of course you were personally responsible for the bloody war!' She could see that her sarcasm had hurt him and that he was shocked by her language as well. 'I'm sorry, but women do swear a lot more these days. That's something else you're going to have to get used to. Think you'll manage?'

He hunched his shoulders then picked up the photograph of his wife again and studied it with misgivings.

'What's she doing now?'

'I don't know, Dad.'

'That same coding job you mentioned?'

'Could be. Maybe they're keeping them on to burn the books! It's all very hush hush.'

'Your mother doesn't have to work, you know that, don't you? I'd be quite happy to—'

'There you go again, you see. Thinking that everything can be solved if you dig your hand in your pocket.' Rosalynde realized that she was sounding like her brother and calmed down. 'She has friends down in London. I suppose that's why she's staying on there, really. It's nothing more sinister than that.'

John Warrington stubbed out his cigarette and gazed once more at the photograph. Old memories stirred inside him.

'I almost wrote to her when he was killed.'

'Your rival?'

'He was a lot more than that, I'm afraid. As for rivals, I had plenty of those before the war.'

'Other men?' She was astonished. 'Did it happen a lot?'

'I'm not talking about lovers, Ros. A woman has other needs than just the physical ones, and it was for thòse that she used to leave me from time to time.'

'Mark resented it, too.'

'What?'

'What you're on about. Her way of shutting you out. Of going out into the garden with her books all the time.'

'Yes, those books. What did she find in those books that we never seemed able to talk about?'

'Did you ever ask her?'

John Warrington shook his head in a gesture of defeat. He was ready to take his share of the blame now.

'I made a bit of a mess of it, didn't I—the family?'

Listening to Ernst's story, Blake had been reminded of certain things in his past and he now found himself talking quite freely about them. He did not stop to consider that he was telling a stranger something which he could not discuss with any member of his family.

'And then we were moved to Germany itself.'

'You had contact with the Russians?'

'Only in the last few days. We pulled back to let them take over the place we'd occupied. They didn't waste any time.'

'So you have met the Russians,' said Ernst to himself. 'You know what they are like. What they can do.'

'I left someone there I cared for very much. . . . God knows where she is now. There were a few letters at the start . . . hasty notes, really, scribbled when she got a chance . . . there's been nothing for ages now. Either she's stopped writing or. . . .' Blake pushed himself up off the fence against which he had been leaning. 'People are being shunted about from one place to another, millions of them. Europe's being sliced up like a cake.'

'Politicians, maps. . . .'

'Yes, I suppose that's it. And the Ruskies will say what the Germans said before them.'

'What was that?'

'The usual excuse. "We were just following orders".'

'I would not like to grow old knowing that I had given some of those orders,' said Ernst, bitterly.

Blake looked up and saw that Jean had come out of the house and was walking towards them. He could see that she was not pleased to find him there and had guessed why he had come.

'I've got my wages. We can go now,' she said, briskly.

'Well. . . .'

'That's what you came for, isn't it? To take me back.'

'I was only thinking of Owen' he replied.

'So you come and spy on me.' She turned to Ernst and her tone changed. 'I'll see you tomorrow.'

'Jean—' began Blake.

'They say I can come,' she interrupted. 'They've been good to me, the Galways. They understand.' She touched Ernst lightly on the arm. 'Tomorrow, then?'

'Yes, tomorrow.' Ernst looked at Blake, trying to say something that would not let itself be said. He settled for one word only. 'Thank you.'

He went off quickly in the direction of the barn, his head bent and his shoulders stooping, the picture of someone who seemed quite without hope. Blake was reminded of that first evening in the house in Germany when he had seen the same despair in the face of a woman.

'What did he thank you for?' asked Jean.

'For trying to understand, I suppose. Let's go back up to the road. Mark's going to give us a lift.'

'Blake. . . .' She caught his sleeve.

'Yes?'

'I'm sorry. I really am.'

'I don't blame you. It's the situation.'

'Owen's your brother, it's hard for you. Hard for all of us, believe me.'

A horn sounded as Mark Warrington rounded a bend in his car and raced towards them. His two passengers waited till he stopped beside them and then got in without a word.

George Hayward had been to check the details of a wage claim with one of the men in the engine shed. Years of working in his clerk's job had taught him that it was far better to chat to the workers on the floor, so to speak, instead of summoning them to the Wages Office like boys being hauled before a headmaster. Having cleared up the misunderstanding with the man involved, he now came out of the door of the engine shed in time to see Blake arriving for the afternoon shift.

'Where the hell've you been?' he demanded.

'I'll tell you later.'

'It's an hour past clocking-on time, Blake.'

'So? I'm a little late.'

'Mercer's been chasing me to find out where you were. You know what he's like about time-keeping.'

'At boiling-point, was he?' grinned Blake, unconcerned.

'Aye, he was. You shouldn't give him the excuse.'

George was far more worried about the situation than Blake seemed to be himself. His son raised his voice as if broadcasting the news to a small crowd of workmates.

'Mercer's an unreasonable sod without any excuse.'

'He's your boss.'

'Siding with the management, are you, Dad?' teased Blake. 'A man of your principles?'

'You shouldn't give 'em the excuse, son.'

'What's an hour, for God's sake? I do my whack when I'm here. As for old Mercer. He doesn't like me because I was a captain in the army. Niggles him somehow. He's got no complaints about the way I do my job.'

'Except when you're late.'

'That's his problem,' Blake laughed. 'When you've nationalized us, he'll still be here, watching the clock. Mark my words.'

George Hayward put his son's survival before anything and the blunt honesty he always showed in political debate was now completely absent. He simply kept repeating the same thing, as if trying to drive it home.

'Don't give 'em the excuse. Don't give 'em the excuse. Use your head, son, just don't give 'em the excuse.'


## CHAPTER EIGHT


Life under a Labour government had not been quite as unbearable as Harry Hayward had prophesied. True, he still railed against its policies and vilified its leaders (Ernest Bevin, particularly) at every opportunity, and he saw each new piece of legislation as part of a systematic attack on everything that made Britain great. Again, he topped up his discontent regularly at the Whitstanton Conservative Club where he could rely on long faces and sympathetic ears—as well as the finest snooker table in the town. As a final monument to his defiance, he kept a collection of political cartoons, snipped with care out of the *Daily Express* and elsewhere, pasted with love into an old exercise book, and shown with pride to Lovett from time to time in a vain attempt to make a boy of thirteen 'take sides'.

Yet despite all this, Harry had to admit that he had actually survived almost a year under the new dispensation without any major change in the quality of his life. In minor instances, his lot had in fact improved somewhat, for although austerity was the norm in post-war Britain, the rationing and the limitations did seem to be easing, albeit at a snail's pace. In his quieter, more introspective moments—out in his boat under a Tory blue sky—Harry confessed to himself that the country was not only managing to 'stand' for the Attlee administration, but that certain sections were even applauding it. All hope that the Labour victory· was to be followed by an early collapse had now disappeared.

It was in such a mood of sour resignation that Harry wandered into the kitchen, saw that someone had been mixing the ingredients for a cake and decided to relieve his political frustrations by helping himself to a substantial taste off the wooden spoon.

Helen caught him in the act.

'Nice?'

'I'm entitled to lick the spoon, aren't I, now that I'm supposed to be in my second childhood?'

'You're entitled to be smacked and sent to your room, if that's your excuse.'

Keir now followed her in from the garden. He had been chatting to her as she unpegged the clothes and found himself being used as a porter. He put the dry things down on a chair and glanced up.

'Owen still in bed?'

'Yes,' said his mother. 'Sleeping like a top. He can sleep in the day somehow.'

'Night's the time for sleeping,' urged Harry.

'Jean says he just can't seem to get off at night,' sighed Helen. 'After all this time, too . . . I can't bring myself to ask him what those Japs did to him but it must have been something terrible.'

'It was,' reinforced Keir, whose duty in the Far East had given him some ugly insights into the matter. 'The Japs think you deserve to die if you let yourself be taken prisoner—not just their enemies, mind, their own selves. Against their code. They're obsessed with the shame of it.'

'Shame!' snorted Helen. '*Them*?'

'I read somewhere that they took three hundred thousand at the start of the war and two-thirds of them died—two out of every three prisoners! Owen's lucky to be alive. To come back.'

'Has he come back?' asked his mother.

'Not as he was, maybe,' said Harry, 'but then none of us is that. We all change. Well, look at your husband, woman. He's changed as much as anyone and he's not been anywhere.'

'George—changed?'

'Aye, he's a damned sight more awkward for a start!'

'That makes two of you, then!' she replied.

'Me? I've changed for the better, I have. Suffered fools gladly—though God knows I'm surrounded by nowt else!'

'Yes,' Helen conceded. 'You are a lot more generous than you used to be. I'll give you that.'

'You've noticed, eh?' Harry was gratified.

'We're bound to, Dad. Aren't we, Keir?'

'What?' Seeing a look in his mother's eye, he agreed at once. 'Oh yes. We've noticed, Grandad. Sticks out a mile.'

'You've been more thoughtful towards others.'

'Aye, it's true . . . it's true. . . .'

'So you're not likely to hang on to something you don't need when someone else could do with it. . . .'

'No,' he agreed, and then realized what she was doing. His generosity vanished. 'We're back to my house again, are we?'

'You could let Owen and Jean have it.'

'Nay. . . .'

'They shouldn't be living with us like they are . . . I mean, you're happy enough in the front room, aren't you?'

'Happy in the front room? How could I threaten him that I'd leave if I'd nowhere to go to?'

'It's only a threat because George cares for you—knows you couldn't manage on your own.'

'Who says I couldn't?' he demanded.

'You've no need, Dad.'

'But who says I couldn't?'

He had forced her to the point where she has to back up a statement that they both knew to be true but Helen did not have the heart to do so. Instead she fell silent and he mellowed slightly.

'I'll think on it. You can't get a house for love nor money these days. Country's bust. Country'll give him nowt for what he's suffered.' He blew his nose into a large red spotted handkerchief. 'Owen can have it.'

'Oh thank you, Dad!'

'I'm glad you said that, Grandad,' said Keir. 'I reckon he's entitled to it.'

'I suppose if you had need of a house you'd think you were entitled to it an' all, eh? Aye, well I'd not give it you!'

'Why not?'

'Because I don't like folk that think they're entitled to summat they've not worked for.'

'Or not had the chance to work for,' he countered.

'There's nobody works where you do—down London,' Harry sneered. 'They just walk up and down street wi' bowlers on, carrying their brollies and looking busy. London! Keep it!' He felt the need of his best friend. 'Where's Lovett?'

'I left them fishing.'

'Got bored, did you? Take Colin fishing, you do, then shove the responsibility for looking after him on to Lovett when you get bored. That's you're bloody trouble, lad. You're a bored generation.' He stamped off to his room. 'A bored generation. . . . !'

'Doesn't get any sweeter, does he?' observed Keir.

His mother chose the moment to worry about the way he lived in London.

'You'd such plans when you were at the grammar school. You were doing so well.'

'Mum. . . .'

'What was it you wanted to do?'

'It was all a very long time ago. . . .'

'But what was it? Some job in Africa?'

'Colonial Service . . . Sanders of the River stuff. . . . It was my childhood dream.'

'What happened to it all, Keir?' she asked, wistfully.

'The war, Mum . . . reality. . . .'

Mark Warrington felt that he needed cheering up. After a rather uncomfortable meeting with his father and a strained car ride in the company of Jean and Blake, he went to the one place where he could be sure of a smile. Peg had finished her cataloguing and was taking a turn at the desk stamping the books taken out on loan. He crept up behind her, put his hands around her eyes, and asked who it was. Though repeatedly telling him to keep his voice down, Peg was delighted that he had called in at the library and accepted his invitation to go for a ride the next day. The soft roundness of her lips entranced him as she talked and his own face got closer and closer. A hoarse female voice interrupted his pleasure.

'Er, when you've finished with Ronald Coleman here, love, could you stamp me books and let me get home to the kiddies?'

His eyes were shut tight as she tiptoed into the bedroom but he was not asleep. She blamed herself for waking him but he assured her that it was not her fault and that he could not sleep without her.

'I'm with you at night and you lay awake till all hours.'

'I go away,' he whispered.

'Away?'

'Not just at night. It happened at work today. In the woods.' He patted the bed beside him. 'Lay down for a while.'

'I should be helping your mother with tomorrow's dinner . . . her thanksgiving . . . all of you together again.'

Owen felt guilty about bringing her nothing but trouble. She assured him that this was not true but she could see that he was unconvinced. Jean lowered herself gingerly down on to the bed.

'Just for a while,' she said.

'Just for a while, then.'

There was a long pause then she remembered his mention of an incident in the woods. He described it and explained how the man had heard him shout.

'Well?'

'I hadn't, Jean.'

'It must have been somebody else, then.'

'But there *was* nobody else—and I'd have heard. Except that I wasn't there. I'd gone away. Like I do at night . . . so it must have been me that shouted.' He reached out for her hand. 'Do I shout at night?'

'You have done. A lot at one time.'

'I should see the doctor.'

'I saw him,' she confessed. 'I told him.'

'What did he say?'

'He was very angry. Not with me—with himself in a way. He asked what could anybody expect—what could they expect?' She leaned over to him. 'You've been better lately.'

'Have I?'

'This last few months.'

'You're not just saying that?' he asked, with an almost pathetic need to be reassured.

'No, I'm not, Owen. I asked the doctor if there was anything that could be done. If there was a cure.'

'And?' He could not understand why she did not go on. '*And*?'

'He said—"Oh yes, there's a cure—make the world a fit place to live in", he said.' Tears welled up in her eyes. 'A fit place to live in . . . that's all. . . .'

Her sobbing became uncontrollable and he wanted to comfort her without quite knowing how. After almost a year sleeping together, he was still unused to even the most casual physical contact with her. His hand hovered above her shoulder.

'Nay, nay . . . don't cry. . . .'

'People want help of me and what do I do . . . nothing . . . I'm so selfish . . . we're all selfish . . . seeking our own ends all the time . . .

taking . . . taking.' She rubbed her hand across her tear-stained cheeks. 'I'd give if I could, Owen, but I've nothing. I'm drained. I've nothing left to give. Forgive me!'

'Nay, what is there to forgive? You rest now . . . just rest. . . .'

For once he was able to put his arms gently around her and feel her relax into them. The pillow made her sobbing seem a lot less distraught than it really was.

Helen was at her usual place in the kitchen when her husband came back from work. George gave her his ritual welcome and she made her ritual complaint about the never-ending cycle of chores that was her lot. Then she asked where Blake was.

'Still there, love. They let us off half an hour early. It was not for such as Blake, though. Only for us that wear a collar and tie.' He grinned. 'Another little privilege to make us different.'

'What's wrong with that?'

'I've told you often enough, woman.' He slipped off his coat and loosened his tie. 'He was an hour late for work this afternoon.'

'Blake?'

'Playing into their hands, that is.'

'He does his job well, doesn't he?' she said, defensively.

'Aye, love, but he might not have got it back all the same. They'd somebody doing it already, you see. Gave it back to Blake when he was discharged because it's law. He got that job by law.'

'A mechanic at the ironworks! Some job for a man that rose in the ranks like he did.'

'Till he's somewhere better to go, he needs it.'

'Oh I've no qualms about Blake. If he loses this job, he'll soon find another.'

'Round here, Helen? What is there round here?'

'You think he might go off. That's why you're fretting, isn't it?' she said, seeing behind his concern for his son. 'You like having him round. Don't want to lose him.'

'Damned if I know why. Rubbish he talks about politics since he came back. He's walked out on us in that sense.'

'Well I doubt if he'll walk out on us the other way. Too fond of his home comfort. Unlike Keir.'

'Keir?'

'Going back to some cheap bedsitter with a gas-ring in the hall that he shares with two others. Our *son*, George!'

Having broached the subject, Helen now unleashed all her anxieties about Keir, pointing out how slovenly he had become and how all his clothes needed mending in some small way. It was the waste of his 'good education' that really got to her, however, and she kept asking her husband to speak to him and try to get him to take a more sensible attitude to his future instead of drifting along without any goal or purpose. ·

'Aye, all right, I'll speak to him. I can't promise that he'll speak to *me*, mind, but I'll try. . . .'

Mercer was waiting for him when he stepped out into the yard. A short, plump, greasy, self-important man in a fading suit, Mercer was not popular with any of the men who worked under him and he seemed to thrive on their dislike. He accosted Blake.

'Going for your wage, lad?'

'Yes, Mr Mercer.'

'They've got something else for you—your cards.' He showed a few teeth between thick lips. 'Not before time in my opinion.'

'Nor mine,' retorted Blake, cheerfully. 'I'd have been asking for them in a week or two, anyway.' He enjoyed the blank amazement on the other's face. 'Have a good holiday, Mr Mercer.'

Mercer was about to speak but checked himself and walked off. Blake let him get a little way then shouted after him.

'By the way!' Mercer turned. 'Thanks. . . .'

They were entwined on the bed, he slightly on top of her in a way that made it difficult for her to get free. He was asleep now at last and seemed to have found the measure of peace that had been eluding him for so long. She eventually disentangled herself and got off the bed with great care so as not to disturb him. As she stood up she saw herself in the dressing-table mirror, hair ruffled, face blotched, eyes rimmed with dark bags, clothes crumpled. She brought her hands to her mouth to muffle the exclamation of pain.

'Oh God!'

'One, two, three, four. . . .'

'Run, Mark. Run. . . .' she urged.

'Seven, eight, nine, ten. . . . Coming!'

'Go on, Lovett,' encouraged his father, taking his son's part. 'You can catch him.'

Encouraged by this and given extra speed by the sheer fun of the chase, Lovett Hayward tore across the sand in pursuit of Mark Warrington, who had been given a ten-second start. The boy soon began to make ground on his quarry and the onlookers laughed.

'Lovett's taken to him,' noted George.

'I quite like him, too,' said Peg, by way of understatement. She hooked her arm inside her father's. 'You don't really *mind* him being a wealthy Warrington, do you?'

'I'll live with it—for your sake. Against you marrying, are they?' She shook her head. 'Thought there might be some reason why you hadn't.'

'There is. He's Catholic. He seems to think it's a choice between me and God.'

George Hayward squeezed her arm for a moment and then looked up as he heard his son's voice raised in triumph. Lovett had finally caught up with Mark and was now being given a ride on his back.

'That's the way to catch your man,' instructed her father. 'Learn to run faster.'

'I can run faster,' she replied. 'The trouble is that people won't let me. Remember?'

Because she had put such tremendous care and effort into the preparation of the meal, Helen Hayward had the satisfaction of hearing the contented chewing of her family and of seeing many hands compete for second helpings. Blake was first to finish and he banged the table like an auctioneer using a gavel.

'My God! My God!'

'Blake—that's blasphemy!' warned his mother.

'It's a hymn of thanksgiving for the best Sunday dinner I've ever had in my whole life, dammit!'

'And so say all of us!' added George, to a cheer.

'It was Jean's doing as much as mine,' said Helen, modestly.

'Nonsense!' disclaimed the other.

'Col enjoyed it, didn't you, Col?' said Owen, still trying desperately to relate to his son in some way. 'He thinks it's Christmas because we're having Christmas pudding.'

'I'm going to die!' announced the boy, holding his stomach.

There was great alarm until they established that he had only swallowed one of the threepenny bits put in the pudding.

'Sick it up, lad!' advised Harry.

'Grandad, don't be disgusting!' scolded Peg.

'Got to come out one end or t'other,' answered the realist.

Colin could take no more of this discussion and raced out with his mother in pursuit of him. Everyone laughed and Harry suggested that half-crowns would have been a safer bet in the pudding. Peg and Mark now thanked Helen warmly and excused themselves from the table to go on what they called a mystery tour. Mark promised that they would be back soon and led her out.

'Can't think why he bothers to go if he's that damn eager to get back!' observed Harry, tartly.

'I thought families were supposed to get together at holiday times,' said Keir. 'Where's Mark's?'

'His mother's in London,' supplied George.

'But his sister's at home,' confirmed Helen.

'And his father,' said Blake.

'Old John Warrington himself?' asked Keir. 'The bloke whose lackey fired you yesterday?'

'It's lackey time again!' moaned Harry, recalling the earlier rows over the word. 'Comes round again like twelve o'clock.'

'Look, nobody fired me, Keir,' insisted his brother. 'I fired myself. Got it? As for Mark there, he calls himself a socialist. God knows why.'

'More or less in the same way that Dad does, you mean?'

'Together again, are we?' said Helen with such force that they all held their peace. 'Can't keep off it, can you?'

She stood up and ordered them all out in a pleasantly sharp way. Owen was helping her to clear up when Jean came back in, pulling her coat on and telling them that Colin was fine now.

'You'll not be long?' asked Owen.

'I'll be back as soon as I can. Where did I leave that shopping I got for the Galways?'

'It's in the other room,' said Helen, knowingly.

Jean ignored the searching gaze of her mother-in-law and went out. Owen continued to move plates off the table.

'I offered to go with her.'

'Best let her go alone, Owen. The Galways are her friends, not yours. There's nothing over there for you.'

'I'd have gone nonetheless, Mum.'

While they continued to clear away the dinner things, Jean Hayward slipped into the living room and found the box that she was seeking just inside the door. Unseen by the three men in the room, who were sprawled out on the sofa and in armchairs, she overheard a snatch of their conversation.

'Is it true, Keir?' Blake was asking.

'No!' asserted George. 'We'd never send them back to Russia to be shot. We just wouldn't.'

'The bloke in the pub said it was definite. He works at the camp.'

'I can't believe it,' said George.

'Poor sods!' sighed Blake.

'Definite, he said. One Ukrainian's topped himself already rather than go back. Others are threatening to do the same.'

Jean could take no more of it and went silently out.

Mark Warrington had driven her along a country road until he came to wrought-iron gates that guarded the entrance to a small estate. Swinging the car in through them, he let it roll at a slow speed down the slight incline and pulled up under the trees in the hollow. They got out and began to walk. Peg was slightly over-awed by it all.

'I came here on a school trip once. Looking at big houses. I wondered what kind of people could live here. Scares me a bit that you're one of them.'

'But I'm not really, Peg. I don't belong.'

'Mark—the house is owned by your parents!'

'By alien people. I don't belong to them.'

'What on earth have they done to you to make you feel that way about them?' she asked, worried by his sardonic tone.

'Nothing . . . they did nothing. . . .'

They followed the curve of the drive and soon got a proper view of the house, set on a ridge above the lake and commanding a superb view on all sides. Peg was duly impressed by the size and impact that the place had and she wondered how Mark could possibly have come to reject such a place as this. From the house and the gardens that fronted it, her eye travelled down to the lake itself and to a cluster of swans gliding over its surface. Then she spotted the small landing stage and saw Rosalynde Warrington inspecting a steam launch with a man in slacks and blazer.

The man turned, saw them and waved. Mark waved that.

'Who's that, Mark?'

'My father. Come on.'


Everyone except George Hayward and Keir seemed to have something to do after the meal. Jean had gone off to keep her appointment. Mark and Peg were at Lake House. Colin, with some reluctance, had been taken by his father to fly his kite. Helen and Blake had decided to take a walk and, with the aid of Lovett, had coaxed Harry into joining them. Only Keir and George remained and the former had fallen asleep in the chair. Eventually, he stirred and looked around for the others.

'All gone out. I said I'd keep you company.'

'Fine company I am, nodding off.'

'I win more arguments when you're like that,' said George.

'Sorry I'm so thorny these days, Dad.'

'Are you thorny?' They laughed. George felt the right time had come. 'How are you making out in London?'

'That means Mum asked me to talk to you.'

'Aye . . . but I care as well, you know.'

'I'm a big lad now. Supposed to look after myself.'

'I can give you twenty odd years but there's scarcely a week goes by when I don't feel like shouting for help.' He ran a hand across his jaw. 'What sort of future do you see for yourself?'

'Not much future for any of us after the atom bomb, Dad. Oh I know the political answers but I can't see any of them coming about. There's so *much* that needs changing!'

'I believe in evolution myself. Revolution cracks too many heads open. Look at. . . .' He let the words die.

'You were going to tell me to look at Russia, then you remembered that I support them. And I do, by and large. All through the war I could see it happening. They were the good old Ruskies, then, knocking the Jerries for six. Not any more.' He sat up and almost shouted the next words. 'Bevin's going to break with them, I know he is! There's an ice age coming.'

'Is that his fault or theirs, son?'

'Not theirs!'

'I don't see it like you, Keir. I mean, look how marvellous Attlee's turned out to be. The work—the legislation—the plans. We're getting somewhere at last. I've felt it all year. I can see the light at the end of the tunnel.'

'Somebody lighting the fuse?' They laughed again. 'You always were an optimist, Dad.'

'It's the one thing Churchill and I had in common. No point in being anything else. So what about you?'

'Tell Mum I'm fine.'

'That's exactly what I shall tell her. Now what's the truth?'

Keir did not want to answer but there was something about his father's willingness to help that he found touching. He conceded one fact.

'I packed my job in.'

'What job was that? You never really told us.'

'Oh it was nothing. And I'll soon find something else. Some piffling thing to keep the wolf from the door.'

George Hayward leaned forward and did the only thing that he could think of in the circumstances.

'I've got a bit put by, if that'll help till you get fixed up.'

'Oh Christ, Dad!' exclaimed Keir. 'You're done more for us than any of us deserve as it is! Drop the load, Dad . . . drop the load!'

George shook his head as if this were not even a possibility, and there was a simple pride in his reply.

'It's a father's instinct to do what he can do, son. I can't turn my back on my nature. Now, can I?'

Keir was glad that he had fallen asleep in the chair.

Their promise to see each other briefly and finally had been broken the minute they set eyes on each other again and they left the Galway Farm together to find a quiet spot on the beach. Haunted by the remarks she had overheard back at her house, Jean talked of them running away together so that they could share their future in freedom.

'Jean, there *is* no future!' he wailed.

'It's happened, hasn't it? What you always feared. They're sending you back to Russia.'

'Rumours.'

'They shoot everyone who fought for the Germans.'

'These are just rumours.'

'They're not!' she cried. 'And you know it, Ernst, don't you! It's the truth.' He could not find the words to deny it and she grabbed at his arms. 'What kind of life do you think I will have with *that* to remember?'

He looked back up the shore and was surprised how far they had walked. The tide was out and they were two dots on a vast expanse of wet, ribbed sand that gave beneath their feet.

'I want you to live on, Jean. To forget.'

'*Forget*?'

'All right, you cannot . . . so remember instead. As I do . . . that, too, is a way to carry on. . . . I remember my mother, my father . . . my brother . . . my sisters. . . . Who is dead and who survived I do not know, but I remember them living when I was young and I did not think too much about politics . . . about war . . . death. . . .'

'I can't live like that,' she said, slowly.

Ernst Sevcenko gazed out towards the sea which was rolling lazily away from them in the distance.

'Sometimes it is all the life there is.'

It did not take Mark long to feel that the visit had been a mistake. His animosity towards his father stirred and was given a slight intensity by the fact that he and Peg seemed to get on so well from the start. While he and Rosalynde sat outside in the garden, his father gave Peg a tour of the library.

'Don't look so gloomy, Mark. Is it because she likes him?'

'She likes everybody,' he said. 'She lives for the day.'

'Who doesn't?'

'There's a reason in her case. Scarlet fever when she was a child. Dicky heart.'

Rosalynde was a little shaken by this news and immediately sympathetic. She wondered if he had forgiven her yet for being the person who told Peg about his religious beliefs.

'That's another problem.'

'Still got those doubts and uncertainties?'

'I'm not using you as my confessor, Ros.'

'Peg is not going to wait forever, you know.'

'I do know, thanks!' he said, as if all too aware of it.

John Warrington now led Peg out to join them. Their interest in books had been a bond at once and Peg had offered to catalogue his library for him, thrilled at the sight of so many antiquarian books and first editions.

'It's a beautiful library. Knocks spots off ours.'

'You've got a library?' asked Ros, surprised.

'Only in Whitstanton—I work there.' They all smiled. 'Your father says you used to spend a lot of time in there with those books, Mark. Is that true?'

'I suppose so.'

Mark wanted to get off the subject of his past as a member of the Warrington family and diverted everyone's attention to the motor launch at the landing stage, asking if it would be possible to take it out on the lake. John explained that the engine had packed in and the mechanic was unable to mend it. Mark recalled his car.

'Peg's brother would soon fix it for you. He's a magician with engines. He's out of a job at the moment, too.'

'A magician with engines out of a job at a time like this?' asked John, with mock gravity. 'With unemployment the lowest it's been for years? What's happened?'

'He got fired from our works.'

'Blake fired himself,' argued Peg.

'The point is that he's out on his ear either way,' said Mark.

'Want me to look into it?' offered John.

'Heavens, no!' yelled Peg. 'And there's no need for Mark to be so embarrassed by it all. Blake's far too good for a job like that. No disrespect to the ironworks but he *wanted* to get himself fired . . . he was getting into a rut.'

'Sounds to me as if he's the sort of young chap we can ill afford to lose,' commented John.

'There is still the boat,' reminded Rosalynde.

'Oh yes. If he could look at that some time. . . .'

'I'll ask him.'

'When we get back,' said Mark. 'Which is now, I'm afraid.'

'Won't you stay?' asked John, disappointed.

All three of them were willing him to agree but something inside him wanted to be away as soon as he could. Muttering thanks and apologies, therefore, he took Peg by the hand and led her back towards the car. John Warrington sighed.

The tide was coming in now and it was building up its momentum with each curling wave. If they stayed there any longer, the sea would soon be all around them. Ernst grew fearful.

'We should go back now, I think.'

'If that's all there is to life, I don't want it!' she said.

'Come!' he advised, taking her hand. She refused to move. 'Jean, please. The tide. . . . Come!'

'I don't *want* it!' she repeated with emphasis. 'I don't want it, don't want it, don't want it!'

Water now played around their ankles and still she would not move. Ernst squeezed her hand and his voice was a plea.

'Come! Come!'

A mile away, on the stretch of beach around the point, two other people had reached a moment of crisis.

'I want to go back.'

'But we've not long come out, Col.'

'I want Mum.'

Owen lifted up the kite which they had brought but the boy would not even look at it. Though he had been talked into coming by his mother, he had found that he could not go through with it and had become sullen. He stared in the direction of the house. Owen scampered towards him with a hopeful smile and took his son by the shoulders.

'You can put up with me for a bit longer, Col, can't you?'

'I want Mum,' whispered the boy.

They were soon making their way, fifteen yards apart, up a lonely beach. It was Owen who brought up the rear, lagging further behind all the time and giving himself plenty of space to think about his latest failure.

## CHAPTER NINE

July was a month of contrasts, a time of alternating sunshine and rain when the narrow streets of Whitstanton were first broiled, then soaked, then dried off with dazzling effect, then spattered unmercifully all over again. One day the town could look bright, almost jaunty, and the next day it was cowed, bedraggled and a picture of misery. August, fortunately, was far more decisive. It made up its mind to provide fine weather and it did not waver from that decision in any way. Whitstanton blossomed and many of its inhabitants found out that it still had a beach. Days were long and warm and even the early morning brought some people out to enjoy the clear summer air.

'Who's the early bird, then?'

'Oh hello, Ros. . . .'

'And I thought I was the insomniac. Looking for worms?'

'No,' said John Warrington, crouched in the shadow of a beech tree. 'Phallus Impudicus.'

'Mind your language, please!' mocked his daughter. 'You'd better make a note of that for when you go to confession tomorrow.'

'Can't you smell it?' Rosalynde sniffed then pulled a face. 'Like a dead rat, isn't it? Pong comes from this mushroom here. The green slime on the cap.'

'Do you *have* to tell me about it just before breakfast?'

'They're commonly called stinkhorns.'

'Very apt.'

'The Germans call the eggs they come from "Devil's Eggs". They used to collect them to make aphrodisiacs.'

'They must have gone to bed with pegs on their noses!' she said and asked him to postpone his lecture until another time.

His mention of Germany made her wonder how her mother was getting on there. For reasons that she was not ready to disclose, Beth Warrington had gone to Germany in the course of her work. Once again her daughter speculated about what that work actually was but she ended up none the wiser. Her father simply said how grateful he was that she had moved back into Lake House with him while her mother was out of the country.

'You're so full of life these days, Ros. I expected you to be bored stiff now that you've given up your war work. Lots of women are bored, I'm told, now they've gone back to having babies.'

'Give me a chance!' she said. 'I have to find a man first. As for this place, I had to help get it ready for you. I'm always happy when I'm making a home.'

'You should be making one for yourself,' he advised. She was about to reply but changed her mind. 'Has he gone back to his wife?'

'There was never any doubt that he would.'

'Because you were both good Catholics?'

'Oh yes, we were good Catholics,' she confirmed, with some bitterness. 'We've confessed our "sin". Well, I have and assume that he did as well.' Her brightness had gone now. 'I don't need any other penance than this . . . this awful nothingness.'

'My poor love!' he said, taking her elbow.

'That was the war, that was. Eat, drink and what have you—for tomorrow we die!'

She excused herself to go and help the housekeeper get the breakfast. Her sadness was proof even against an August glow.

At the Hayward House that morning, George and Harry sat down to their usual meal of egg, fried bread and reflex banter. It was a Saturday morning and Harry was critical of the fact that Blake, now in business on his own as a mechanic, was still in bed while every other working man in the country was getting ready to go to his job. George felt that his son could do as he wished.

'He's anticipating the five-day week that we shall all want when the country is back on its feet.'

'That'll be when Nelson gets his eye back!' opined Harry. 'I want never gets, your mother used to say. Only union she ever joined was Mothers' Union. Six days shalt thou labour . . . know where that's written?'

'Aye—Conditions of Employment, Whitstanton Works.'

Helen came over with a breakfast for Colin and chided him for reading his comic at the table. The boy was moody and preoccupied and did not even raise his head when Harry spoke.

'Important day for you, Col. Moving house. And you're going to a better place than this: 42, Betsy Street, my old house. You'll like it there, lad. I can vouch for it. I lived at peace there.' He laid his knife and fork on the empty plate. 'Amen'.

Seconds after he had gone out of the room they heard him calling out that it was 'Eight bells' and then ringing his own bell eight times to prove it.

'Damn bell!' moaned George. 'Two years in the navy during the Boer War we owe that to. That racket'll stir Blake, anyway. And Jean, if she's asleep.'

'I'll take her up a cup of char,' said Owen, jerking out of his reverie at the mention of his wife's name. He poured the tea then turned to Colin. 'Ready to help me with the big move, Col?'

'If I have to,' muttered the boy.

Owen left and Colin was told off by both his grandparents.

'But I don't want to go,' he replied, helplessly.

'You'll have a house of your own,' argued Helen. 'Everybody wants a house of their own.'

'*This* is my house.'

Colin decided that he could eat no more, excused himself and left. His grandparents tried to understand why he was so afraid to leave the family house.

'Maybe it rubs off from Owen,' suggested George. 'He's only going because he knows he must. A man with a child's fear of the dark, that's Owen.'

'He's not been afraid of the dark when he's gone out at night in search of poachers.'

'Another kind of dark, Helen. The kind that makes you run to your mother and bury your head where it's warm and safe. . . . Maybe that's what Col sees in Owen—the child not the father. Competition for a place to hide.'

Helen considered this and shook her head in bewilderment. Then she remembered another aspect of the story.

'The last of them left the camp yesterday.'

'Ernst went last week. I called there to see him off and they'd taken him off.'

'Does she know?'

'I daren't ask.'

'You read nothing about it in the papers, George.'

'No . . . it's all morale these days. Shame's not good for morale. And what we're doing is shameful. Handing them back to the Russians to be executed! And all in the name of justice.'

'Owen should know about it all,' she said, reaching for an argument she had used many times. 'She should tell him. Jean committed no sin. She thought he was dead.'

'He's not up to it, love. Not Owen.'

'But he seems well enough.'

'In his body, maybe. But what about his mind?'

It was a question that neither of them could answer, although to some extent it had answered itself. Before they could rehearse their worries about Owen, Peg came in briskly with the mail. She handed a letter to Helen and a bill to George. There was also a letter for Blake from Germany.

'From one of his mates in the Army out there,' said George and went off to get ready for work.

'Give Blake a shout for me, Dad. Mark's calling for him.'

'Right.'

'This letter for him . . . looks like a woman's handwriting,' said Peg with a sly grin. 'What's yours, Mum? I never get any letters myself—only fair that I should share everybody else's.'

Helen Hayward was transfixed by what she had just read, but when she spoke it was with a casual tone, as if this kind of thing happened to her all the time.

'It's from the radio . . . that audition I did. . . . They want me to broadcast. . . . They want me to sing Brahms.'

John Warrington was still reading *The Times* when she came back into the living room to tell him that breakfast was almost ready. He fell back on his usual technique of asking one of his children to tell him about the other.

'How's Mark getting on at the estate office?'

'Haven't you been there?' There was some reproach in this.

'The ironworks have taken up all my time since I got back, Ros. Been more or less tied to the office at Silport.'

'Hiding away!'

'You said that with such aggression. . . .'

'Sorry . . . but you've seen Mark yourself. Haven't you asked him direct?'

'Couldn't seem to get round to it.'

'He loves the new job. What he loathed was the office—the one where you spend all your time. I'm glad you didn't try to pressurize him into carrying on the family name at the ironworks.'

'I think I appreciate how he feels, Ros. I inherited a double responsibility, you see—the ironworks and the estate. I know where *my* real interest lies, but he's different. Envy him in a way.' He folded his paper and put it down. 'Is he still keen on that girl?'

'Peg? They're inseparable.'

'So?'

'One big snag. . . .'

'She won't become a Catholic?'

'Mark doesn't think that she should have to. Peg waits while he agonizes.' She shrugged. 'You might as well know . . . I fancy we're going to lose him. First, politics, now religion. He won't even talk to Father Ross.'

'If he loses his faith it will be my fault.'

'No, it won't, Dad!' she protested. 'For heaven's sake, get rid of that hair shirt! It's not your fault any more than it was when you and Mum separated.'

'No hold on. . . .'

'I don't want to open old wounds but she *was* unfaithful to you. She did give you cause.'

The old wounds had been opened and they bled in silence for a minute or so. He asked how his wife took the death of the man with whom she had lived. Rosalynde told him how shattered her mother had been and how she had never recovered from the blow.

'Did you ever meet him?' he wondered.

'No. She wanted me to but I couldn't. Mark wouldn't have done it either. He belongs to a family for all that he likes to pretend otherwise.'

She reminded him that Blake Hayward was coming to mend the motor launch that day. It would give him an opportunity to meet another member of Peg's family. John's eyes twinkled.

'That's another obstacle we've to surmount, isn't it?'

'Class, you mean? Isn't it supposed to have gone out now? A Labour Government with a liberal quota of ex-public school boys.'

'At least they must know something of the class they represent. I know more about Bantu then I do about the British working class. Appalling ignorance, really.'

'Now's your chance to learn.'

Not realizing that he was to take a part in the education of John Warrington, Blake sat on the edge of the bed without moving. He had read Herta's letter so many times now that he knew the words by heart.

> It is almost impossible to go now from a place which is occupied by Americans, British or Russians to one or the other. Now I am in the British sector but for some few weeks only. Soon I must return to the East where my father still is. This will be the last letter I write to you.

Blake was at once pleased and depressed, delighted that she had managed to get in touch with him and yet mortified that this would be the last occasion, relieved that she had somehow survived at the same time as he realized what that survival must have cost her.

'Can I have the stamp?'

'Stamp?'

'On that letter.'

'Letter?'

Blake had been miles away when Lovett came into the room that they now shared. He tore off a corner of the envelope and handed the foreign stamp to his younger brother.

'Mark's here for you.'

'Who? Oh yes, of course. I'm more ready than I look. Just make the bed and then I'll be off.'

'I'll make it for you,' announced Lovett, somnolently.

'Thanks. I'll take you up on that offer.'

Blake finished getting dressed and asked why his brother had got up so early that morning. The boy told him that he had been for a long walk along the beach.

'We all seem to be having long walks these days. Maybe we're trying to get the war out of our lungs.'

'I think we probably are,' said Lovett, seriously.

'And what sort of war did you have, then?' asked Blake, amused.

'Boring. Missed it all by being too young.'

'You missed nothing, believe me!'

'But I'll always feel that I have, won't I?'

There was an element of despair in his voice that was quite out of character. It astonished Blake.


If the prospect of moving house had made Colin Hayward surly and resentful, it had turned his mother into a bag of nerves. She was pacing up and down in the hall among bags and boxes and suitcases, wondering why the van was taking so long to arrive and finding a dozen other things to worry about. Helen could see her agitation and tried to calm her. Owen was up in the attic, searching for various odds and ends that had been put away up there. She opened the front door and showed her mother the pile of furniture and the packed tea chests that were standing in readiness.

'I can't think why Owen wants to take so much,' she said, fidgeting. 'It's only a small house and most of Grandad's furniture is still there.'

'You're taking the bed, I see.'

'Yes.' Jean became guilty. 'Do you mind?'

'Don't be silly.'

'Owen insisted. He likes everything he's been used to.'

'Of course, love. And we can manage without it. We'll move Lovett's bed back into your room if he'll let us,' she added. 'Something's making him so irritable these days. And he's not the only one. It's catching.'

'I'm sorry, anyway ... Owen would take the wallpaper if he could!' Jean paused as she remembered what he had once told her. 'Yes, well I suppose that's it.'

'What is?'

'Owen ... this need. ... He said that he used to lie awake at night in the camp he was in ... just thinking about the pattern on the wallpaper in that room. If only walls could speak. ...'

'It's better this way, Jean,' assured her mother-in-law.

'Is it?'

'Place of your own. Fresh start. It'll help you ... both of you, I mean.'

Jean seemed unpersuaded. She drifted back into the living room and gazed around fondly as if she were seeing it for the last time. Helen came in and stood beside her.

'You'll be able to come back as often as you like. ...'

'I'm glad Ernst was able to visit this house ... just that once,' said

Jean. 'He loved you all. I think you reminded him of his family.'

'We weren't on our best behaviour that day,' recalled Helen, grimly. 'Peg was to blame, stirring it up.'

'Ernst didn't mind. He loved you. . . .' Her voice sounded faraway now. 'The prisoners from the camp have all gone.'

'I know, Jean.'

'And do you know what will happen to them in Russia?'

'Well. . . .'

'Perhaps he is with them now . . . his family . . . the dead. . . .'

'You mustn't assume that, Jean.'

'I wanted to die too, you know. Ernst wouldn't let me.'

Helen took her by the shoulders and spoke softly but with great intensity.

'He was right.'

Jean could not bear even to think about it any more and changed the subject at once, resorting to a frantic brightness.

'I'm glad about your news.'

'News?'

'The radio. Your great triumph!'

'It's hardly that.'

'You deserve it. I shall miss hearing you sing and play the piano—and I don't know a thing about music. I shall even miss those dreadful children you give piano lessons to.' She gave a brittle laugh. 'Does George know about this thing?'

'Not yet. He's always been a bit odd about my singing . . . as if it came between us. "What about your politics," I always say, but he won't listen. I shall tell him in due course.'

'He ought to be thrilled. Any other husband would be!'

'Yes. But I shall tell him . . . when I feel up to it.'

Rosalynde Warrington was descending the steps from the house when she heard the distinctive sound of her mother's car. Surprise and delight made her run to meet it.

'We thought you were still in Germany!'

'Got back last night. When you weren't at home, I assumed you might be here. But perhaps I shouldn't say that?'

'What?'

'Calling my place "at home". You may feel that being at Lake House is that. And don't worry, I've not come to drag you away. Just to see you.'

'You're very welcome, you know that!'

'Thank you. Is your father here?'

'Down by the landing stage. Mark's brought a friend who's going to take a look at our motor launch. It conked out.'

'Talking of which, has your father got any extra petrol coupons, by any chance? I've run out.'

'I thought you got extra rations because of your work?'

'I do but I've driven rather a long way. Should have used the train, really, but I have to go back from a different airfield at the end of next week.' Beth Warrington got out of the car and started to walk towards the house with her daughter. 'Has he any idea what I've actually been doing in Germany?'

'Not really—and I haven't told him.'

'Good.'

'He's made a few remarks. Thinks you might be entertaining the occupation troops. That's one thing he's always been impressed by, you know. Your theatrical career.'

'Such as it was. . . .'

'Now don't be modest. Shall we join them?'

'Why not?'

'Just one thing. . . .'

'I know . . . behave myself.'

'I was going to say . . . be kind to him. You only knew the pre-war John Warrington, remember.'

'Is the post-war model so very different?' asked Beth, at her most arch. She relaxed. 'I'll do my best, Ros.'

'Thank you. After all, you haven't spoken to each other for more than five or six hours in as many years.'

'If that,' conceded the other. 'If that. . . .'

They walked past the house and went down through the garden at the rear. In the distance they could see four figures against the glassy calm of the lake. Blake and Mark were examining the engine aboard the launch while John was chatting to Peg on the landing stage. The women were too far away to hear what was being said or to notice the shadowed resentment on Mark's face as his father and Peg laughed. Mark decided to break up their conversation and walked up the landing stage towards them.

'Blake's having a spot of trouble, sir. I think you should have a word with him.'

'Right, I will,' said John, obligingly. 'Excuse me.'

As soon as he was out of earshot, Peg turned to Mark in some surprise, her eyes faintly mocking him.

'You called him "sir"!'

'It's a class habit. Respect for one's parents should be shown even when it no longer exists. Like a lot of other things, it dies hard.'

'Old sourpuss!' she said, reprovingly.

'But you were laughing with him just now, Peg.'

'Not him—I meant *you*!'

Mark accepted the rebuke with grace and ran an affectionate hand through her hair. He was about to take her in his arms when he spotted the two women approaching him. A new uneasiness kindled inside him though he could not quite understand why.

Unaware that his wife was only thirty yards away, John Warrington peered down into the engine aboard the launch.

'Mark says you're having some trouble.'

Blake, arms black with oil to the elbows, sat up and nodded.

'We're going to need a new one of these, Mr Warrington.' He held up a long bolt with a small wheel attached to its end. 'It's broken clean through, as you can see.'

'Must have had a fault.'

'It was made at your ironworks,' Blake commented, neutrally. 'They could make you another one easily.'

'See to it, then.'

'I can't. Not allowed on the premises. One of your managers gave me the sack.'

'From what I hear, it was the other way round. You don't seem to be too heart-broken by it.'

'I'm not!'

'Our loss—your gain. Peg tells me you've set up in business on your own.'

'Yes. . . .'

'Good. It's what the country needs. It's hope for the future.'

'Is it what we deserve, though?' asked Blake.

'We stood against Hitler,' said John, proudly. 'Virtually alone in the early days. Don't we deserve something for that?'

'We got medals for that . . . but then that happened after the first lot, didn't it? And you soon had men pawning their medals to stay out of the gutter.'

'I doubt if we'll go back to that,' came the bland assurance.

'Oh I don't intend to. . . .'

'Am I butting in?' asked Beth, standing beside the launch.

'Beth!' Her husband was thrilled.

He leapt up. Under pressure, Beth agreed to stay for lunch and then asked him to go across to the others so that Peg could take a photograph of him. With that same reflex affability that Blake had first noted in his son, John went off to join the others. Beth was left alone with Blake for a moment.

'He assumes we've already been introduced—I'm Beth Warrington. Mark's mother.'

'Blake Hayward . . . Peg's my sister.'

'I didn't need telling that,' she smiled.

'You've been in Germany, haven't you?' he asked, with interest.

'I've just come back from there, actually.'

'What's it like?'

'You seem very keen to know. . . .'

'I've been trying to get there myself for the last twelve months. They say it's impossible.'

'It is for most people,' she agreed.

'And you?'

'That's rather different. Why do you want to go to Germany?'

'I have a friend there, Mrs Warrington.'

'English?'

'German.'

'German?' Her curiosity was aroused. 'It must be someone important if you've made repeated efforts to get over there.'

'It is.'

A call from the others brought the conversation to a halt. Beth was wanted for a photograph by Peg, who was holding a box camera and experimenting with positions. Blake found himself alone again and addressed himself to his job of stripping down the engine. As he knelt beside it, trying to loosen a nut with his hand, he heard some footsteps behind him.

'Pass me that half-inch spanner, will you?' he asked without turning around. A wrench was put into his grip. 'Didn't they teach you anything at that public school that you. . . . ?'

His voice tailed off as he saw Rosalynde Warrington standing beside him. He apologized but she waved this aside. 'I'm Ros—Mark's sister. I can see that he's been binding to you about his public school education.'

'Ever since we met in Germany just before the end.'

'The end!' she repeated, dramatically.

'Well, that's what it was.'

'Doesn't feel like the end to me and over a year's gone by since Adolf shot himself. We could still be at war, really. Same grey old wartime world here. If we're not careful we shall get too fond of it.'

'Yes.'

'There is something new, of course.'

'New?'

'Peg and Mark. . . .'

'Oh that. The working girl and the boss's son.'

'It would never have happened before the war. They realize that.' She regarded him quizzically. 'Do you approve?'

'I hope I'm not a snob,' he said, levelly.

'Ah—the boot's on the other foot now, is it?'

John Warrington interrupted them to tell them that lunch was ready. Rosalynde hoped that Blake would be able to join them.

'Love to,' he grinned, wiping his hands on a rag. 'Always wanted to know how the other half eat away from the Officers' Mess.'

She led the way up towards the others, arriving in time to have the briefest word with her mother.

'Interesting family,' was Beth's aside.

'Like us, mother. No two the same.'

Rosalynde walked on past her and fell in beside Mark. Beth waited for a chance to speak to Blake again. There was something about him that made her want to help him.

'Engines your speciality, Blake?'

'Yes. Anything that makes the wheels go round.'

'Still want to get to Germany?' she asked, casually.

'Do I!'

'I think I can arrange it.'

'You?' Amazement and gratitude lit up his face.

'Get Mark to bring you to the cottage. I'd rather not talk about it here.'                    •

Harry Hayward had known for some time that the boy was troubled. All the signs were there and when Lovett even passed up the chance to go out in the boat with his grandfather, the old man could refrain from comment no longer. He invited Lovett into his room and chatted to him gently until he had created the sort of atmosphere in which the other might be ready to confide in him. Harry and Lovett had spent so many happy times in that room amid the accumulated rubbish of a lifetime. It was the one place in the house where the boy was able to relax somehow.

'Out with it, then,' said Harry, at length.

'Out with what, Grandad?'

'Now don't think you can pull the wool over my eyes, Lovett Hayward. I'm not like your parents. I watch you careful.'

Lovett offered a few token protests of ignorance and then put a hand into his pocket. He fished out a letter and handed it across to his grandfather. Harry raised his spectacles so that he could squint beneath them and he read the typed words, his brow crinkled with concentration.

'Told anyone else?' he asked, sitting back.

'No.'

'Why ever not? Anybody's think you were ashamed, lad. You've won a scholarship to a good school. You should be proud. How long have you kept it to yourself?'

'Since last day of term when they gave me the letter.'

'I don't understand you, Lovett. What's all the secrecy for?'

'I don't want to go.'

'Eh? But Why?'

'I just don't, that's all. I just don't.'

Lovett Hayward put an end to any further discussion by letting himself out of the room.

## CHAPTER TEN

The town was just inside the British sector and they had given her a small, rented room in a bomb-damaged house not far from the main street. Through broken panes in the window, she was able to look out on the broken lives of those below her, frightened people who scuttled past about their business between khaki uniforms and loaded rifles. For her as for many other Germans the war had not so much ended as entered a new phase, and they were now suffering all the indignities and abuses of military occupation.

'I'm sorry about the room,' he said.

'I would not have any other,' she replied, looking around at the cracked plaster, the bare floor, and the iron bed. 'He is coming today?'

'Today or tomorrow. Travelling is so unpredictable these days.'

'Oh yes!' she said with feeling. 'I know. I know.' She went right up to him. 'Thank you. For what you did, thank you.'

'Only too glad to be able to help.'

Captain Waters had changed very little in the past year and he had the same cheerful straightforwardness. Herta Wenkel, by contrast, had changed a great deal in the time, her cheeks becoming hollow and the lines around her eyes and mouth deepening into a bitterness that seemed permanent. Her hair was long and unkempt, her clothes dowdy and her chin, so often held high in the old days, was now much nearer to her chest. Twelve months of trailing around the Russian sector had taken its toll and Waters was not pleased to see what it was. What he noticed first was that her spirit seemed to have been broken, too, another incidental casualty.

Herta walked around the cramped room and examined every detail of it as if it had a special significance for her. Then she spoke.

'If only I had come to the West when Blake had wished me to!' she sighed. 'It would have been so much better.'

'I doubt it. Things are just as bad here.'

'You have been to the Russian sector?' she asked, sharply.

'No, no . . . I haven't. . . .'

The challenging anger in this remark persuaded Waters to back down and apologize. Herta Wenkel was in the town to attend her father's funeral and it was Waters who had made it all possible.

'When does your permit expire?'

'In a week. I could always just disappear, of course.'

'Don't do that!' he warned.

'I will not embarrass you by making a run,' she assured him, with a rare smile. 'I have to go back. You know why. And since I have to go back, I shall not see him.'

'But it's the reason Blake is coming!'

'When my father is buried I shall go. I must go back. You do understand?'

Waters took account of all the factors in the situation and agreed, albeit reluctantly, that she was taking the only course open to her. Hurt on behalf of a friend, he told her that he understood.


'When will they let us on board?'

'It's always like this. One simply has to wait hopefully.'

'The voice of experience.'

'It was worse in the war, of course.'

'You flew during the war?' Blake was astounded.

'To France. It's no longer a secret.'

'Except from your husband.'

Beth Warrington and Blake Hayward were standing by the side of the runway with their luggage, waiting to board the Dakota plane that was standing some fifty yards away. Like most other wartime airfields, this one was small, makeshift and restricted to basics. Passengers had to forego such luxuries as an airport lounge where refreshments might be served.

'We're separated,' she said, in answer to his comment.

'Mark told me.'

'It must be pretty obvious, anyway.'

'It isn't, actually, not when you're together. That day we all had lunch at Lake House, for instance.'

'How much can you know of people simply by seeing them together? Not a great deal. . . .'

The wind was starting to get troublesome now and Blake wished that he had brought a thicker jacket. Beth seemed unconcerned as her hair was tossed about.

'Why don't you want him to know about all this?'

'John? I have my reasons.'

'In other words, mind my own business.'

'No, I don't mind telling you, Blake. I've a feeling I can trust you not to tell him. There was another man, you see.'

'Mark did touch on that as well.'

'What Mark doesn't know is that I first met the man in Germany. I speak fluent German and worked in a theatre there before the war. I played several of the major cities, in fact. John met the man, too, as it happens. Briefly. But he won't remember and I wouldn't want to rub salt in old wounds.'

'And this refugee thing you're involved in now?'

'That arose through the same man as well, though he was dead when they asked me to do it. It's sort of . . . in his memory. . . .'

Blake had been staggered to learn about the work that she had done during the war and he was equally staggered to realize how important a position she now held.

'And you're involved with the government? I mean, you run the whole thing?'

'You sound as disbelieving as my husband. I shall say no more. My turn to be question master now.'

'Fire away,' he invited.

'This German friend. How did it come about?'

'We met on V.E. Day. . . .'

'Romantic!'

'Sounds like the title of a novel, doesn't it? But it wasn't quite like that. When we pulled back behind the Yalta line, she stayed in the Russian sector. She thought her father was there.'

'And she's been there ever since?'

'Yes.'

'Well, that's how it is in Germany these days.' She watched him for a moment. 'You have sympathy for them?'

'A certain amount . . . not for Auschwitz, Belsen and the rest of those places. . . .'

'That's going to be a problem for *them*, too, living with it. My friend—the man I was telling you about—was in the German Labour Movement before the war. The leaders fled eventually to America and so on . . . some stayed and perished in those camps.'

For the first time since he had met her, Blake could believe that the elegant, poised lady and the deeply committed organizer of relief for refugees were one and the same person. He began to have a new respect for the Warrington family.

'It's very good of you to help me like this.'

'Ah but I have an ulterior motive, Blake.'

'Do you?'

'Yes. I'm hoping that when you see what it's like out there, you'll stay and help us. We need your skills.'

'Mrs Warrington!' called a voice from the plane.

'Take-off,' she said. 'Come on, Blake.' He picked up the luggage and followed her towards the Dakota. She had one piece of advice for him. 'Hold on to your stomach. They call it the Flying Duck.'

Sunday was no day of rest for Helen Hayward and she spent the morning, as always, in her kitchen. The demands of family kept her shackled to her work and yet she was curiously unwelcoming when someone offered to loosen those shackles slightly.

'I don't need any help, Jean.'

'All us to feed at table—of course you need help. By the way, I brought a few things. Spuds, carrots. . . .'

'When I want you to bring anything I'll ask,' said Helen.

'Still the same, aren't you?' smiled the younger woman. 'Now shove over from that sink and I'll peel the spuds while we chat.'

Realizing that she would have to accept help, Helen made the most of it and she was soon talking happily to her daughter-in-law again, wondering how they had settled into the house.

'We like it. I do, anyway. And I think it'll help us, living there. Unless I make a mess of things.'

'You won't.'

'You hope, you mean.'

'You won't,' repeated Helen with confidence.

'I nearly did . . . that time. . . .'

'It's behind you now, Jean. Forget it.'

'I can never forget it, Mum. Never.' She had filled the bowl with water now and put in the potatoes. She reached for a knife. 'Did you know that I'd finished at the Galways?'

'No, but I'm glad. Too many associations.'

'They were very good about it. They liked Ernst, but they felt that I'd done the "right thing". God, the right thing!'

To prevent her from brooding on it, Helen talked instead about the room that they had occupied before they had left. Helen had not even had time to clean it properly since their departure but she would have to get in there soon as Blake was going to move into the room when he got back from Germany. All that Jean could recall about it was the wallpaper on the walls and the great importance this had held for Owen during the long nights in a Japanese prison camp.

It had been a tremendous effort for her husband to leave the family house, even though they had not moved very far away. Though he said little about it—as about everything else—she knew that it had been a wrench and that he was still far from settled in the new place. Still peeling away, she returned to the eternal problem.

'There's a lot goes on inside his head and he'll not even mention it. I still fear to push him to tell me what happened to him, what they did to him out there.'

Harry Hayward lurked in the hall like a conspirator in search of a conspiracy. Colin went past and was given a curt nod, Peg went by and collected a guilty scowl, Owen ambled through and gained a non-committal grunt. When he saw Lovett approaching through the front garden, Harry actually dodged back into his room and stayed there until the footsteps died away. Only when George Hayward walked along the passageway did his father show any signs of being sociable. Finger on his lips to command silence, Harry hauled his son into a room that the latter had never been allowed to enter before without the rigmarole of using the ship's bell. Once inside the door, George opened his mouth to speak but did not get the chance. A letter was thrust into his hands and his father gesticulated that he should read it. The words had an immediate effect on George.

'How long has Lovett had this?'

'Since his last day at school.'

'Why didn't he tell us?'

'He left it here o' purpose, I reckon, hoping that I'd break the bad news to you.'

'Bad news?'

'Scholarship to a public school. Your own lad. You, a pillar of the Labour Party round here. What is it you once called public schools— "Breeding grounds for privilege. . . ."'

'It's an achievement for Lovett all the same. No reason to hide it from us.'

'Unless he wants to go and fears to tell you because you'd tell him nay.'

'We can't afford,' replied George, simply.

'It's a scholarship.'

'He'd need things we couldn't provide if he was to stand his ground. And there's no more money coming into this house than there was before the war. Keir stays in London without a copper to spare us, Blake's gone off and might never be back again. Even the bit we had from Owen and Jean living here has been taken from us.'

'Aye well, it's a better excuse than a principle,' said Harry, going on to the attack.

'It's not an excuse, Dad, it's a reality!' retorted George. 'I know what respect you've got for principles. . . .'

'I've principles of me own, maybe, but I don't expect others to pay the price for 'em, though.'

'Look, it's not the reason. . . .'

'Pull the other one!'

'It's not—though it's a good enough reason even so. I'm local secretary of a party that's pledged to reform education, to carry on where Butler's act left off.'

'Butler! Butler! I'm sick of hearing about Butler!'

'He's a bloody Tory!'

'Shame on him, then!'

George burst out laughing at the sheer absurdity of this but his father's next remark checked his mirth at once.

'You think I'm ignorant, don't you?'

'Why do you say that?' asked his son, trying to mollify him.

'I am ignorant, I know I am. I did better for you than was done for me. It's up to you to do better for him. That's how life goes forward. Not with ideals. Ideals can blind you to facts. What you believe today is in the rubbish can tomorrow but there's them that'll go on believing it regardless. . . .' He grabbed hold of George's arm to emphasize his point. 'It's *his* future we're talking about, not yours!'

When George Hayward left his father's room, his mind was buzzing and his resolve was not quite as firm as it had been.


Alone in the empty bedroom which he had shared with his. wife, Owen Hayward stared at the wallpaper with total fascination. He went across to it, touched it to make sure that it was real, and then let his eyes focus on one small area of the fern pattern. Voices began to make themselves heard inside his head, at first indistinctly, then audibly, then loudly, then with deafening insistence. Mesmerized by a jungle that was growing on a bedroom wall, Owen Hayward put frantic hands to his ears in a vain attempt to block out noise, but the collective tauting and yelling of Japanese soldiers continued till he thought his skull would crack. Only when another voice spoke did the clamour fade.

'Owen . . . Owen. . . .'

It was Lovett, sent to fetch his brother, puzzled by the anguish on the other's face.

'Dinner's ready,' he said. 'Are you coming?'

Owen squatted down until his face was level with that of Lovett and then he reached out to touch it gently.

'Never leave home, Lovett . . . never leave home. . . .'

Swooping down through low cloud, the Dakota circled the airfield once and then came into land on its single runway. It was a bumpy landing but a safe one and the passengers were duly grateful to the pilot when the plane taxied to a standstill near some low buildings. Beth Warrington got out and Blake Hayward came after her carrying their joint luggage.

'What do we do now?' he asked.

'Wait again, patiently. A truck should come, if it doesn't break down. I'm afraid they're always breaking down. That's why I need your services.'

'Will it come to this actual spot?' he said, grunting under the weight of her bag. She told him to put it down and rest. He said, 'What's in it, for God's sake? Lead?'

'Something that's immensely valuable.'

'Gold!'

'Much more valuable than that—cotton.'

'Cotton?'

'We use it to make shoes from old tyres. You can't beg, borrow or steal it in Europe.' She looked up into the sky to see the cloud drifting away to allow the sun through. 'It's a lovely day!' she decided, and promptly sat down on the grass.

'Can't we wait in one of those buildings?'

'They're derelict if you look close. No—this is fine.'

'You've got more patience than I have, Mrs Warrington. I couldn't just lie out on the grass like that.'

'When you've seen the accumulated misery of five years of war in the faces of certain people, and realize that it won't be wiped away in a day, a year, a lifetime for some—once you've accepted that, you've learned how to wait.'

Blake looked around in time to see the plane wheeling around in order to take off again. With a roar of its engines, it was soon airborne and clear of German soil again. They were quite alone now. He took her advice and settled down beside her.

'Been doing this since the war ended?'

'More or less. I was in Prague a few weeks ago: I went to an internment camp for German civilians. I acted in Prague before the war. A beautiful old theatre, destroyed now, of course. . . .' A flash of pride made her eyes sparkle. 'Masaryk came to one of our performances.' She became sad.

'They showed me a room where the German prisoners were hung with wire after a trial in which all that was said was "You have not been granted mercy." It was a very clean room—white tiles, a hose to wash down afterwards.'

'You learn to forgive the hard way, don't you?' he commented.

'What other way is there, Blake?'

'I could tell you,' he offered.

'Listen . . . in the room next to the one I described there were dying babies, some of them born to Czech women who married Germans. They were alone, left to die alone, no one even to sit with them in this world in which we all have to live!'

'The sins of the fathers. . . .'

'You wonder why I'm still a Catholic, don't you?'

'After all that, yes.'

'It's *because* of all that, Blake.'

She then asked about the friend who had arranged for Herta to be allowed in to the British sector of Germany and Blake talked with offhand affection about Waters and their time together in the army. The welcome sound of a truck was heard at last and they both got to their feet. Beth had one last piece of advice for him.

'Don't hope too much. In Europe now a little hope has to go a long, long way.'

Herta Wenkel sat on the edge of the bed and stared ahead of her, wrestling with her conscience. She did not really hear what Waters was saying to her about going off to meet Blake until his final question.

'Didn't you say that your mind was made up?'

'It is.'

'I think not, Herta.'

'You know my mind better than I do?' she asked.

Waters still suspected that she had severe reservations about her decision but he did not want to risk her ire. There was something in her desperation that told him it would not take a great deal to make her explode completely and that was the last thing he wished her to do. In a delicate situation like this, all he could do was to reason softly with her.

'Then you want me to tell him that you won't see him?'

'No! Only that you do not know where I am.'

'I told him that I had found your father. I told him that I was trying to fix it so that you could come here. He'll want to know what went wrong.'

'Say that I cannot see him—not won't—that I *cannot*.'

'He'll ask why, Herta,' persisted the other, gently.

'Invent something,' she pleaded.

'Me?'

Even in the middle of her own gnawing uncertainties, she could appreciate the position that she was putting him in. She shook her head and got up from the bed.

'No, no, it will not work. I ask you to lie for me and you do not wish to lie. In your heart, you cannot lie.'

'I'm such a bloody awful liar, to be honest!'

'I remember. . . .' For a moment, she remembered other things as well, all beginning with kindness shown towards her on V.E. Day. It had its effect. 'I will see him, then. I will see him.'

Waters breathed a sigh of relief and talked to himself.

'Thank God for that!'


Any pleasure that his parents may have taken from the news that Lovett Hayward had, against stiff competition, won a scholarship to a public school was destroyed by the fact that the boy had felt it necessary to conceal his success from them. George Hayward had decided that it was just not possible to let his son take up the place, though his own father had made a frontal assault on that decision. It was now Helen Hayward's turn to visit the room with the ship's bell guarding its door.

'George is right, Dad. . . .'

'Your husband is *never* right!'

'We couldn't afford it . . . unless. . . .'

'Unless what?'

'I could earn. . . .'

'You? Nay, lass, you'd have to give piano lessons morning, noon and night to bring in a tenth of what's needed.'

'I've had an offer.'

'This radio thing?' he asked.

'No, nothing to do with that. George'd hate it. He'd never let me do it, anyway.'

'*Let* you?' Harry bridled. 'Have you no life of your own? He said nowt against women working in't war, did he? In't factories, everywhere. Wrens, A.T.S., Waaf. . . .'

'You were more against all that than him, you old humbug!'

'Me?' he said, a picture of innocence in the dock.

'And women in trousers!' she remembered, teasing him. 'You'd have thought they were stripping off not covering up!'

'Getting back to Lovett. . . .' he began.

'Getting back to Lovett, I have this idea, Dad.'


While they were getting back to Lovett in the room below, George Hayward was in the boy's bedroom trying to discuss the whole subject with him. It was nearing the end of the school holidays now which meant that Lovett had kept his news secret for well over a month. George could only guess at the effort it had taken to get through that time with a letter from school burning a hole in the boy's pocket.

'Why didn't you tell me, Lovett?'

'Don't know.'

'Don't know or just won't tell?'

'Don't know . . . honest,' he insisted.

'Anything to do with me and politics.'

'A bit, maybe. . . .'

'And the rest?'

'I don't want to leave here, Dad. This house. I like it here.'

'No need to sound so defensive about it, son. There's nothing wrong in wanting to stop with your roots.'

'Unless I got like Owen. . . .'

'Owen?'

'He's frightened to go anywhere. Won't even go to Silport.'

'Who says he won't?' asked George, alarmed.

'I heard Jean tell Mum.'

It was an impeccable source and his father could not gainsay it. He simply wondered why his wife had not passed on the information. Then he tried to take some of the questioning strain out of the other's face.

'It's what the war did to him.'

'Will he always be like that?'

'I don't know, son. As for the other—my politics—I named you, as I named all my sons, after a well-known Labour man.'

Yes, Dad. William Lovett. I looked him up in the school encyclopaedia once. Said he was a Chartist or something . . . William Lovett.' He recited the other names. 'Then there was Ramsey from Ramsey Macdonald, Keir from Keir Hardie, Blake from William Blake, the poet and revolutionary. . . . I looked 'em all up.'

'That'll have done you no harm,' said George with approval, adding warningly, 'except in Macdonald's case, of course. The point I was making, though, was this . . . I named you but what you are, what you become, is up to you. I've nothing against that particular school you've won the scholarship for. It's got a good reputation—but then so it should have. It's paid for out of the profits that come from the sweat of honest folk. It's public in that sense.'

Lovett Hayward was too familiar with his father's arguments for them to have any real effect on him, just as he was too familiar with the opposing views held by his grandfather. When he ignored the prejudices of his elders and consulted his own heart, he chose his course with a firm voice.

'I think I should go.'

'If it's what you want.'

'I think I should, Dad.'

After breathing heavily a few times, George said, 'That's it, then. No more to be said.'

Helen Hayward now tapped on the door and saw from their expressions that something had been decided. She found an excuse to get rid of Lovett, who was only too keen to escape, and then turned to her husband for the news.

'He wants to go.'

'I'm glad.'

'Five years of war with all but one of your lads away and now you want him gone! You're a funny woman, Helen!'

'It's cost you more than me, George.'

'Principle, you mean?'

'We shall afford the money side of it, somehow or other.'

'I wish I knew how. I suppose you think like him down there in his cabin? That God'll provide?'

'Happen he thinks like me about one thing—that you've done enough. . . .'

Taking advantage yet again of a glorious evening, Rosalynde Warrington was pruning the roses on the trellis with a pair of secateurs. At the bottom of the garden, near the ornamental pond, Mark and Peg were having an animated conversation though they were too far away for any of their words to be heard. John Warrington watched his daughter snip away with ruthless precision and then asked her if she knew when Beth was returning from Germany. He was told that it was at the end of the week. Without even waiting to absorb this information, he delivered some news which he had been saving all day, letting it come out almost tentatively.

The Conservative Party, still smarting from its wounds inflicted at the General Election, had resolved to make a better showing the next time round and they had approached John to stand as prospective Parliamentary candidate for the constituency. Rosalynde reminded him that the Labour member might well sit for another four years but was told that the incumbent was in fact rumoured to be quite ill. The demands of the job were proving too taxing and an early by-election in Whitstanton was being predicted by more than one commentator.

Seeing that his daughter was not going to make any observation about his potential career in politics, he switched his attention to the mime at the bottom of the garden. Rosalynde let him in on the secret that Mark was actually proposing to Peg and had already bought an engagement ring to offer her. From the gestures that were taking place she did not seem too keen to accept it. John Warrington was pensive, fearing that it meant his son was lost to Catholicism for good, but rallying when Rosalynde pointed out that there was a gain, in the person of Peg Hayward herself. Her father agreed, qualifying his agreement by saying that Peg, whom he liked enormously, was trying too hard to bridge the gap between herself and Mark. He then referred to another gap that remained to be faced— the Warringtons, as a family, had yet to meet the Haywards. Rosalynde announced that she had tried to do this but Mark had baulked her, almost as if he was ashamed of his own family.

Their discussion had taken their attention away from the couple in the distance. When they glanced up, only Mark was left down by the pond. Peg, face red and jaw set, was approaching them with all the speed she could muster.

'Ros, could you give me a lift home, please?' she asked.

Mark Warrington stared into the water beside him and fingered the engagement ring that was still in his pocket.


The accelerating numbers of dead during the war had quite outstripped the facilities for burial. Cemeteries in many towns were full to capacity and they often overflowed, as in this case, into an adjacent field. Token efforts were made to incorporate the field into the precincts of the cemetery itself but all too often, again as here, the place remained defiantly what it was—a piece of land, set aside for another use altogether, hastily designated as yet another annexe for the burial of German dead.

Blake Hayward stood some way off from the tiny funeral party with Waters, talking in undertones.

'What did her father die of?'

'Malnutrition, old age, defeat. . . . The usual erosion, speeded up. People are dying too quickly. There aren't enough graves, Blake.'

'Why did you stay on, Waters?'

'To learn.'

'About what?'

'Survival. It's a fascinating study; almost every instinct of life becomes subordinated to it.'

The brief service was now at an end. The priest, together with the bearers, departed slowly. Herta Wenkel was left alone to stare down into the hole in the earth where her father's coffin lay. When she had seen enough, she walked towards them without looking up until she was almost upon them.

Her eyes met Blake's as they had done all that time away and for a second, notwithstanding the circumstances, both of them heard a Beethoven piano sonata being played.

In hunting country, where the traditions are as weathered as old oak, the shooting of foxes is frowned upon; on the Warrington estate, which had no Hunt to cross it with horse and hounds, the only way to kill the animal was to shoot or trap and Owen Hayward did both with a zeal that would have offended the gentry in other counties. Owen had not reared his pheasants to provide two meals a day for a predator and he did his best to track down a fox the moment he became aware of its presence on the estate. .

'These are old droppings,' he said to Mark, pointing to the pellets of dung. 'Hasn't been here for two or three days. I'll be after him, though.'

Mark, also with a twelve-bore under his arm, asked how close they were to his mother's cottage and was surprised to be told that they were very close indeed. He was surprised about something else as well.

'That farm where Jean worked. . . .'

'The Galways?'

'Didn't realize it was part of our estate.'

'Aye, belongs to your Dad.'

'They must be the only tenants we've got who aren't moaning about their problems. Must take a run over there one day to see how they manage to cope so well.'

'I was round home yesterday,' said Owen, artlessly direct as ever. 'Peg came home in a temper from your place. Why was that?'

'I gave her a ring. She gave it back to me.'

'Why?'

'I told her I'd stopped being a Catholic. She said if I could give up caring as easily as that, I could do the same with her.' Mark almost shouted. 'But I damn well did it *for* her!'

'Contrary, that's women . . . contrary. . . .'

'I've been fighting it out with myself for years. Now I finally make the break, this happens. It doesn't make sense, Owen. It just doesn't make sense.'

Peg Hayward, not worried about the apparent senselessness of her actions, opened the front door of her house to find a stout, balding man standing there. Jack Bassett was Labour Party agent for the

constituency and he had come for a word with her father. Peg showed
him in, taking him past a door which was slightly ajar so that Harry
could hiss silently as his enemy walked by. George gave his colleague
a warm welcome and sat him down in a chair in the living room.

'Can't stop,' said Bassett, glancing round to make sure that they
were alone. 'Will it be safe for me to bring someone to see you later
this week?'

'Safe?'

'Don't want too many to know about it, George. Happen we'd
better use back room at the Working Men's Club. We can slip in
quietly through rear entrance there. I'll give you a ring when I've
heard from her.'

'Her?' He was mystified.

'When she's ready to talk, I'll be in touch.'

Bassett was on his feet again and moving towards the door.

'Hang on a tick, Jack. . . .'

'No time. Now keep this to yourself, won't you?'

He went out into the hall in time to see the furtive figure of Harry
Hayward darting back into his room. Bassett left and George
scratched his head, wondering who the woman was and why her
arrival in Whitstanton had to be treated with such secrecy.

It was very different from their last time alone in a bedroom. Then,
it had been warm and intimate: now, it was cold and polite.

'You said your letter would be the last,' he accused.

'Because you did not write to me.'

'But I did, Herta! All my letters came back!'

'Oh!' She recoiled slightly as if from a blow. 'I thought you had
married some nice English girl—to live as other people live.' She
sounded beaten. 'How is it in England?'

'You'll see for yourself—I'm taking you back!'

'My permit expires soon. I must return to the East.'

'Oh no you won't!'

'You are like my father, Blake. Always promising to do things.
And my mother would always say "Yes, love, yes, yes . . ." because he
would never accept what she knew to be impossible.'

'He was right.'

'Do you know why I came here to this place? Because this was his
room. He lived here for a year, with nothing. Twice I was allowed to
visit him. This is all he had,' she said, indicating the cup, pan, knife
and remains of a candle on the table. 'I have to go to the hospital
now for his things, what he wore. In the old days they would have
burned them. His poor, worn-out shoes are now things of value.'

'I'll come with you,' he offered.

'No, no, there will be papers to sign and it will take many hours. It will be very boring.'

'But I want to be *with* you, Herta!'

'I will see you here in the evening, and Waters will come, perhaps. We shall sit as we did in the house where we met ... as I will always remember ... like a family. ...'

She could hear the Beethoven sonata once again but Blake Hayward could not hear it at all now.


Mark Warrington found it difficult to discuss almost anything with his father and a chat about his religious beliefs was something that threw him into a frenzy of embarrassment. John did not waste any words and came straight to the point.

'Have you seen Father Ross yet?'

'No.'

'Do you intend to see him?'

'No.'

'So you're just going to leave the flock and head for the hills?' Seated opposite him in the armchair, Mark looked more uncomfortable than ever. 'Well, are you?'

'I've already done that,' admitted the other. 'I realize you're going to find it difficult to accept.'

'It seems I'm not alone. After that incident with Peg yesterday—'

'That's between us!'

'Yes, of course it is—but do you fully understand how she feels?'

'No.'

'That's honest, anyway. ...'

'I suppose you think you do understand?' challenged Mark, who was getting annoyed by a hint of complacence in his father's manner. 'That you know more than me?'

'But I do, Mark. I'm in a rather better position to understand, you see.' He paused and tried to break the news gently. 'Peg has been seeing Father Ross for the best part of a year now. She didn't want to become a Catholic simply because of the marriage problem. She wanted to find out if there were better reasons.' The paradox brought a wry smile to his face. 'It seems that Peg was well on the way to finding those reasons when you lost yours.'

Mark was stunned for a few minutes then asked how his father came to know all this. John said that he had been told by Peg herself.

'I was faced with a choice, father.' He shrugged. 'I'm sorry. I'm a poor Catholic.'

'No poorer than many of us. You're not alone in your doubts.

"Lord, I believe . . . help thou mine unbelief. . . ." I think you should go and talk to Peg.' Mark looked up at him hopefully. 'Well, don't just sit there. She's in the next room waiting for you.'

When Blake arrived at the shabby little room, Waters was there alone. Herta had decided not to see Blake again and she had asked Waters to explain why. There was an awkward silence and then Blake asked why she could not have been there to give her own explanation.

'Maybe she thought you might persuade her to do what she'd like to do more than anything, go home with you, marry even.'

'She was afraid of *that*?'

'I'm afraid she's married already, Blake.'

'Married?' He was visibly shaken.

'A German in the Russian sector, some sort of Communist Party official . . . quite high up, I fancy.'

'That's what she's gone back to?' asked Blake, incredulous.

'More than that.'

'More.'

'A child.'

'His?'

'Yours.' Waters let the shock take effect before he said anything else. 'She didn't know she was pregnant until we'd left that sector and the Russians moved in. By the time she discovered her father was in the British zone, it was too late. She married the German to protect the child.'

'My child?'

'You weren't there, Blake,' explained the other. 'You were at home. They were living in the Dark Ages here in Europe. It was all Herta could do.'

'My child,' murmured Blake, head spinning. 'My child. . . .'

'Her husband kept it with him to be sure that she went back. Would you have had her do otherwise?'

Mystery had been the order of the day at the Hayward house. Peg had been mysterious about what had happened when she went back to see Mark at Lake House. Lovett had been mysterious about his true feelings regarding the scholarship. Helen had been mysterious about her evening out, getting into her Sunday best but telling nobody where she was going. And Harry Hayward, whose life was a voyage across a sea of mystery, spent the morning behind his bolted door.

George Hayward, heading that evening for the meeting at the

Whitstanton Working Men's Club, was both the creator and victim of mystery. He had gone out of his way to conceal where he was going though he himself had no real idea what he was going to find when he got there. Slipping in through the back entrance of the Club, he made his way to the room where Bassett was waiting alone and glancing at his watch.

'Look, what is going on, Jack?' he demanded.

'I'd sooner she told you herself.'

'Why me? Why not the rest of the selection committee?'

'I told you. There's a personal interest involved.'

'I can't think what. . . .' George had at least worked out why the woman was coming. 'All a bit previous, really. He might see this Parliament through yet.'

'A year I'd give him, at most.'

'He'd expire tomorrow if he knew the party had lined up some woman to take his place.' He wandered restlessly up and down. 'I'm not against women in politics, within reason . . . not like I'm against the way they've taken to using pubs.'

'You're old-fashioned, George.'

'Maybe, but it's one of the reasons I rarely use this Club any more. Some of the turns they get in—honest!'

'I've no objection,' said Bassett, with a grin.

'Women with screeching voices trying to make theirselves heard because nobody wants to listen; those blokes just want something to gawp at while they sup their beer . . . somebody flaunting her sex.' George's contempt was complete. 'I despair of my class sometimes when I see what they rate as culture.'

There was a knock on the door downstairs and Bassett went off to see if it was their guest. Left alone, George began to brood on what he had just said when a sound from another part of the building made him prick up his ears. He crossed to the door and opened it wide. The sound was more distinct now and quite unmistakable. A fine contralto voice was singing a familiar piece from Brahms and it made George hurry out.

When Bassett arrived with the mystery visitor, there was no sign of the secretary of the Whitstanton Labour Party.

'He must have gone down the passage a minute,' said Bassett. 'Won't be a tick . . . uh, sit down, Mrs Warrington.'

'Thank you.'

Beth Warrington sat down at the table and waited patiently. It was something at which she had had a great deal of practice.

Further down the corridor, George Hayward was opening the door to the concert room at the Club, only to be transfixed by what he saw. Here was no gathering of working men supping their beer and turning dark eyes at some woman on the stage. It was something very different. To the accompaniment of her pianist, Helen Hayward, in her Sunday best dress, was singing a selection of her favourite songs before an audience that was silent, respectful and quite enraptured.

## CHAPTER ELEVEN

Hope had first begun to offer him its subtle blandishments early in July, 1946. Safe behind the locked door of the one Tory room in the house, he had scissored his way through a page in the *Daily Express* to add yet another Giles cartoon to his collection. It had shown a baker's van, guarded by a man with a shotgun, to whom the baker himself was saying: 'Now don't forget—anyone hanging round with a wistful look in their eye—let 'em have it—bang, bang!' The advent of bread rationing had revived Harry Hayward's belief in the forth-coming demise of the Attlee Government. That cartoon, he had felt, with its promise of the ultimate act of rationing, was the beginning of the end.

From that moment on everything had seemed to confirm his diagnosis. Stricter rationing all round produced howls of complaint, housing shortages led to the large-scale occupation of disused Army camps and empty London houses, and industrial unrest started to bubble like a cauldron. Harry Hayward was able to score political points off his son at random across the kitchen table and when the Big Freeze hit the country that winter he was, literally, in his element. Snow and ice were, to him, the heaven-sent means of unseating the Labour administration.

Like every other part of Britain, Whitstanton came virtually to a standstill and faced a fuel crisis that almost closed down the iron-works. Roads were cut off, houses held in an icy grip, factories, shops and offices places of woe rather than work. Freak disasters along the railway lines that led to the town meant that no mail or newspapers reached it for over a week. Harry Hayward alone seemed to welcome the blizzards and the biting cold, chanting a slogan that had now become quite famous—'Starve with Strachey, and shiver with Shinwell'.

After the snow came the long, slow thaw, bringing with it a whole new set of tragedies as floods displayed their awesome power of devastation. Even as late as spring, 1947, there was still a moat of sludge around the Hayward house and it brought a lot of problems to Helen.

'Boots!' she ordered.

Harry removed his boots at the door so that the liquid mud could drip off. He knew that she was making a special effort to keep the place clean and tidy because Blake was returning home that day, calling for Keir in London on the way.

'Comes back home with nowt in his pocket, I'll be bound!' said Harry.

'It was voluntary work he was doing over there, Dad,' reminded Helen. 'He did it for his keep. To help others.'

'God helps those who help theirselves.'

'Old skinflint!' she said, amiably.

'Who is?'

'You are—but Blake won't be completely broke. He's got that car he was doing up to sell. That should fetch in a few bob.'

'We need more'n a few bob, woman. Does he know what straits we're in because of the Great Labour Freeze-up? Aye, you could tell it was socialist snow because it was distributed more evenly! Voluntary work, was it? Well, he can do some here now! For us!'

A rare break in the grey clouds had tempted Beth Warrington out into the garden of her cottage to assess the jobs that had to be done. She was examining the damage to a hedge when George Hayward strolled up the drive and greeted her.

'Bassett said I should keep in touch, but that's been the devil's own job these past nine months. Every time I've rung or called, you've not been here.'

'Sorry, Mr Hayward. I did come back from Germany just before Christmas, actually, but I stayed in the south.'

'Very wise. Murder up here. First of January we nationalize the pits and two months later we're told there's not enough coal to go around.'

'You're not joining in the popular chorus against Manny Shinwell, I hope?' she asked.

'A neglected industry, worst winter this century . . . an Act of God, I'd call it.' He realized what he had said and apologized. 'I'd forgotten you were Catholics.'

'You think God's got it in for the Labour Party, do you?'

'Dad does. Anti-Christ, he calls us, and that's from a man that never even goes to church!'

The two brothers staggered along the track under the weight of the heavy suitcases, neither man wanting to be the first to ask for a rest. It was a long time since they had seen Whitstanton and both were warmed by the sight of the beach and the rocks and the great sea wall, familiarity breeding affection. Eventually, Blake dropped his case down and used it as a seat.

'Let's have a breather, Keir.'

'Why not?'

Blake found a packet of cigarettes and offered one to his brother. Through wisps of pale smoke, they looked out to sea and spotted a small boat zigzagging its way towards them.

'Wouldn't mind being in that boat,' said Blake, enviously.

'You'll have missed that in Germany.'

'I missed a lot of things.'

'You're an odd bod!' Keir decided.

'You reckon?'

'Helping the Krauts in their hour of need after five years of fighting the sods.'

'I'd a reason to be there.'

'Not after your Frau was back out of bounds in the Russian sector, surely?'

'You should see it, Keir. It'd dampen your enthusiasm for violent revolution, I can tell you. It's always the proletariat that suffers.'

'They sacrifice themselves for the future,' argued Keir.

'Not if they're asked, they don't.'

Keir was about to reply but changed his mind, feeling that he could not fall out with someone who had paid his brother's fare to Whitstanton with his last pound.

'God, I hate coming home broke! Why did I let you persuade me?'

'Because you wanted to come, really.'

'I'm twenty-seven, Blake. Even if you knock off five years for the war, I'm still too old to be living off the family. Dad's going to think he'll never get shot of me.' He put the cigarette in his mouth and spoke with it still there. 'Got anything in the bank?'

'No.'

'Snap!'

'I've a car at the yard that I've been doing up. Should get a hundred quid for it. At least.' His optimism quickly became a rather shame-faced bitterness. 'Look at us, Keir. War heroes. We're neither of us shining examples, are we?'

He stood up to stare at the sailing boat.

'Someone you know?' asked Keir.

'Impossible to say at this distance, but yes . . . it could be. . . .'

In the living room of her cottage over a mile away, Beth Warrington confirmed his identification. It was indeed her daughter who had gone out sailing. As she told George Hayward, Rosalynde had got bored with the life of idleness after working so hard during the war, but could not seem to find anything to interest her for any length of time. George took the cup of tea that was handed to him and touched on the subject of Mark and Peg.

'I gather they haven't set a date yet,' said Beth.

'Looking for somewhere to live first, I think.'

'Who isn't these days? Part of the universal shortage—food, coal, houses, everything.' She became practical. 'Do you think we'd win a by-election if it came?'

'Last year I'd have said there wasn't any doubt—what with the gains we made in the local elections and the legislation that went through the house. The winter set us back.'

'They still want me to stand, I assume?'

'Those of us that know about it do. There was mention of two union-backed candidates from somebody on the selection committee. But you can forget them. They'll cut one another's throats. You'll be asked to stand.'

'I'm not exactly well-known in the constituency.'

'Neither was Stafford Cripps and look what happened there. Anyway, your local connections'll count in your favour.'

'Tory husband, local industrialist?'

'Aye, but you're separated.'

'Supposing we weren't, Mr Hayward? By the way, do I have to go on calling you that? Can't I call you "George"?'

'I'll not take exception to that,' he said, smiling.

'Supposing we weren't separated, George?'

'Your husband's not active in politics now. It might make a difference with the committee. Hard to say.'

'Do you know John?'

'I'm a wages clerk in his works.'

'Has he made no effort to get in touch since Peg and Mark got engaged?'

'None,' said George, easily. 'I daresay I shall meet him at the wedding itself.'

'John is very English, I'm afraid. America must have been a terrible shock for him, quite apart from depriving him of the pleasure the English take in being uncomfortable.' She sipped her tea and put the cup down. 'He's a very private man, George. If you phoned him and asked him to meet you for a drink, he'd probably come like a shot, but he'd never make the first move.'

'That's not come easy to me.'

'I'm thinking of Peg . . . and Mark, of course.'

'Then I *should* contact him?'

'Be generous. Show him that you're not going to let class come between you—between the families, I mean. It could be a very good thing for all of us.'

George pondered this for a long time then asked if John Warrington knew about her intention to stand for Parliament. She explained that they had been apart for seven years now and lived in their own worlds. Consequently, he did not know.

'What made you want to stand for Labour?'

'What makes you ask?'

'It's getting fashionable among the upper crust, that's all. People's reasons interest me.'

'In other words, mine may be the wrong ones.' She took a deep breath. 'I'm a socialist for the same logical reason that I'm a Catholic —it appeals to my reason.'

'I know nothing of religion,' he said.

'New worlds are opening up for all of us—the world of the Bomb, living with what was done in the concentration camps . . . yes, and what Aneurin Bevan said in *Tribune*—the hope of an organic Federation in Europe.' She leaned forward in her chair. 'I've been all over Europe in the last two years—I know what he means and why it's necessary—and yet people have such short memories. Is Blake home yet, incidentally?'

'Blake?' he asked in some surprise. 'Coming home?'

'He was on the plane with me this morning. He's been a godsend to us out in Germany—mending our old trucks when they conk out. And such an enigma.'

'Oh yes, he's that. Went to war a socialist, believing all I taught him and came back an enemy . . . well, not an enemy, maybe, but he'll not vote for us when the time comes.'

'We'll see. Oh, I wish I could come out in the open and declare myself now. Is all this secrecy necessary, George?'

'I'm afraid so.'

'The sitting Member?'

'A sick man. Bassett talked to his wife on the quiet. She feels it might destroy him altogether if he knew we had a successor limbering up on the sidelines . . . but he is a sick man. Lobby fodder.'

'Staggering into the divisions, the light of socialism in his eyes. Or am I being unkind?'

'Not really.'

'In that case, I shall have to wait, won't I? It's just that, although

we're separated, I wouldn't want my husband to think I'd deliber-
ately not told him of something that's bound to be a big embarrassment for him.'

The bang of the front door announced the arrival of Rosalynde
Warrington and she soon appeared in her sailing gear, dripping wet.
She surprised her mother by greeting the visitor as 'George' and
saying that she was across at the Hayward house most weeks to see
Peg. Before she soaked the carpet too much in sea-water, she then
took herself off to change. Beth Warrington was left to reflect on her
daughter's situation.

'I'm glad she didn't rush into marriage when the men came home,
as so many others did. But I do wish Ros could find some fulfilment
in life. It's still a man's world, isn't it, George? And I resent it—I
think I always have.'

'You'll have to change it, then, won't you?'

They laughed together.


Four people were seated at the table but one of them was eating as
much as the other three put together and doing so in such a voracious
way that his family just watched him. Helen was upset, Blake
remembered Herta falling on that first meal in three days, and
Harry put manners first.

'It's not a trough, Keir. I say it's not a trough. . . .'

'I'll take it where it'll not offend you to see me eating then,
Grandad,' said Keir, picking up his plate.

His mother tried to stop him but he flounced off with his food.
Expecting a rebuke, Harry turned to his daughter-in-law.

'Go on then—flay me!'

'What a thing to say, Dad!'

'Eating like a pig!'

'That's enough!'

'They cost nowt, don't manners. If I did at table like that, you'd
soon tell me. You've spoiled him! You tiptoes round this house for
years to give him quiet to work in and what's he done with his life?
Nothing. I know why he's back. Spent up, that's why!'

'It's none of your business, whatever it is!' she shouted.

It was Harry's turn to take offence and stalk out. Helen noted how
much more irritable the old man had been since Lovett had gone
away to school.

'Keir was eating like he was starved, though.'

'Don't think he's been getting much food, Mum. His last job
packed up a month ago.'

'What was it?'

'Something in the kitchen at one of the Lyons Corner Houses. Washing up, I suspect.'

'A Higher School Certificate to wash up!'

'I'd to follow him to three addresses to find him. He'd flogged his typewriter to raise cash but still owed two weeks rent.'

'You paid it?'

'I'd just enough to pay for the tickets here.' Blake avoided her eyes. 'We're both a bit of a let-down, aren't we?'

'I've no worries about you . . . it's him. Still trying to be a writer, is he?' Blake nodded. 'What was it like where he lived? And I want the truth.'

'It was what they call a semi-basement, Mum. Down some steps, bars on the window, flagged floor, gas ring, few bits of furniture. . . .'

'Dirty?'

'Filthy!' he said with a grin.

'What's so funny about it?'

'In the circles that Keir moves in, it's the only respectable way to live. They don't starve in garrets these days—they rot in semi-basements.'

Helen asked what they were going to do about him but Blake's only advice was to feed him up before he went back to a life that he had actually chosen.

'I had such hopes for him!' she sighed.

'You're a fine one to talk!' he teased. 'Singing in clubs to help keep Lovett at that school. Dad got used to the idea yet?'

'No. He'll not let me go without him. It's like having a bodyguard. As if I'm going to get admirers at my age!'

'I'll bet Dad has to fight 'em off!'

'Nonsense!' she said, but took it as a compliment. 'That girl of yours in Germany—you've lost her?'

'The barbed wire's gone up since Bevin started to thump the table at the Russians. And Herta's on the other side of it.' He spared her a few moment's thought, then turned to someone else. 'Did Ernst get back to Russia?'

'We heard nothing more, Blake. Nothing.'

'How are they—Jean and Owen?'

'They keep going. I think she accepts now. I think she does. . . . What about you . . . and this girl?'

'No, Mum. I *don't* accept. I don't go in for resignation. Sorry if it worries you. I know you'd like to see me married . . . settled. . . .'

'It's what all mothers want. Then there's Keir—Oh that war!'

Blake got up from the table to help clear the plates away and told her that they could not blame the war forever.

'I may learn it in time . . . to accept. There are just some things I know that make it harder. Maybe it's better not to know, like Owen. He's safe now—in his ignorance. Isn't he?'

'Only the Galways know about Jean and Ernst, so, yes, Owen is safe—in his ignorance.'

Shotgun under his arm and dog trotting at his heels, Owen Hayward was heading towards the Estate Office when he saw something that made him halt a distance away. John Warrington had emerged from the building with a large bunch of flowers and almost bumped into his son who had just arrived. Even from where he was, Owen could detect the father's embarrassment at being caught with the flowers in his hand. The men talked for a while and then John got into his car and drove off. Owen joined Mark.

'What did your Dad want?'

'Asked me if we'd found anywhere to live yet. Offered me the stable flat up at Lake House—no thank you! He wanted to know if we'd set a date as well so I told him it would be autumnish.'

'He seemed a bit . . . uneasy.'

'We're always like that when we're together, Owen, but there were other reasons this time. He's getting nervous about your family.'

'Why?'

'He's wondering what the form is. Whether he ought to meet them since Peg is going to be his daughter-in-law. I told him to do whatever he thought best.'

'It is odd—the way you and your father are together.'

'Odd but unavoidable, I'm afraid. We're all prisoners of our past, Owen.'

'Prisoners?' The word pricked him.

'Father had one piece of news,' said Mark quickly, to cover the awkwardness. 'The tenants at that farm near us—the Galways. Seems their barn was burned down last night. Insurance problems. I'll go in the morning. Come with me.'

'All right,' agreed Owen. 'I'd like that.'

Keir Hayward had retreated to the spare bedroom, the one formerly occupied by Owen and Jean. Slumped in a chair, he had no time to stare at any wallpaper patterns. He was so caught up in his own depression that he saw and heard nothing, not even the door opening and the tread of slippered feet.

'Pssst!'

'What is it, Grandad?' he asked, seeing the old man at last.

'Mad at me, are you?'

'Serve you right if I am. You've got a nasty habit of telling the truth.'

'It's my age.'

'What's that got to do with it?'

'You can afford to speak the truth at my age and you've nowt to lose.' He chuckled to himself. 'I could lie with the best when I were younger. Harry Hayward could tell a real tale! . . . eh, I found something in my chest.'

'Have you been to the doctor?'

'Not that chest, you fool, that in me room! Been out away for years. Saving 'em for your twenty-first, only you'd been called up when it came and it sort of slipped me mind till now. Hold out your hand.'

Keir took the four gold sovereigns and was astonished. He began to protest that he could not take them but Harry would hear none of it.

'Don't you dare say nay. I've same put away for Lovett. Your Blake had his afore the war, and Owen. I'm in his bad books at the moment an' all.'

'Owen's?'

'Yes.'

'But he never gets riled about anything, does he?'

'He did about this, Keir. I papered this room here for your mother, see, when she were out one day. I were in Dickie's Meadow with her for summat or other—I forget what. Thought I'd best get right side of her and I'd never liked the pattern on the wallpaper in here. So I found a new one.'

'Why did that upset Owen?'

'God knows but it did. Came in while I were in t'middle of it. First time I've seen him come to life since he left that camp. Raged at me, he did. Went out and slammed the door. Nobody saw him for hours.' Harry was upsetting himself by recalling the incident and he made a pathetic attempt to explain it away. 'They lived in here, him and Jean, from when they were wed. It'd be sentiment, I suppose. Funny thing is sentiment. . . .'

'I can't believe it somehow, not Owen.'

'Nor me. Especially after I'd given him and Jean my own house. I mean, you expect some gratitude, not to be sworn at.' He moved on from a subject that was clearly still painful to him. 'I miss young Lovett.'

'Yes, I suppose you do.'

'Nobody to go fishing with. They'll not let me take Col. He was my mate, Lovett. Stood by me.'

'I'll go fishing with you, Grandad,' offered Keir.

'I didn't give you four gold sovereigns just so's you'd go out in a boat with me, you know.'

'Of course not. And that's not why I'm coming.'

Harry Hayward was satisfied now and padded off happily. Keir was left to examine the coins and then to peer closely at the wallpaper, wondering what there was about it that could give such offence.

One of the major attractions of a visit to the Hayward house was that the patch of grass outside the garden gate made an ideal football pitch. Colin Hayward had brought his ball along and he was now enjoying its feel as he flicked it into the air, caught it on his instep, flicked it up again and then, as it hit the ground, drove it hard towards the corner of the goal. Owen made a token drive, missed the ball, and rolled over laughing. Colin had a strong suspicion that the goalkeeper had not been doing his best.

'You don't have to let 'em in, Dad. I can beat you any road!'

'Yes, Col. I believe you could.'

The result of the match was of far less importance to Owen than the fact that they were actually playing together. At long last Colin seemed to be accepting him in the role of a father. Such a thought was also passing through the mind of Jean as she watched them from inside the gate and asked what the score was.

'Five–one to Col.'

'Hey, look, it's Blake!' The boy's attention was distracted by the sight of a boat approaching the shore. 'Can I go out with him if he'll take me?'

'Well. . . .' Owen was reluctant but fought it. 'If he's a life-jacket aboard you can.'

'Thanks, Dad!' yelled Colin, and raced off.

'You didn't really want him to go, did you?' asked Jean.

'No, but he's warmed to me so much over the last six months or so, I don't have the heart to deny him.'

'He'll be all right with Blake.'

'You fear for 'em even so.'

'Like your mother did when you went off to the war.'

'And *you*?'

'Yes, Owen . . . and me. . . .'

Peg Hayward now came out of the house and strolled down to join them, addressing her question to Owen.

'You've not seen Mark at work by any chance?'

'Aye, at the Estate Office. Coming over here later on, he said.'

'That's all right, then. I thought he'd forgotten.'

'As if he would!' Owen remembered something else. 'Have to be up early in the morning. We're off first thing to look at a barn that's been burned down.'

'I hope it's not the one I want Mark to look at tonight. I thought maybe we could convert it and live there.'

'Which barn is it?' asked Jean.

'Not the one Peg is on about. No, it's over towards his mother's place. Galways' Farm. Where you used to work, love.'

Jean Hayward swallowed hard. She knew at once that it would lead to trouble.

When the bell rang and she opened the door, he was standing there rather sheepishly with the bunch of flowers. She chided him for being so formal in ringing the bell and invited him in. Though she would have loved the flowers for herself, Rosalynde Warrington realized that they were a homecoming present for her mother and she was impressed by the romance of the gesture.

'Are you missing me up at Lake House?'

'Of course, but I do understand, Ros. You must be here when she's home because she'd never cope otherwise.'

'You've really got to stop thinking about her like that, you know. You're deceiving yourself. In fact. . . .' She shelved what she was going to say. 'Oh it's all so nonsensical! You up there, lonely . . . us down here.'

'You started to tell me something . . . "In fact . . .". Go on.'

'All right,' she agreed, plunging in. 'Marriages sometimes break up because people sometimes find out they're married to someone else. They've married the person that is—not the person as they want them to be. You don't just marry a body: you marry a head as well.'

'Are you saying that I undervalued your mother?'

'Underestimated, anyway, which is slightly more forgivable.'

Mark came in, announcing that he was hungry and wanted some tea before he went out. Noting the flowers, he was about to make a sardonic comment when his mother came in, welcomed her husband and thanked him very much for his present. To Mark's annoyance Beth sniffed the flowers, offered to take over the making of the tea and took John off to the kitchen with her.

'Flowers!' he sneered when they had gone.

'And very nice ones, too.'

'You know the old saying—"Beware of Greeks bearing gifts".'

'What a suspicious mind you have, Mark Warrington.'

'You're not that naive, Ros. It's his Jesuit upbringing!'

'And what about yours?' she countered. 'The beliefs that Peg's accepted so that she can marry a Catholic—or are you only pretending nowadays because she *did* accept them?'

'It's not as easy as that! I wish it was! Anyway, she didn't accept those beliefs because of me, she accepted them out of a need for certainty because of that damned heart trouble of hers. How would you have felt at her age, hanging on to life by a thread?'

'Is it that serious?'

'It's far more serious than the rest of us have to live with.'

'You still resent the fact that she went to Father Ross without telling you, don't you? The fact that she owes her certainty to him?'

The truth of this caught him on the raw and his retort was immediate and bitter.

'Father Ross is not God!'

'Mark we're Catholics,' she continued, falling back on reason. 'We live with it as well as for it. Those two in there, for instance, living unnatural lives apart. Can you wonder that there's a compulsion for them both together again? To live a natural life that they couldn't otherwise live without sinning?'

'Mum doesn't want it,' he said, bluntly.

'How do you *know*? Have you thought that maybe it's you that doesn't want it? Have you thought of that?'

Harry Hayward leaned casually against the table and spoke into the telephone as if he used it every day. The instrument had been installed by Blake when he had set up in business on his own, but his grandfather reserved the right to take advantage of it when it suited him.

'Nay, don't come here,' he was saying. 'I'll meet you there. And say nowt to nobody.' He heard footsteps coming towards the hall. 'Right then. I'll be seeing you.'

He put the telephone down nonchalantly as Helen came out of the living room. She reminded him who had paid for the instrument.

'Blake did. And now he's nowt left to pay for it, I daresay they'll come and take it back.'

Helen ignored this, much more interested in his phone call. It was the first time she had ever caught him ringing anyone and she was curious to know who it was.

'Who do you know on the telephone, anyway?' she asked.

'You'd be surprised.' He opened the door to his room and beamed at her. 'I keep me own counsel, I do. I move in mysterious ways my wonders to perform.'

Harry Hayward vanished into his room again and she was left to reflect how irritating he could be when he really put his mind to it.

## CHAPTER TWELVE

Blake Hayward sat on the wooden bench outside the back door of the house and polished his shoes with a soft cloth. He did not notice that the kitchen window, some four or five feet to his left, was wide open. He was still enjoying the pleasure of being home again, of settling back into the comfortable groove of family life. His father came up the garden towards him.

'Talked to Keir yet, Dad?'

'No, not in the way you mean. It'll keep.'

'He's got problems.'

'Who hasn't? But I'm glad he came back with you. Hoped you'd persuade him when I knew you'd gone to London.'

'Yes, that's what I couldn't work out,' said Blake. 'How did you know I was going to see him? Come to that, how did you know that I was definitely back in this country?'

'Ah well. . . .' George Hayward's manly chuckle explained it all. 'Understand now, lad?'

'She's back, then?'

'Aye. . . .' There was real pleasure in his voice.

'And you've just been to see her?'

'I have an' all. But you'll know better than to let it get about if you've talked to her. I suppose you will have?'

'I talked to her, yes. Out there.'

'You'll know all about it, then?' asked George.

'I know roughly what's going on between you two, yes.' He grinned at his father. 'But you know my views. I can hardly approve.'

'I don't need your approval, Blake. Just keep your mouth shut about her, that's all.' There was a sense of amiable conspiracy. 'I've got every reason to keep it dark, as you can imagine.'

Hearing all this from inside the kitchen and completely misinterpreting it, Helen Hayward went the colour of beetroot and began to tremble slightly. When Jean came up behind her and spoke, Helen swung round on her, mouth agape, eyes rolling.

'Are you all right?' asked Jean.

'Yes, fine . . . fine. . . .'

'You don't look it.'

'The chill. Not really warm enough to have this window open so wide.' She closed it noisily. 'That's better.'

'Have you seen Owen and Col?'

'Owen and Col?' She went blank for a second, then recovered. 'Oh yes, still on the beach, I think. I'm sorry, Jean, but you've caught me on the hop. What with Blake and Keir rolling up, then the tea to make, I'm all of a dither.'

'We won't stay. You've enough on your hands.'

'But you must. I can cope now. . . .' Helen shook off her own anxieties by concentrating on someone else's. 'I know you've worried about tomorrow. Owen going to the Galways.'

'It was such a shock, Mum.'

'It will be okay, you'll see. They're nice people, the Galways. They'll not say anything about Ernst, I'm sure. So stop worrying.'

'It's guilt . . . conscience.'

'If you'd known that your husband was still alive—'

'I'd not have let it happen. Quite. But it *did* happen so it's always there between us . . . the deception, silence. I'm only being silent for his sake. Am I right?'

'I've always thought so till now.'

'You have doubts?' she asked in a way which showed that she had several herself on the subject. 'Well?'

'Sometimes . . . only sometimes, mind, I've thought it might be better to tell him. To clear the air, so to speak. And then I've looked at Owen and thought . . . could he bear it?'

'He couldn't.'

'There's your answer, then.'

'It's what I feel. It would hurt him so much. Destroy what little we have managed to build up between us since he came back. He's still not quite with us, Mum. Even now. . . .'

Helen nodded, her mind straying back to what she had overheard minutes earlier and her control weakening. When Peg breezed in and asked about tea, therefore, she got a reply of uncharacteristic sharpness from her mother and she retreated before the barrage.

'Oh dear! What's happening to me!' gasped Helen.

George now came in with the expansive smile of a hungry man who knows he will soon get some food.

'Tea ready, love?'

'Would you mind going out and coming back in again?' said Helen between gritted teeth. 'And saying something else. . . .'

Having finished the ritual cleaning of his shoes that he had learned from his first day in the Army, Blake Hayward got off the bench in time to meet Owen returning from the beach with Colin. The boy was sent on into the house and Blake had a moment with his brother.

'You're back, then? For good?'

'If I can earn a living to keep me here. I managed to pay the rent on the yard while I was away so that's still there.'

'Blake Hayward, Mechanic, Limited. . . .'

'And car salesman,' said the other. 'I'm going to sell that car at the yard that I did up, then I can buy a second one and start all over again.'

'You'll be another Lord Nuffield!'

'Why not, Owen? Somebody's got to get the country back on its feet again.'

'They'd nationalize you!' warned his brother.

'They'd be welcome if they paid me the compensation they paid the coal owners.'

The two men laughed and neither saw Harry Hayward slip out of the door behind them and head off in the opposite direction.

'There's been talk of Warrington's being nationalized,' noted Owen, bringing his brother up to date. 'Ironworks as well as the mines. Different Warringtons that own the mine, aren't they?'

'They'll be related somewhere along the line.' The socialist in him flickered briefly once more. 'They've had too much for too long round here.'

'That's what Dad says.'

'And yet it'd only be another lot running us from London if Dad had his way,' complained Blake, cynically. 'I had enough of being told what to do in the Army.'

'So did I. . . .' muttered Owen. 'Funny to think of it all going on while we were away. Whitstanton, I mean. . . . Them thinking I was dead and me still alive.' He grinned. 'And now I'm here as if I'd never been away . . . everything the same as it was, after all that. . . .' He looked serious and put a hand on his brother's shoulder. 'I am all right now, you know.'

'Of course you are, Owen!'

'I am all right,' he repeated, as if trying to convince himself as well. 'They told me I was.'

Afternoon tea had been polite, civilized and unrelaxed. John Warrington's natural reserve kept getting in the way, Beth's fierce sense of independence made itself quietly felt, and Rosalynde's efforts somehow to bring them closer together over the almond cake were far too obvious to have any effect. Because all three of them wanted something different from the occasion, none of them ended up satisfied.

As Rosalynde loaded the tea things on to a tray, John studied some of the many books stacked neatly on the shelves. Given pride of place in the alcove beside the fire was the complete Standard Edition of the works of Bernard Shaw and he was quite surprised. Indeed, the more he looked along the shelves, the more amazed he became at the range of his wife's reading, admitting that he had never really taken the trouble to find out what her taste was before. Beth pointed out that she had kept certain of the books tucked away when she was living with him because she thought the sight of so much radicalism on display might embarrass him. She then took out the tray and left the others alone.

'I thought Peg was going to catalogue *your* library.'

'We decided to wait until things are more settled,' he said.

'You decided? You and she?'

'Yes.'

'Because you thought Mark would object, I suppose. Yes, you two have got quite a relationship. Needs watching.'

'Why do you say that, Ros?'

'Because Mark might get the idea that you're using Peg to drag him back into the bosom of the family.'

'That's rubbish!'

'We know that—but does Mark? He's very touchy.'

'You don't need to tell me that, Ros,' he said, smiling.

'Have you told him about the flat at Lake House?'

'Yes. Today, as a matter of fact.'

'Cool reception?'

'Only to be expected.'

'What about Peg?' she asked, watching him carefully.

'Well, yes. I think I may have mentioned it in passing. . . .'

'Which means you have—probably before you spoke about it to Mark. You'll have to watch it. With respect, you're just not very good at this sort of thing.'

'What sort of thing?'

'Conniving!'

John Warrington was about to protest but decided against it. He let his eye wander along the bookshelves again, taking out a copy of the Left Book Club Edition of Morton's *A People's History of England* and skimming through the first page before returning the volume to its place. Rosalynde perched herself on the edge of the table and tried to sound as if she was merely passing on gossip.

'Did Mummy tell you that Peg's brother is back, by the way?'

'Brother?'

'The one who started mending the engine on the launch until he was press-ganged into doing charity work in Germany.'

'Oh that one! What's his name again?'

'Blake,' she answered, rather too quickly.

'That's it . . . Blake Hayward. One of four brothers.'

'You say that as if you knew them all. Don't you think it's high time that we got acquainted? Officially, as it were. Your son is about to marry into their family.'

'I know,' he muttered. 'I've been very remiss about it.'

'That's not the word I'd use!'

'The truth of it is that I've been hoping the approach might come from them. I have dropped hints to Peg. . . .'

'Trying to work through her yet again, are you?'

'Ros—'

'The Haywards are very proud people, in the right sort of way. Well, I approve, anyway. So it's going to have to come from you.'

'I've not been holding back for reasons of snobbery,' he said, defensively.

'I know. Would you like me to help?'

'How?'

'Well, I could get that brother to come and take another look at that engine. It's still not right after all this time.'

'Would he come?'

'I get the impression from his mother that Blake . . . that he'd be glad of the work. So, yes, he'd come to you. After that, the ball is in your court.'

'Yes, I suppose it will be.'

She had gone across to the window and was staring out. In the far distance, the sea was rolling gently and she decided that she would sail again the next day at first light. He warned her to be careful of the tides which could be treacherous.

'Don't be an old fusspot!'

'I'm entitled to be one, Ros. It seems that you're the only family I've got left.'

The barn was completely derelict and the countless sheep who had slept under its inadequate roof had left ample evidence of their tenancy. It had no appeal for Mark but it clearly fired Peg's imagination. She stood in the middle of the floor area pointing in turn to where the kitchen, lounge, hall and bedroom might be, and blithely ignoring the vast amount of work that would need to be done to effect the conversion. When she applied to Mark however, he told her that he could see nothing but trouble if they took the place. From a practical point of view, it was just not feasible. Peg was deflated and her comment was ironic.

'Oh well! I daresay something'll turn up in the next three or four years or however long we have to wait. . . .'

'There's a flat,' he said.

'Where?'

'Lake House.'

'Oh. But you wouldn't want that, though, would you?'

Mark Warrington led her out of the barn and considered the problem for several minutes as they walked slowly back to the car.

'I'll take you to see it tomorrow,' he decided.

The yard was small and cobbled and at the rear of a house in Whitstanton. One end of it was under the protection of a sloping roof of dark slate and it was here that Blake Hayward's car had been kept and repaired and polished up. His absence in Germany had meant that the vehicle had been neglected for a long time and had acquired a thin film of grime, but its engine was still in excellent condition and started, on full choke, almost at once.

Moxon was as much interested in the appearance of the car as in its mechanical soundness. He kept moving about to view it from different angles as Harry Hayward waited patiently and threw in the odd remark from time to time.

'Looks well enough,' conceded Moxon.

'Just wait till it's been cleaned up proper, Jim. You'll be able to see your face in that bodywork—if you can stand the shock.'

'Tidy motor and no mistake.' He circled it yet again. 'Yes, it's a tidy motor, Harry.'

'You and the missus'd look grand in it.'

'We'd best not live past seventy, then. The money that'd pay for this is what we'd set aside for retirement. It'd not get us past seventy.'

'You'll not live past seventy!' assured Harry.

'Put it in the guarantee, will you?' asked the other, drily. 'We'd just retired when war started, see. Never been anywhere much. Saved every penny we could for the day.'

'You know what they say about thrift.'

'Thrift! I wouldn't do it again, I can tell you. All the things the missus and me did without until we were too old to enjoy 'em! You feel life's let you down, don't you?' He sighed and rubbed his chin. 'I never fulfilled my ambition either.'

'What were that, Jim?'

'To become a cowboy.' He patted the car with affection. 'I shall call it Trigger. . . . How much did you say?'

'Fifty quid.'

The friends adjourned to the bar of the Whitstanton Conservative Club to discuss the matter over a glass of diluted beer.

He waded out into the water and gave her a hand to pull her boat up on to dry sand, both of them panting slightly from the effort. Blake explained that he had seen her from his house.

'I noticed you were in trouble. Always sensible to beach round here if you're having problems when you're single-handed.'

'Who said I had problems?' she asked, needled.

'The tide's on the ebb.'

'I know. I was beaching because I was coming here.'

'Oh, to see us?'

'You obviously don't remember me,' she said, trying not to show her disappointment. 'I won't play guessing games. I'm Mark's sister.'

'Of course!'

'You said that very convincingly.'

'It was the sailing rig that threw me. Yes, we met at your father's house when I came to mend that launch.'

'He does remember!' she said, pleased.

'I've been abroad. Only got back yesterday.'

'So my mother told us.'

'Half of me must still be in Germany . . . sorry. . . .'

'That's all right. My father's finally got round to having that part made. For the engine. Been keeping it until you got back. He's wondering when you could do it.'

'You'd better come up to the house,' suggested Blake.

They made their way up the beach, sauntering easily and starting to enjoy each other's company. Inside the house, their approach was a signal for Helen Hayward, still in her dressing gown while she made the breakfast, to bolt out of the kitchen. Peg raised an eyebrow.

'Your mother thinks she's not fit to be seen,' explained George, from behind his copy of *Reynold's News*. 'She's gone off to put her tiara on.'

Blake brought Rosalynde into the kitchen, where she was given a warm welcome by the others.

'You'd not say no to a cup of tea, I daresay,' decided George, finding her a cup.

'Thanks—it's damned cold out there!'

'Mark still in bed, I suppose?' asked Peg.

'Oh no. He was up at the crack of dawn. He's gone off to some farm on the estate.' She fished a little. 'He was rather quiet this morning. You were looking at a house, weren't you?'

'A sort of house, Ros. A barn in need of conversion.'

'No good?'

'Mark didn't like the bedroom; we're looking at something else today, though.'

'Oh what's that, Peg?' wondered George.

'A flat up at the Lake,' she said, turning to Rosalynde. 'Near your father's house.'

'The old stables flat. So that was the plot!'

'There was no plot, Ros.' '

'Tell the truth and shame the devil!'

'You don't approve?'

'Of course I do, Peg. I hate Daddy being up there when Mummy's at home. He's all on his own.'

Blake had listened to this exchange with interest and he did not notice Harry Hayward standing in the living room, trying to beckon him through with graphic gestures. Rosalynde Warrington felt that it was a good moment to speak to George.

'I think he'd like to meet you, by the way.'

'He knows where to find me, then,' replied George, simply.

'Why don't the two of you have a pint together somewhere? That might be the best way. Where do you drink, George?'

'Working Men's Club. . . .'

'That's where he'll meet you, then,' she said.

'Nay, nay, we can find somewhere better than that. Er, I could be at the pub at the harbour tonight, if he wants. Eightish or so.'

'I'll tell him.'

'Aye . . . aye . . . well, right. . . .'

George was too embarrassed to say anything else and walked out. Blake watched him and caught a glimpse of Harry waving to him. He excused himself and went off to see what his grandfather wanted. Rosalynde turned to Peg.

'What's wrong with the Working Men's?'

'He'd have to live it down.'

The women settled down to enjoy their cup of tea and chat.

Blake Hayward, meanwhile, had been led by his grandfather into the relative privacy of the hall. The old man was evidently pleased with himself. He tapped Blake on the chest.

'You did yon job for your keep, I hear.'

'Something like that, Grandad.'

'You'll be a bit short, then?'

'A bit. . . .'

'Till you've sold yon car.'

'Yes, well, there is that . . . if I can find a buyer.'

S.W.—F

Harry's face cracked into a grin as he produced what he thought was his trump card.

'I've already done it, lad.'

'You what?'

'Sold it. I've got the money here, look.' He took out a wad of notes and handed them over. 'Not easy things to sell these days, cars. Nobody's got any cash to spare. But I managed it. Sold it to a mate of mine because he never got to be a cowboy.'

Blake had finished counting the money and was shaken.

'Fifty pounds!' he exclaimed.

'Thought I'd happen surprise you,' said Harry, complacently.

'That car was worth more than a hundred, Grandad! It'll cost me more than fifty to get another one that's in bad nick. You've *really* been a help!'

Harry Hayward gulped. His immediate vision was of Jim Moxon driving along the main street of the town and saying 'Whoa! Trigger' as he pulled up outside the shops.

Owen Hayward strolled around the farm buildings out of interest, scattering a few chickens as he did so and collecting a surly glare from the bull that was tethered in a loose box. He wandered into the yard in time to see a battered old van draw up. The farmer who got out was short, wiry and dressed in faded working clothes. His flat cap had been spattered with everything from milk to mud and the face beneath it was scored by years of hard manual work.

'Estate Office?' asked Galway.

'Aye,' said Owen. 'I'm with Mr Warrington. He's having a look at your barn.'

'Beams are charred to jiggery. Bad for sandstone, a fire. Weakens your inner leaf. If I've a mind to break through a wall at any time, it could fetch the lot down. . . .'

'What started the fire?'

'Carelessness! Useless, is the chap I have now. Not a patch on the Ukrainian chap I had helping me out during the war. Happen if he'd wed the lass we had working here then like they wanted, they'd not have shipped him back to Russia.'

'Russia?' Owen's mind was swimming.

'Ernst was a P.O.W. He and the lass might have made a go of it if her husband that she thought was dead hadn't come back from the Japs.'

Galway went off towards the barn without realizing at all what he had done.

Keir Hayward took the last of his things out of the suitcase and threw them on the pile on the floor. His father spoke from the open door.

'Unpacking, lad?'

'Mum's been pestering me for my washing. I'm ashamed to let her see it, honest. Filthy!'

'Can't be like home, living on your own,' said George, coming into the room. 'Will you go back down there?'

'Eventually. When I've got myself together, sorted myself out. There's work at the mine, they tell me.'

'You're an educated lad!' argued his father, hurt.

'Above labouring with my hands and working up a sweat, is that what you mean? I'm surprised at you, Dad. What's happened to "the dignity of labour" all of a sudden?'

'Nothing, Keir ... but the world needs brains as well. Do we aspire to nothing better than the toil of animals?'

'Don't worry about me having aspirations,' said the other, sitting on the bed. 'Aspirations are about all I have got. I eat, sleep and feed on aspirations.'

George Hayward glanced down at the shirts and underclothes that lay in a dirty heap on the floor. They seemed to symbolize the kind of life that Keir had lived in London.

'This writing you do, lad. What's it about?'

'Politics, mostly. History of the working classes dressed up as fiction.' His tone was deprecating. 'Pretty awful most of it. When it's not tub-thumping, it's mawkish. There's not much I haven't torn up. You think I'm wasting my time, don't you?'

'No, I don't think that, Keir. I can do nothing to help you, that's what I think.'

'A stretch of honest toil might give me something to write about, Dad. I mean, what do I really know about the proletariat that I'm always preaching about?'

'Life's a mix, Keir,' said his father, philosophically. 'You've to look at it in the round, not isolate any one class. I married your mother, more than a cut above me. I've to meet Warrington tonight that'll be Peg's father-in-law. I was to meet him in pub, but I've asked to go to his place instead because I'm embarrassed to be seen with him.' He shrugged his shoulders. 'That's the way it is. Nothing to do with the man that he is, just that life's set us apart.'

John Warrington was looking forward to the interview with some trepidation as well, albeit for different reasons. As Mark and Peg quizzed him about the key to the stables flat, he poured himself a stiff whisky and gulped it down. Peg was amused.

'Dutch courage?'

'Are you surprised?'

'Dad'll be far more nervous than you.' She waited until Mark had gone off to open up the flat. 'Will you promise me something?'

'What?'

'Promise me that you won't offer to help with the wedding. He's very proud about things like that.'

'But aren't the circumstances rather unusual?'

'Because we're poor and you're not, you mean?' she said, in a teasing voice that was tinged with bitterness. 'We'll do our best not to embarrass you and your posh friends.'

'I don't have many, you know ... friends. Posh or otherwise. I've always been a bit of a recluse in a way. There are relatives, of course but I don't much care for them. One or two, perhaps ... the ones who wouldn't give a damn anyway.'

The sound of a door opening in the hall made him pour himself another drink. Peg laughed at his discomfiture and assured him that his tie was straight. After a moment or two, Rosalynde Warrington brought in the visitor who was walking stiffly in his best suit.

'George, this is my father,' she introduced.

'How do you do?' said George Hayward.

'I'm extremely pleased to meet you,' returned John Warrington with equal formality.

They exchanged a token handshake.


While her husband was paying a social call at Lake House, Helen Hayward was wiping off the kitchen table with her dishcloth. Keir was surprised that she had not been invited as well.

'Men only this time,' she said.

'You mean, you get inspected later.'

'I do wish you wouldn't!'

'Wouldn't what?'

'Make life such a battleground. These versus Those.'

'I don't make it like that, Mum. It just is so.'

'Look, I'd sooner she married someone her own kind as well, believe me. But I like young Mark and so I'll live with it.'

'That's the spirit!' he chortled.

'What is?'

'You looking down on them.'

'I look down on nobody, Keir,' she asserted vehemently. 'It's a difference, that's all.'

'Oh yes. It's a difference all right! Where's Blake, by the way?'

'He's up at Lake House as well. Fixing an engine or something.'

'Everyone gets an invitation except us!'

Helen announced that she had to go off and practice. Her singing engagements were an important part of the family income and it meant that Lovett could be kept at boarding school. But there was pleasure as well as work in it for Helen and she did not talk about her next concert in Silport without enthusiasm. Her only worry was that her earnings would néver be able to pay for her daughter's wedding. Keir was nudged into saying something.

'I'll not be a burden on you. I'll be working soon.'

'So your Dad was telling me.'

'I've disappointed you, haven't I?'

'You're as you are, Keir. More like your Dad than anybody—trying to take all the aches and pains of life on yourself.' Mock anger informed her voice. 'And where's that washing?'

'Upstairs. You're not going to like it.'

'I'll have to wash it all the same. And when you've fetched it down, go and cheer your Grandad up. You'd think it was him that was fifty pounds down, not Blake. There's another that thinks he can put the world to rights. . . . What a family!'

Jean Hayward came bustling in with Colin in tow. She asked if Owen was there and was disappointed to be told that he was not. She could not understand it. Owen had gone to work that morning with Mark and had not been seen since.

Keir excused himself to go and get his washing, leaving the women to get on with their joint anxiety. When he opened the door of his room, however, he discovered that he had a visitor. Owen Hayward was sitting on the bed, quite motionless, hands on his knees, face drawn, head down. His brother watched him for some while, then was moved by the expression of quiet suffering on the man's face.

'How long have you been here, Owen?'

'Noboby here when I came.'

'What's wrong, old lad?'

'Grandad changed the wallpaper.'

There was a pause and the sound of Helen's voice could be heard drifting up from the room below where she was now singing to her own accompaniment. Owen continued with an effort.

'When I was dead . . . life went on . . . when I was dead. . . .'

'Keir!' called Jean from the bottom of the stairs.

'It's all right—he's up here!'

Owen did not look at his wife when she came in with Colin. He simply took the boy in his arms, as he had done once before on the platform of Whitstanton, and hugged him so tightly that Colin was afraid and complained that his father was hurting him. Owen let go.

Jean stepped forward to comfort her son and then looked into the dark, turbulent eyes of her husband.

'You know, don't you?'

'Aye. . . . Aye, I know.'

In the room below the piano continued to play.

## CHAPTER THIRTEEN

Some more rubbish was thrown on to the fire and she watched the sparks fly up into the gathering darkness.

'The days are drawing in.'

'Aye, we're well into autumn. Winter before us. Let's hope it's not like the last.'

'It could never be that, George,' she said.

'Butter and meat rations cut again, bacon ration halved, potato rationing on its way. It'll be a hard winter, whatever the weather does with itself.'

He poked the fire with a stick and she held her palms out to enjoy the fresh burst of warmth. Rosalynde Warrington felt curiously at home when she was at the Hayward house, even if she was only watching George burning rubbish in the garden. There was an explosion of laughter from inside the house and she was able to identify it for him at once.

'They're addressing the invitations for the wedding. Mark must be describing some of our relatives.'

'Or Peg could be describing some of ours,' suggested George. 'They'd get a laugh anywhere. Every family has 'em, doesn't it?'

'I suppose so. Have you seen Father lately?'

'Mark took me up to the house a couple of weeks back when we talked about the wedding. Grand place.'

'And you don't mind the reception being held there?'

'Part of me does,' he admitted. 'The part that wants the best for Peg accepts it.'

Rosalynde bent down and threw a few twigs on to the blaze, and then inhaled, enjoying the distinctive smell of burning wood.

'I'm glad you two get on,' she commented.

'We're still on opposite sides of the fence,' he reminded her.

'Does it matter?'

'It's one of those questions that only ever comes from your side somehow,' he noted, amused. There was another outburst of laughter from inside the house. 'They seem to be enjoying theirselves in there.'

He picked up the broom and began to sweep the dried leaves into a large pile ready for the fire.

Seated around the table in the living room, Peg, Mark, Blake, Helen, Harry and Jean had been engaged in the important business of addressing the wedding invitations. Owen, also present, was very much the outsider, watching and smiling but taking no part whatsoever in the conversation. Helen, as usual, was having trouble with her father-in-law.

'I shall wear a dickie bow,' he insisted.

'You'll wear what I tell you!'

'You wouldn't think she was old enough to be me mother, would you? Trotting down the street in me short trousers, holding her hand. "What a big lad he's grown into, Mrs Hayward", they'll say, patting me on the head.'

'*I'll* pat you on the head in a minute!' threatened Helen.

'Who's your best man, Mark?' asked Jean.

'Blake,' he said.

'Very appropriate choice,' agreed Blake.

'Balloon head!' called Peg.

Mark collected in all the envelopes and stacked them neatly in two piles. Harry noted that there were more invitations for the Warrington family than for the Haywards and felt that this was unfair.

'It's quality that counts,' answered Mark.

'I'm sure your relatives are all very nice,' said Helen, not realizing that he was joking.

Peg now decided that it was time for her and Mark to go in order to see how much the decorators had done to their flat. Blake cadged a lift from them because he had promised to go sailing with Rosalynde up at the Lake. Helen watched the three of them leave, then found something encouraging to say about her son.

'Blake's sold another car. Bought another one to work on.'

'He'll do well,' mumbled Owen. 'He'll make a go of it.'

'I wondered when you'd have something to say for yourself,' Jean added, not intending it to sound as hard as it did.

Helen looked back over the year and saw things for which she was grateful. During the long, punishing winter, her one thought had been how to survive it. Now that they all had, everything seemed to be getting back to normal.

'War seems years away in spite of rationing still being here.'

'The Labour Party'd ration the shirt on your back!' moaned Harry, who related every single complaint to this one source.

'We get by, Grandad,' said Jean.

'And it's the same for all of us,' argued Helen.

'Force of habit's a terrible thing, though. You women won't know what to do with yourselves when you don't have to queue no more.'

'Oh yes I will!' replied Helen.

She then remembered that Keir would soon be home and went off to get his tea, aided by Jean who followed her to the kitchen. Owen was staring at the clock on the mantelpiece. Harry was meditating.

'Two more weddings to go and you'll all be settled,' mused Harry, picking at his teeth. 'That's what your mother's thinking. They dote on weddings, do women. Blake . . . Keir . . . they'll stay single if they know what's good for 'em. I sometimes wish I did.'

He got up from the table, put his hands into the pockets of his cardigan, and slouched back off to his room. Owen remained in his chair, still watching and listening to the regular ticking of the clock. Now that he was alone to concentrate, the sound seemed to be amplified, growing louder and louder so that it was almost as if he were inside the clock itself, a tiny cog in its complicated machinery. It was only when the noise reached its peak that he realized he could not hear a clock at all—it was the steady clack of army boots he could hear as the Japanese soldiers came marching towards him in terrifying numbers.


Peg, Mark and Rosalynde climbed into the car while Blake tried to persuade someone else to join them on the journey to Lake House.

'Come on, Dad.'

'Five of us in yon motor! No. I like the man well enough, son, but I never feel right up there. Not like you. Taken to it like a duck to water, haven't you?'

'Officers' Mess gave me a taste for it.'

'Don't keep us waiting!' yelled Peg from the car.

'You'll be turning Catholic soon, happen?' observed George.

'Is that what you think?'

'It's what we might guess. You never properly told us what went on in Germany, yet.'

'That's all behind me now, Dad,' he said, firmly.

Keir Hayward came in through the garden gate in his work clothes, a bag over his shoulder, but a grin shining through the dirt on his face. There was a toot on the car horn.

'They want you, Blake,' he said.

'See you later.'

Blake Hayward vaulted over the stone wall and ran to jump in the car. It was soon tearing off with its four passengers, the horn punctuating the noise of its engine.

'Warrington clan are all the same,' commented Keir. 'They like to let you know they're there.'

'Mark's not like that, Keir. He's just in high spirits, that's all. Because he's marrying your sister.'

'Blake looks set for a merger, too. What price the ties of flesh and blood now, eh?'

'Flesh and blood?'

'Your grandson in Germany. Out of sight, out of mind.' Keir waited until the full impact had hit his father and then said, with an attempt at surprise, 'Didn't you *know*?'

George Hayward was white with anger.

'You know damn well that I didn't!'

Although it was a bright enough day outside, there was a pervasive gloom inside the restaurant. It had once been the Grill Room of a first class hotel but was now a somewhat seedy place with the scars of war still upon it in such features as wooden beams that supported a cracked wall, and a ceiling that had lost some of its plaster mouldings.

Waters was already there when she arrived. He was smart, amiable, reassuringly gallant. She rattled off her apology.

'I am sorry. I am late. I wanted to be sure that my husband had gone out on his business before I came.' She sat down on the padded chair which he had drawn out from the table for her. 'Thank you.'

'You look well. Beautiful as ever.'

'Ah my polite English gentleman!' she said, then bitterness intruded. 'But of course I look well. We all look well in the Russian sector. The State provides!'

'Does it?'

She evaded the question though her appearance was in some measure an answer to it. Though she looked healthy and well-fed, there were all the signs of suffering and anxiety upon her. The dress she was wearing was the same one that had done duty at her father's funeral over a year before and it looked even more faded and unbecoming.

'How is it in England?' she asked.

'They fear another winter. The lights going out. Men at work in their offices in overcoats to save the heat—working for the new Jerusalem!'

'The rest of Europe is even worse off, though?'

'Much worse, I think.' He had been studying her with care and sounded quite sad. 'You're getting like them, aren't you?'

'Them?'

'All the others in the Russian sector. I've met dozens. They give you no answers—just ask questions. If you ask them if the State really provides, they always say "How is it in England?" '

Herta Wenkel weighed her words before she spoke.

'My husband is communist. Where we come from, he is an important man. He is reliable. Only important men who are reliable are allowed to come here to the British sector on business. I ask him questions, also. I ask why we cannot bring my son. We know, both of us, that my son is left behind to make sure that I go back. Yet I ask still.' She reached out to take his hand. 'Does the father of my son know you see me?'

'I've written to Blake but your own letter didn't reach me until the day before yesterday.'

'You think he will come?'

'I think it's impossible, Herta, even if he could get here before you go back. He only managed it before because he had a job helping the DP's.'

'Is what I thought.' She clasped her hands together and stared ahead of her. 'I wrote to him. A friend of mine brought the letter here to send. I do not know if Blake has had my letter. It was like the telephone call you make to someone at home when you are far away. Asking. Wanting to know. "How is this one? Or that?" And then, into the long silence when there are no more words, to someone you almost certainly will not see again . . . the question to which even the answer you wish to have gives you pain . . . "Do you love me still?" '

Waters reached into his pocket and offered her his handkerchief.


Shirt sleeves rolled up well beyond his elbows, Keir Hayward washed his hands and arms in the kitchen sink. Jean watched him in silence but Helen chided him.

'We're one of the fortunate few round here, you know—we do have a bathroom!'

'There was somebody in it when I went up. I'll eat mucky if you like.'

'Eat mucky! What a thing for a gentleman to say!' She went out, repeating the words to herself with disgust. 'Eat mucky!'

'Hear what she called me? "Gentleman"! She hasn't got the message yet, has she? Either that or the wedding's gone to her head.'

'Is the job getting you down?' asked Jean.

'You're really asking me if I'm up to it, aren't you?'

'Well, you were brought up to study, Keir, not to be a manual worker.'

'I wish to God it'd been the other way round!' he exclaimed.

'I thought you believed the working man was badly done for?'

'Jean, I don't draw a line between working with your head or with your hands. Not in that way, I don't.'

'Yes, well, what suits one doesn't suit another,' she said, with a trace of glibness. 'Owen likes his job. It suits him. He works on his own mostly.'

'Is that what he says?'

'Suits him, he says.'

Keir Hayward grabbed the kitchen towel to dry himself, then rolled down his shirt-sleeves. He asked how things were between Jean and his brother.

'You mean, now that he knows about Ernst? He understands, he says, . . . that we thought him dead . . . that life goes on. . . . I wish I'd told him myself, though. Instead of him finding out.'

'That was a fluke, really.'

'It happened, Keir.'

'You've heard nothing of him since—the other one?'

'No.'

'Another one thought dead?'

'I never think about it,' she said, tight-jawed. 'Like Owen says, life goes on.'

She looked into the oven to see if his tea was ready and told him that it would need five minutes or so to warm through. He went into the living room to wait in comfort. Owen, still facing the clock on the mantelpiece, was sitting with his head in his hands like a marble statue.

'Owen. . . .'

His brother did not stir at once. When he did, he seemed to have come out of some sort of trance. He saw the clock.

'It's after five. Where's Col?'

'Does he know you're here?'

'Jean'll have told him. She came to help with the wedding cards.'

'What do you think to it all, then?' asked Keir chattily, trying to get the other to relax a little. 'This marriage, I mean?'

'I like young Mark. I work with him.'

'Peg turning Catholic! That's the bit that bugs me.'

'Don't you believe in God?' asked Owen.

'Oh yes. Created by man in his own image . . . a sort of super-human to make us feel safe when things go wrong.'

Jean came in from the kitchen with George and told her husband that it was time to go. Still asking everyone where Colin had gone to, Owen let himself be led out by his wife. George gave his son an affectionate pat on the back as he left, then turned back to Keir.

'Jean says he's taking it well, knowing about her and that Ukrainian. What do you think, Dad?'

'Why should I think any different to her.'

'You've eyes.'

'Aye . . . that I have. . . .'

'It's the change I can't get used to. From how he was before the war. Full of beans, playing about, noisy . . . but now. . . .'

'There's a book in Whitstanton library. Came out this year. By a chap that was a P.O.W. in a Jap camp around the same time Owen was. I read a quarter of the way through then got Peg to take it back. I just couldn't bear to read on, Keir. Wonder is that he's alive, not that he's changed.' He stiffened slightly. 'You've not changed much, though, have you?'

'Me?'

'Dropping bricks on people from a great height like you just did to me in the garden. This thing about a grandson—is it true?'

'You don't think I'd invent a thing like that?'

'It was the sort of thing you'd do before the war. Anything to create a stir . . . now what's the truth?'

'Ask Blake.'

'I'll have to ask him now you've brought it up, won't I?' said George, hotly. 'It's my bloody duty to ask him!'


Down on the beach where the light was failing fast now, the cries of Colin Hayward competed with the sound of the waves as he squirmed in his mother's grasp. Because her son had not come when he was called, Jean was slapping him hard and ignoring Owen's half-hearted order to stop. When Colin's yelps got too loud, Owen eventually stepped between mother and son, telling her that she had hit him enough.

'I have to do it, Owen . . . you won't, so I *have* to. . . .'


'The light'll be going by the time we get it rigged,' said Blake Hayward, indicating the boat that was moored nearby.

'There's the moon.'

'I like to see where I'm going.'

'You just don't like my boat,' complained Rosalynde, pouting. 'You prefer that old wreck of yours.'

'Wreck!'

They were sitting idly beside the lake in which a crescent moon was already starting to dance. It was peaceful, autumnal and, to one of them at least, more than faintly romantic.

'Oh well. We don't need to sail. I'm happy enough staying right here where I am.'

'Are you?' he asked, quietly.

John Warrington disturbed them and suggested that they might like to go to the flat to see what the decorators had done that day. Mark and Peg were in a mood to show the place off. Blake announced that he would put the boat away and hauled it off towards the small boathouse down beyond the landing stage. John settled down beside his daughter and ignored the chill of the evening air.

'I don't think George is altogether happy about having the wedding reception here.'

'Don't you?'

'I have the feeling he bowed to practicalities, Ros.'

'He did.' She became cross. 'I don't see why we have to have all those damned relatives of ours. Half of them aren't even speaking to each other!'

'I didn't want people to think we were running away.'

'From *what*, for heaven's sake?'

'From wholehearted approval of the marriage of my son to the daughter of one of my wages clerks.'

'But you do approve.'

'I want to be *seen* to approve.'

'By the family, or by Mum?'

'Both, I suppose. Your mother's in Germany again, I gather? What's she going to do with her life when there aren't any refugees to work for?'

'That day will never come, unfortunately.'

John Warrington leaned back on his hands as he recalled something that had struck him as rather odd.

'She seems strangely radical these days. I don't just mean on her bookshelves. We can all be armchair reformers . . . no, the last time we met, I made some passing criticism of Attlee and she really went for me.'

'Free country,' reminded his daughter.

'She certainly wasn't radical before the war.' His voice became more sombre. 'I suppose she got it all from that chap.'

'I believe he was involved in politics in some way—not that she ever talks about him. I think it was through him that she met Morrison.'

John sat up as if he had been stung by a bee.

'Herbert Morrison, the Labour man? I hope to God she doesn't throw it around at the wedding, especially if your Uncle Hugh's there. He'd have a fit. I can remember him telling me about his first day in the House when Labour came to power . . . how they sang "The Red Flag" and the Tories just sat there appalled, thinking the revolution had come.'

The memory made him chuckle and she was glad about this. She was even more glad when he said that he felt it was just what the country had needed to jolt it out of its complacency.

They got up and began to stroll back towards the house, Rosalynde peering into the dark to see if Blake was coming yet. Her father sensed her affection for the visitor.

'This friendship between you two. . . .'

'That's exactly what it is,' she replied. 'A friendship.'

'Oh.'

'Disappointed? Do you want to take the Haywards over completely?'

'I like them enormously as a family.'

'But they're not Catholics—is that it?'

It was something that mattered to him and he saw no point in disguising this, telling her that he did not believe that Blake would ever become a Catholic as Peg had done. Rosalynde assured him that the problem was an academic one. She had been through a similar situation once before.

'I'm not likely to go through it all again, am I?'

The living room was bare but large and decorated with taste. The lingering smell of paint was pleasant and redolent somehow of a cleanliness and newness. Mark surveyed it all without enthusiasm.

'When's the furniture coming?'

'When I've finished choosing it. There's just so much to choose from. . . .'

'Been going around the house with him, have you?'

'Mark, don't,' she pleaded, softly. 'Don't be sour about him. I like your father. That should be good.'

'You like him because he spoils you to get at me.'

'No! He spoils me to *please* you!'

'To ingratiate himself!' he sneered.

'Mark!'

He was about to sneer at his father again but instead he took her impulsively in his arms and held her tight. It was foolish of him to let anyone come between them but Mark was somehow drawn headlong into this folly every time he thought about John Warrington.

They were standing by the window now and he could see a light on the ground floor of Lake House.

'That's his study over there, Peg. It worries me that we're so close to him.'

'Forget him. You did it for *me*, didn't you? Not for your father. You came to this flat for my sake.'

'Of course.'

'And it wasn't easy, was it?'

'No, it damn well wasn't!' he confessed.

'Then I owe it to you—not to him. Thank you, Mark. I love it here. I know we're going to be happy together ... always. ...'

He held her even tighter and their kisses lasted a long time.

'It's too much for him, isn't it?' she asked in a whisper. 'The work.'

'It's what he seems to want. ...'

'*Want*? To work down a mine?'

'A means to an end, that's all ... to earn his living while he feels his way towards whatever it is that he really wants.'

'To write?' There was an element of suppressed scorn in the way she said this.

'Aye. To write.'

'It's not a real job, George.'

'It's what he wants, love. It's in his head. He'll not be moved from it.'

They were sitting in their living room and conversing in undertones because Keir himself was asleep in his armchair only a few feet away. Totally exhausted after another day at the mine, he had dropped off as soon as he had settled down after his meal. Helen Hayward gave vent to her feelings in a controlled hiss.

'A family of donkeys, that's what we've bred!'

'They're all late starters because of the war, that's the pity of it.' He cleared his throat, approaching the topic with care. 'Has Blake told you anything about this woman he met in Germany?'

Before she could answer, the sound of hammering came from Harry's room. Both of them looked across at Keir to see if it had woken him but he did not move. The hammering stopped and George returned to his question.

'Has he?'

'No. Precious little, anyway. That's another thing they are—secretive.'

'Secretive donkeys, eh?' He was amused by the idea. 'Old Keir there looks like a secretive donkey, I grant you.'

'Hee Haw!' obliged Keir, opening an eye.

'He's got donkey's ears as well!' said Helen.

'Well how can I kip with that racket going on in Grandad's room? What the hell is he up to?'

'Making his coffin, he said, and serve me right for asking! Now . . . where was I?'

'Secretive donkeys,' nudged George.

'Hee Haw! Hee Haw!' brayed Keir, holding up his fingers as ears.

'Oh yes, there's our Peg an' all,' continued Helen.

'What's she done, Mum?'

'Only turned Catholic without so much as a word to us. There's Methodist families round here'd turn blue if it happened to their daughter.'

'Blue Methodists!' Keir found the vision an appealing one.

'Aouw!'

The yell that had stopped their talk had come from Harry's room. He had clearly hit his thumb with the hammer and Helen rushed off to scold him and help him at one and the same time. Keir became more serious about what had happened to his sister.

'Has Mum cottoned on to the real worry of Peg being a Catholic?'

'She's said nothing if she has.'

'You have, though?'

'Aye, Keir . . . I have . . . I have. . . .'

They walked to the parting of the roads and then paused. Piles of rubble still marked the places where houses and shops had once stood and there was a general air of helplessness in the face of destruction. Herta offered him a pale smile.

'Better I go alone from here.'

'They watch you, do they?'

'It would be new for me if they did not. We are used to it, Waters. We have been watched in Germany since Hitler came. First, by our own kind, then by you English, now by Russians. In our zone, the socialist parties became united last year. The Soviets wished it so. Dissidents were purged. . . . Perhaps one day my husband also will be purged. He is not a hard man. There will be things he will not be able to agree with, I think.'

'If ever I can help. . . .'

Herta looked at him as if trying to decide how much she could ask of him and then she spoke out.

'In some weeks from now, maybe, we will come again. Then you might help me.'

'Anything.'

'Tell me. If when I come, I am willing to leave my son . . . could you get me to England?'

The request took his breath away and he could make no answer.

Mark Warrington could remember little about his stag party beyond the fact that it had started when someone handed him a glass of beer that had quite clearly been spiked. Even in a time when breweries were having to dilute their beer and distillers to sell a weaker brand of whisky, Mark's friends had concocted a drink with a kick like a mule. From that point on it was an endless riot of singing, dancing, play-acting, drinking to excess and being sick in the bathroom. Inevitably, Mark was the butt of many jokes and the whole subject of his forthcoming wedding was treated with amiable obscenity.

It was enjoyable while it lasted, he felt, but he was glad when the party finally began to break up in the early hours. His friends staggered off into the night, leaving the newly-decorated flat looking as if a tornado had been through it. Someone had made coffee and Mark managed to pour himself a cup and slump into a chair when he had a visitor. She was not impressed by what she saw.

'Not a very good idea, Mark.'

'Mum! What are you doing here?'

'I came back from Germany for the wedding . . . saw the lights in here as I was passing. Heard the yells. *Whatever* was going on?'

'My stag party. . . .' He made an effort to rise but failed dismally.

'Look at the mess! They've wrecked the place, Mark.'

'They had a bit of fun, that's all. Anyway, Father said he'd send someone round in the morning to clear up.' He made a second vain attempt to stand. 'I'll sleep here tonight.' He finished the coffee then waved the empty cup around. 'Vandalism apart, what do you think of our palatial residence? Rather grand, hm? Dad let Peg have whatever she wanted from the house.'

'That was good of him,' said Beth Warrington.

'He likes to be liked. Especially by Peg. He's charmed her. She actually thinks he's a nice man.'

'He is, Mark.'

'Not nice enough to keep his wife on the straight and narrow.'

'I'll put that remark down to the drink,' she replied, sharply. 'And forget it was said.'

He apologized and tried to pull himself together but his antagonism towards his father kept spilling over. Beth decided to tackle him head on.

'What's the crux of your complaint? That we sent you away to school?'

'I didn't know what a family was until I met the Haywards . . . but it wasn't you—it was him.'

'It was both of us, Mark. It was what we were brought up to believe at the time. The importance of "a good school" and so on. I don't happen to believe in such schools any more or in their inherent "goodness"!'

'Does he?'

Mark's mind was slightly less fuzzy now and he asked her a question that suddenly seemed to him to be of great significance.

'You're a real Catholic, aren't you?'

'How I wish I was!' she said, wistfully.

'I'm only a Catholic because of Peg now. . . .'

'It's amazing. For someone who's seen so many die in war, you've stayed remarkably young. . . . Even war doesn't mature us, does it?'

Mark thought about this for a moment then hauled himself to his feet, managing to stand there without falling over. He crossed to the window, looked out and saw a light in his father's study. Still swaying, but now much more in control, he turned around and spoke like a boy in need of his mother.

'I think I'd like to go home now.'


## CHAPTER FOURTEEN


Frantic activity enlivened the Hayward house on the morning of the wedding. In the best tradition of such an occasion, there was a last minute panic about a missing tie, a broken shoelace, an empty jar of Brylcreem, a shortage of buttonholes, a stain on a trouser leg, and and an ominous parting of a seam on a dress. People rushed to and from mirrors, up and down stairs, in and out of rooms, washing, shaving, brushing, combing, polishing, powdering, laughing, bickering, searching, borrowing, stealing, cajoling and queueing up to use the lavatory. Yet Peg Hayward herself, the person most entitled to succumb to the pressures, remained cheerful, relaxed and unhurried —an island of calm in a sea of hysteria.

Jean stood on the front doorstep and saw something that did not help her jangled nerves in the least.

'Look at that, Keir!'

'What?' He joined her to stare at the beach.

'Down there.'

Some distance away, Owen Hayward was trying to stop his son from playing on the wet sand and getting himself dirty before they all went off to church. Owen's ineffectual gestures showed that he was not managing to persuade the boy, who, after a short while, went running in the direction of the sea until his best shoes were caked.

'Typical!' sighed Jean.

'It won't hurt the lad to run off a bit of steam.'

'I sent Owen out to fetch him back in and what happens? Col does what he likes when his father's around. Owen will try to reason with him when what he needs is a good slap now and again.'

'There could be a reason why Owen won't hit him.'

'Yes, he's too soft!'

'Maybe it's because he's seen enough violence, Jean.'

'That's not violence. It's just . . . being a father.' She hurried purposefully out. 'I'll go after him before he gets mucked up to the eyes.'

Keir watched her break into a dignified trot as she held up the hem of her dress, then he went back into the living room where Blake was having difficulty with a cufflink.

'Dad ever belt you?' asked Keir.

'A couple of times, I think.'

'Never raised his hand once to me.'

'Ah, but then you were so perfect!' mocked his brother.

'God, I'm going to *hate* this day!' warned the other, pacing.

'Seeing your little sister married?'

'You know what I mean, Blake . . . all those damned Warringtons looking down their noses at us. I could stomach it for myself, but the thought of them looking down on Mum and Dad. . . .'

Harry Hayward, trying to assume a nautical air, strode in and overheard the rest of the conversation.

'For heaven's sake, keep it cool,' ordered Blake. 'If you really want to upset Mum, start a political demonstration. She'd love that!'

'I suppose the other lot'll be there, too, the ones that own the bloody mines.'

'I doubt it. Aren't they supposed not to have spoken to each other for years?'

'Ah, but they fly the flag on a day like this,' said Keir, bitterly. 'A display of unity. They may hate each other's guts but they don't want the world to know.'

Disappointed that neither of them had turned to admire him in his best suit, Harry drew attention to himself with a quiet groan.

'Eh, I wish Lovett was here. What's this "isolation" he's got? Never heard of that complaint before.'

'I'm not surprised,' laughed Blake. 'You've got hold of the wrong end of the stick, Grandad. Lovett's got measles and he's in isolation because of it.'

'Oh . . . I see. . . .'

Helen Hayward came dashing in and rifled a drawer in the sideboard to find a safety pin. She then dashed out again, only to reappear at once.

'Are you three respectable? Let's have a look at you.'

'Line up for inspection, lads!' called Blake.

'Have you washed behind your ears, Grandad?' teased Keir.

'You speak for your own, lad!'

Helen had run a shrewd and searching eye over all three of them, clicking her tongue occasionally but otherwise quite impressed. She smiled as she saw how Harry had wet his hair to stick it down.

'Will we pass, Mum?' asked Blake.

'Never in your life have you brushed the back of your shoes, have you, Keir? You and Blake'll do, though, I suppose.' She headed for the door once more, firing her parting comment at Harry. 'But I told *you* to wear a white shirt.'

'Women!' snorted the old man. 'Blue's more naval.'

Inside the marquee that had been set up on the main lawn at Lake House, John Warrington, at his most distinguished, moved between the trestle tables that were loaded with food and drink, making a final check that everything was in order. A waiter with dark trousers, white shirt and shining red jacket, stood by and watched, relieved when given a nod of approval by John.

Mark came hurrying in, a recent haircut making him look more boyish than ever. His voice managed to convey calm and agitation at the same time.

'We're off to church in ten minutes.'

'Everything seems to be all right at this end. . . .'

'I suppose we had to have it here,' said Mark, his reservations surfacing again.

'Your future father-in-law seemed to understand . . . accept my reasons. He did have the option, you know. I wouldn't have been able to dragoon him into this.'

'I suppose not.'

'What probably persuaded him was the fact that Peg wanted it.'

'She said so?'

'Yes, standing in the garden here one day—"What a lovely place for a wedding!" I took the hint.' He lowered his voice. 'Anyone who stands so bravely at the edge of life as she does deserves whatever can be given her.'

'I don't need you to tell me that,' snapped Mark.

'I wasn't telling you so much as reminding myself.' The waiter had vanished now and John took the opportunity to confide in his son. 'I'm glad you're marrying Peg. Very glad. I know so little of the people who work for me. America opened my eyes to a certain extent, made me aware of just how class-ridden our society is. I don't think the war's made all that much difference, and I don't think this government will survive clearing up the mess . . . but perhaps—with you and Peg—we're building a very small bridge that might help in the future. . . .'

Beth came towards them and gave Mark the chance to break away.

'I'd better go and give the ring to the Best Man.'

'Ten minutes,' Beth called after him. 'I thought there was talk of her brother being Best Man at one time?'

'Blake? There was . . . they changed their mind.' He gazed around the marquee in the hope that the sight of the small banquet might give him the feeling that he could do something right at least.

'Doubts?' she asked, reading his face.

'I'm beginning to feel a failure in this brave, new, post-war world, Beth.'

'Mark?'

'We don't even begin to communicate.'

'He's very young still, in many ways.'

'Yet he's seen men die. . . .'

'I told him that last night. War doesn't mature people.'

'All I could do was to make some pompous speech at him about building bridges to help the future!' He tried to shrug off his annoyance with himself and turned to admire her startling and elegant dress. Then he said, 'You're a busy woman these days.'

'I suppose I am.'

'What you're doing at the moment . . . is it what you want?'

'It'll do for now, John.'

'And when it's over?'

'I shall do something else, I expect.'

'I'm lonely in this damned house, Beth,' he confessed. 'I was so happy here before the war.'

'Were you? I suppose I was, too, in a way. And yet it always seemed temporary somehow . . . as if I knew that it couldn't go on. Like the Empire on which the sun never sets! I think I saw the end in sight even then.' Feeling that she was in danger of saying too much, she switched to another topic altogether. 'I'd like to look round the ironworks some time.'

'The works?' He was amazed.

'In all the years we were married, I made only one visit—to the offices. Are women supposed not to be interested in their husband's work?'

John was baffled but delighted and told her that she could have a guided tour whenever she wished. Beth thanked him and admitted that her reasons for wanting to look around the works were somewhat confused. She promised to explain to him more fully what they were at a more convenient time than the morning of their son's wedding. When she went off to find the hat that would complete a stunning outfit, John Warrington smiled properly for the first time that day. His daughter came into the marquee.

'You're looking pleased with yourself.'

'Am I? Don't give up that dream yet, Ros.'

'Dream?'

'The one you have about us all being a family again. On a day like this I could believe in miracles!'

He sneaked a sandwich from under its covering cloth and nibbled at it happily. He was ready for the trip to church now.


Peg Hayward waited with mounting impatience but her father remained silent. In the end, she resorted to outright command.

'Say something, Dad!'

'Eh?'

'Do you like my dress, for heaven's sake?' she demanded, swinging around in a circle to show it off. 'Well?'

'You'd look good in a sack!' he said.

'Well, if that isn't typical.' Peg was immensely proud of her dress, which represented endless hours of work. 'Most of it's made from your clothing coupons, you know.'

'I thought it looked familiar,' he joked.

George Hayward was far more nervous about the impending marriage than he would have thought possible. Apart from all the social implications to a man of such stern political principles, there was the simple human fact that he was losing his only daughter. Peg looked beautiful in her wedding dress but it was not stubbornness that prevented him from saying so. It was a recognition of how delicately poised her life still was in some ways. Paradoxically, now that she was at her most radiant, she also seemed to him to be at her most vulnerable.

He wanted to kiss her on the forehead but hid behind his grin instead. The interruption rescued him.

'Mum says can you come and talk to Grandad?' It was Owen who brought in the bad tidings. 'He says he's not going.'

'Not going!' Peg was horrified.

'Blake and Keir put him into a white shirt and it got ripped right down the back.'

Helen Hayward came in herself to reinforce the message and George went off with her to tackle his recalcitrant father. Owen told Peg that the shirt would be completely hidden by Harry's coat, and that there was no real need for the crisis. Peg was not listening to him. Her mind was on something else.

'I can remember your wedding, Owen.'

'Can you?'

'I'd not been long out of hospital with that scarlet fever that'd left me with this silly heart. . . .'

'It's a grand heart!' he said, chirpily. 'Last you a lifetime.' He could not understand why she began to cry. 'What have I said?'

'It's not you, Owen.' She groped for a handkerchief.

'Should have had more sense, making jokes at a time like this.'

'It's all right . . . all right. . . .'

She was still searching in her handbag, tears streaming.

'Sure?'

'Yes. . . .'

'Here, take this,' he offered, pulling a large white handkerchief from his pocket. 'Dry your eyes, Peg.'

She thanked him and dabbed at her face, smiling and crying at the same time like someone with too much happiness to contain.

'You're back again!' she said. 'Just like you were before the war. Always joking, making us laugh. Dear Owen! Dear Owen!'

Ignoring any creases she might get in her dress, she reached out and hugged his tight, sobbing afresh. Owen stood rigid and perplexed. George and Helen came in at speed and saw the embrace.

'What on earth's happened to your face, girl!' scolded her mother. 'You look like the Colorado Desert!'

'You've never even seen the Colorado Desert,' said George to his wife. 'Now, off with you. Car's waiting.'

'I can't leave her like that, George.'

'You've no option, woman. You'll hold up the entire works if you don't get moving.'

Torn between her urge to stay and her need to go, Helen wavered for a second. Peg, who had repaired the worst of the damage now, turned back from the mirror to see her mother. Helen plunged forward and locked her daughter in an embrace.

'God bless you, Peg! Good luck, love!' She broke away and hurried to the door, pausing only to aim a last warning at George, 'I shall hold you responsible!'

Owen winked at his father then followed her out to the waiting sedan. George, who had just had to bully his father into going to the wedding, hoped he had no other crisis on his hands.

'Seems I'm responsible for the entire Colorado Desert,' he said, with a jocularity that hid his concern. 'What was all that about, then?'

'Oh—just me and the day. I haven't hurt you, have I, Dad? Marrying a Warrington?'

'Only one thing in your life could really hurt me, Peg—that you shouldn't be happy. Are you?'

'I am! I am!'

It was George's turn to be involved in a tearful embrace now. Trying not to show how moved he was, he fell back on jocularity once more.

'Now don't start irrigating that desert again or you'll get me shot!'

When Peg had seen to her face again, he took her proudly on his arm and led her outside to the waiting car.


Whitstanton Parish Church was packed to capacity with members of the two families, wedding guests and the army of the uninvited. Any wedding in the town was an event, but when it involved the son of John Warrington and the daughter of one of his wages clerks it took on a special lustre. The atmosphere during the ceremony itself, therefore, was quite electric and it affected all present. Before the priest had even called upon the couple to take their vows, many handkerchieves were sodden and as many necks cricked from straining to see what was going on.

John and Beth Warrington sat in their appointed place in the front pew, Rosalynde alongside them on the aisle seat, looking demure and self-possessed in a smart suit. Directly opposite her across the aisle was Blake Hayward, cool and relaxed in a charcoal grey suit that transformed the mechanic who was usually seen in a pair of oil-stained dungarees. Beside him sat his mother, nervously happy, and beside her was Harry Hayward in a turmoil of embarrassment and discomfort. Forced into a white shirt against his will, he was convinced that the torn garment was hanging down below his jacket at the back and so kept putting an exploratory hand there every few minutes. Keir, immediately behind him, found this diverting, as did Colin, seated in the same row between Jean and Owen.

At the climax of the service when emotions were running high throughout the congregation, Keir saw the tip of the white shirt peeping out from beneath the jacket in front of him. He was unable to resist reaching out to tug it down. Colin sniggered.

Unaware of this incident, or indeed of much that was going on directly in front of him, Blake Hayward was instead lost in a reverie that was brought on by the whole notion of a wedding. As his sister swore to love, honour and obey her husband, Blake heard the voice of someone else repeating the words from her latest letter.

Perhaps you write to me still but your letters do not reach me so I do not know. This is my last letter I will write you, although in my head and heart and in our child we are married. . . . It is you to whom I am married and not this man who claims me and will not let me go. . . . I need that we should be together. I cannot live from words on paper. I will not write again. We must live as we can. . . .

The elegiac note in all this moved him deeply and then his head turned across the aisle. Rosalynde Warrington was looking at him steadily, almost as if she, too, had received some kind of message that was to be a turning-point in her life. Neither of them looked away until the organ music began to swell.

After much initial awkwardness, the two families came together under the generous and undiscriminating cover of white canvas. The wedding breakfast itself was a sumptuous affair and it was rounded off with some speeches and with the ritual cutting of the cake. It was at this point of the proceedings that Harry Hayward, having tasted a quality champagne for the first time in his life, realized that he had actually enjoyed himself.

'That was a grand spread, that was,' he announced to his immediate neighbours at the table.

'Wherever did they get the coupons from?' asked Helen, always thinking of the practicalities.

'Coupons are for the poor, Mum,' sneered Keir.

'Here we go!' sighed Blake.

'Don't you dare, Keir!' ordered Helen, bridling. 'Not even a cross word! We're being watched!' Her frown was gradually erased as she realized that the same thing applied to her. Blake laughed. 'What's so funny?'

'You?'

'What a family!' she smiled.

'We're a match for them any day,' asserted George, lighting his pipe. 'Some real toffee noses among that lot! Eh, where's Uncle Ted?'

'They've sat him over there in the corner, Dad,' said Keir, indicating an ancient man in an old suit and blotched pullover, wheezing as he lay back on a folding chair.

'I hope to God he doesn't take out his jew's-harp,' moaned George. 'He usually does around now.'

Helen Hayward caught the aroma of tobacco smoke for the first time and told her husband to put his pipe away, feeling that he was letting them all down by taking it out. As he was about to protest, George caught sight of John Warrington bearing down on him with a pipe in his mouth as well.

'I seem to have left my tobacco up at the house, George, and you and I are the only addicts here. . . . I don't suppose you could oblige?'

George Hayward handed over his tobacco pouch and shot his wife a sidelong glance.

Blake was lost in thought once again but was not displeased to be brought back to reality by Rosalynde Warrington. She suggested that they went out into the garden and he agreed at once, ignoring the polite crudity of Keir's warning to him as he left. The bride and bridegroom now came up, working their way around all their guests to thank them for their cards, presents and best wishes. Peg was still glowing and Keir could not resist feeling happy for her. Mark, also equipped with a permanent grin, asked Keir what he thought of the Warrington relatives.

'Don't throw any of 'em out, Mark. They'll be worth a fortune in twenty years.'

While Keir was busy widening the grin on the bridegroom's face, Jean Hayward was telling her son that he could not leave the table and go off to play. Owen interceded and the boy was allowed to run off. Jean returned to a theme that was becoming well-worn now but which had great importance for her.

'I know you care for him, Owen. I know you want to make him care for you. But you're making a rod for your own back. Don't you understand?'

Her husband seemed too preoccupied to understand anything.

They met in the same restaurant and shared the same bottle of cheap wine in the gloom. The brief passage of time since their last meal together had not made her view of the future any more sanguine.

'As he grows up, the State will take him from me . . . my child . . . Blake's son. Perhaps even they will send him to Russia as they empty our factories of machinery by which we might live.'

'The spoils of war. . . .'

'Children also . . . are they the spoils of war?'

'Their bones were used to make fertilizer in the concentration camps,' he said, ruefully.

'How can our minds live with such things?' she asked.

'They have no option, Herta. They're up against historical fact. Reality. We look in a mirror and there it is. Though we hope that the mirror lies, of course.'

'Of course.' She became tense. 'You have heard from Blake?'

'Yes. He had a letter from you saying that you wouldn't write again. Did you say that because you hoped to be seeing him again soon? Did you tell him?'

'No! Did you?'

'No.'

'I know why, Waters. You say nothing because you do not believe that I will go on with this.'

'Perheps.'

Herta Wenkel owed a tremendous amount to him and had a great fondness for him as well. It made her anxious to have his good opinion.

'Do you condemn me?'

'No.' He regarded her, almost shyly. 'No, I don't.'

'You have made the arrangements?'

'Yes.'

'Tell me.' Her hands were trembling. 'Please. . . .'

'You must stay here. They close in an hour but I have arranged that you can stay. Were you followed?'

'No.'

'Are you sure?'

'Quite sure. I have been very good since we last meet. I have seemed to accept. He believes this . . . my husband. I have said everything he wishes to hear. Before now sometimes I felt there was someone watching me all the time. Now, I do not feel it.' He nodded and stood up. 'You go?'

He told her that he would be back in three or four hours with the man who would be taking her and that she would simply have to wait. Sensing a disapproval behind his brisk recital of the details, Herta clutched at his hand and told him that he was giving her a new life.

'It might seem so to you.'

'I shall lose my son in any case,' she argued. 'To the State. Don't look at me like that, Waters. Don't make me feel guilty.'

'If you feel guilty, it is not because of me, Herta, it is because of what you're doing.'

He was about to leave but she clutched him even tighter. She wanted to know what Blake had said about her in his letter. Waters was evasive at first but she pressed him.

'Blake said that you were right to want to stay with the boy, his son, because the child would need you. . . .'

Captain Waters strode out quickly and left her to reflect on what had been said by the man she was giving up everything to see.

The wedding itself was over but the celebrations were dragging on well into the afternoon. Owen had found a local landowner to talk to and was astonished to hear that there were still wolves running wild in one part of Britain. His attitude towards his companion was polite to the point of being obsequious and it never occurred to him that the story of the wolves might be put down to too much champagne. Before Owen could question the man further, Jean rushed up to say that their son had got himself caught up a tree and was in some danger.

Owen charged off as fast as he could, the run reviving memories of another dash he had once made through wooded terrain. By the time he arrived in the clearing where Colin was, he was breathing stertorously and his head was a cavern of noise. Another boy, who had been playing with Colin, fled when he saw the adults coming. Colin himself was dangling from a branch some ten or twelve feet from the ground, gulping with fear. Owen touched his son's feet and then talked him slowly down, catching him in his arms.

Jean was relieved, Colin was grateful, and both wanted simply to go home now. But Owen was in another world where justice was harsh and filthy clothes were punishable by beating. Yelling out the same Japanese word again and again, Owen told his son to 'Look, look, look!' at the state of his clothes. He began to slap the boy unmercifully and Colin screamed in pain. Jean was horrified at the manic way in which her husband was administering the punishment and she begged him to stop. When he did so, he ran off into the woods, gasping and sobbing. Jean called after him then turned back to Colin.

'You see what you've done . . . what you've done. . . .'

Tom Poster, a genial, white-haired man in his sixties, propelled himself forward in his wheelchair until he trapped Beth Warrington in the corner of the living room.

'Got you at last!' he shouted.

'I was just looking for you,' she said.

'Brave man, your husband.'

'Because he married me, you mean?'

'Because he invited me here—a Labour Member of Parliament at his son's wedding. That takes courage. Even if I am an insignificant back-bencher.'

'There's nothing insignificant about you,' she assured him.

'Thank you. This damn chair has held me back a bit, though. Still, I should be out of it next week.'

'Marvellous!'

'Thought you'd be disappointed,' he said, with an artful grin.

'Disappointed?' Beth was puzzled. 'What an odd thing to say!'

'There's something I know that you don't know I know.'

In the chat that followed, Beth Warrington realized how wrong she had been to accept the notion that the Member of Parliament for Whitstanton was completely in the dark about something so vital as the nomination of his successor. Tom Poster had known all along.

'It was you who nominated me to take your place in the House, wasn't it?' she said, stumbling upon it.

'Whatever gave you that idea?'

'Woman's intuition. I've seen you watching me out of the corner of your eye when the German Committee meets.'

Tom laughed, warned her that he was not ready to retire just yet, and talked about the severe problems facing the government.

'Did you read Orwell's correspondence in *Tribune*?'

'Zilliacus? Yes. . . .'

'A few on the Left would like to rock the boat. Watch 'em.'

Beth told him how well she got on with George Hayward and how the family tie would be a useful cover for their political meetings until her candidature was made public. She also mentioned her proposed visit to the ironworks.

'Does John know?'

'Hardly!'

'Be like a small atomic bomb on the Warringtons.' His glee faded and he became serious. 'Any chance of you two getting back together?'

'Ros wants it. I think John does, too. For myself, I'm not sure. I do get lonely—on the rare occasions when I have time. But what could I offer him? I have precious little private life.'

'I see what I see, Beth. You're Catholics. What sort of life is there for you apart? Guilt-ridden if you stray from the straight and narrow. Like you were with Peter Fraser.' He continued quickly as she looked startled. 'Oh yes, I knew! All due respect to him now that he's dead, but Peter only opened a door that anyone could have opened.'

Beth Warrington was glad that she had saved the most important conversation of the day till last. George Hayward joined them and Tom gave him a warm welcome.

'We're like foreigners among this lot, George. Aliens!'

Waters opened the door and let him in after him. They went straight to the table where she had been sitting when he left. There was no sign of Herta. Waters told the man that he would not be needed. As he went back out through the door of the restaurant, the man did not see the slight smile around the other's mouth.

After he had seen Mark and Peg off on their honeymoon in the car, Blake Hayward returned to the stables flat. Rosalynde Warrington was looking down at the discarded morning suit that Mark had worn for the ceremony.

'Back to Moss Bros,' he said.

'I don't know why I suddenly couldn't bear to see them off.'

'The sight of so much happiness, perhaps?'

'I don't despise happiness,' she replied, with feeling. 'By God, I don't!'

'That wasn't quite what I was saying, Ros. Love's an illusion, or so I keep telling myself.'

'Even an illusion is a reality to the one who has it.'

'More Catholic double-talk?' he taunted.

'At least I've got that, Blake. What keeps you afloat?'

'Only a refusal to sink. Try it some time. You could have your Sundays free.'

'I don't need temptation.' She picked up the grey top hat that had been worn by her brother and ran a hand around the rim. 'I only hang on because God let me go.'

'Lost sheep?'

'Yes. Lost in the war.'

'That makes two of us.'

The look which had united them across the aisle of a church now shone in their eyes again. He moved towards her, took the hat from her grasp, set it down, then touched her arms very gently. She felt the need to make a token protest.

'We've nothing in common but sailing.'

'We have. Keeping afloat. . . .'

With nothing more to guide him than his pain and confusion, Colin Hayward ran through the trees in the most densely wooded area of the estate. The ground was a carpet of wet, yellowing leaves and there was a sense almost of decay all round him. He suddenly stopped.

Ahead of him was a brick building that looked like the rear wall of Lake House itself. It appeared that he had been running in a huge and futile circle. Then Colin looked more closely and realized that this was a different building, flat, solid, imposing, climbing out of the banked lawns that fronted it with real purpose. It was only when he got right up to the building that he saw how deceived he had been. It was a folly, a one dimensional structure put there to satisfy the whim of a previous owner, an architectural joke.

The boy in Colin was aroused. Forgetting his fear and his panic, he opened the door of the building and went through to find a flight of stairs, open to the sky. As he climbed these, lost in his own awe, he tried to work out why such an extraordinary structure should be erected. Then he reached the window and looked out.

'Dad! . . . Dad! . . . Dad!'

His scream could be heard by everyone.

'Dad!'

From his position high up, he could see his father's legs dangling from beneath a large over-hanging tree. There was nobody who could reach up and help Owen Hayward to safety now. Overcome by remorse, he had taken the only escape he knew from the voices inside his head.

'Dad! Dad!'

Disturbed by the noise, a flock of snow geese rose gracefully out of the grass and were soon flying together across the shimmering emptiness of the lake.

# Fontana Paperbacks

Fontana is a leading paperback publisher of fiction and non-fiction, with authors ranging from Alistair MacLean, Agatha Christie and Desmond Bagley to Solzhenitsyn and Pasternak, from Gerald Durrell and Joy Adamson to the famous Modern Masters series.

In addition to a wide-ranging collection of internationally popular writers of fiction, Fontana also has an outstanding reputation for history, natural history, military history, psychology, psychiatry, politics, economics, religion and the social sciences.

All Fontana books are available at your bookshop or newsagent; or can be ordered direct. Just fill in the form and list the titles you want.

FONTANA BOOKS, Cash Sales Department, G.P.O. Box 29, Douglas, Isle of Man, British Isles. Please send purchase price, plus 8p per book. Customers outside the U.K. send purchase price, plus 10p per book. Cheque, postal or money order. No currency.

NAME (Block letters)

ADDRESS